DRAGON SLAYER

CHARLES RAY

NORTH POTOMAC, MD

For information about this and other books by this author, contact him at: charlesray.author@yahoo.com or charlesray.author@gmail.com.

Printed in the United States of America.

Cover illustration by the author.

DEDICATION

To the gallant men and women of the U.S. Foreign Service, with whom I had the honor of serving for 30 years. They labor in relative obscurity in order for the rest of the world to enjoy peace.

Chapter One

June 21, 1978, Dirksen Senate Office Building
Washington, DC

"Mr. Chairman; distinguished members of the committee, I am honored to have the opportunity to appear before you today." As David Morgan leaned forward, his hands, fingers interlaced, resting in front of him on the dark blue cloth covering the long table at which he sat. His throat felt dry, and he was afraid his voice would crack, but he didn't dare pour water from the crystal pitcher into the tumbler at his left hand, fearing he might spill it and look like a bumbling fool. "I am also honored to have been nominated by the President to be the United States Ambassador to the Republic of Naganda, and if confirmed, I will do my utmost to carry out our nation's policy, and protect its interests there."

Morgan paused, looking up at the four men sitting behind the long, curved desk. Two Democrats and two Republicans – members of the African Affairs Subcommittee of the Senate Foreign Relations

1

Committee, they held his fate in their hands. Sitting here in the fourth floor hearing room of the Senate Dirksen Office Building, just northeast of the Capitol, he could not help but be awed by his surroundings. The medium brown wood paneled walls and high ceilings; the darker brown – a mahogany – of the dais behind which the committee members sat, elevated so that they could look down upon those called to appear before them; the stern, uncompromising looks on the faces of the six white men who were sitting in judgment on him; it all combined to give him a hollow feeling in his gut.

Discretely, he removed a handkerchief from inside his dark blue suit jacket, and wiped at his dark brown brow. He took a deep breath, looked down at the neatly typed notes, and resumed.

"The nation of Naganda is currently at a crossroads," he said. "One of West Africa's poorest nations, it has recently suffered a coup d'état, with former army captain Musa Gweru overthrowing the former ruler, Joshua Saidu. While Saidu was a despotic, often violent, ruler, we expressed our concern at his extra-legal, unconstitutional removal from power. The new leadership has committed to improving Naganda's human rights record, restoring democratic government to the country, and complying with international norms of behavior and rule of law. As American Ambassador, if I am confirmed, I will continue to monitor events, and as appropriate, recommend actions to assist Naganda and its people return to the fold of civilized nations." He was aware that he shouldn't talk too long – just make a brief opening statement and shut his mouth. The rule of thumb he'd been given at State over in Foggy Bottom during the weeks of preparation for his hearing was, talk 25% of the time, listen 75%. They're not there to hear your views, but to express their own. "Thank you again for the opportunity to appear before you. I will now be pleased to answer any questions you might have."

He took a deep breath and sat back in his chair. He could feel the people behind him, sitting on stiff backed, but not too uncomfortable chairs. Staff of the State Department's Africa Bureau, mostly the West African office and the Naganda country directorate. They'd worked with him for weeks, cramming his head with names, dates, events relating to the country of Naganda, a poor, landlocked former British colony in central West Africa. In the front row of spectators seats, between State Department Deputy Assistant Secretary Jason Symington and Naganda Country Director Ed Harris sat the only three people he considered friends. Lee Kennedy, a senior agent in the Diplomatic Security Service (DSS), his sixteen-year-old daughter, Rachel, and Alison Chambers, an analyst in the State Department's Bureau of Intelligence and Research (INR), were there for moral support. Morgan had met Kennedy and Chambers three years earlier when he was serving as deputy chief of mission at the American embassy in Dagastan, and they'd become friends. He'd met Kennedy's daughter, Rachel, when he was called back to Washington to after being nominated to be ambassador to Naganda. Kennedy and Chambers, he'd learned, had, after over two years of an on-again, off-again relationship, recently married. The three of them made a picture-postcard family group. The two women – and Morgan had quickly learned that Rachel, like her father, was mature for her age, and a very serious person – had a close and intimate relationship, unlike many step-parent, step-child lash ups. Even without looking back over his shoulder, he knew that they were smiling at him, while the rest of the group would be looking anxious, worried that he'd flub his responses to questions despite the stack of index cards with talking points they'd prepared for him. Truth be told, he worried about that himself.

It wasn't lost on Morgan that the room, though dealing with the business of a black African country, was overwhelmingly white. Except for himself, and two junior desk officers, neither of whom dealt with Naganda, everyone in Dirksen's Room 419 was white, including the two men who sat to either side of him. On his right, Senator Jonathan Appleby, a democrat from North Dakota, had insisted on appearing in his support, even though Morgan wasn't from his state. The man had been a strong supporter from the beginning, and was in all likelihood the reason he'd been nominated in the first place, despite some objection from a few in the State Department bureaucracy who resented his independent streak. Senator Leland Kirk, the junior senator from Maryland, Morgan's home state, sat on his left. Never very interested in politics, Morgan had never met the man before, but he seemed an affable sort, and had quickly agreed to present him to the committee. Both had extolled his abilities and virtues, with Appleby, as the senior legislator in time served, going first – ensuring the committee that the country couldn't have chosen a better representative than David Morgan, a decorated military veteran and an accomplished diplomat who had served his nation in some most challenging assignments.

Now that he'd finished his short presentation, it was time for the main event. Beginning with the committee chairman, each of the six members of the committee would make a speech, highlighting the contributions each had made to American foreign policy, supporting or taking potshots at the administration, depending upon their own political party, and then asking him one or two questions. He'd been assured that it was all a pro forma exercise, and because the Senate would soon be going into the July 4th recess, his confirmation would come speedily.

The committee chairman, a gaunt man with stooped shoulders and flowing white hair, was the junior senator from Connecticut. A democrat, he'd been the ranking member until the democratic takeover of the Senate. He cleared his throat and looked down at Morgan, his thin lips turning up in a half smile.

"The committee welcomes you, Mr. Morgan," he said in a deep, resonant voice that was out of character with his appearance. "We also welcome the presence of our two colleagues, the gentlemen from North Dakota and Maryland." Appleby and Clerk nodded and mumbled their thanks at being allowed to be present. "Now, Mr. Morgan, I want to thank you for your many years of service to your country, especially your service in the military." He went on for several minutes about the importance of service and his pride in his own service as a young lieutenant during World War II. After mentioning the emphasis the administration placed on human rights, he cleared his throat again. "To that end, Mr. Morgan, can you tell me what your actions will be in Naganda to improve that country's human rights performance?"

It wasn't exactly a softball question, but he'd been well prepared and anticipated that at least one member of the committee would ask it. Among the many issues of his campaign, the president, a democrat and former state governor, had placed respect for universal human rights as enshrined in the United Nations Charter high on the list. American diplomats around the world had now to include this topic in the list of issues they took up with the governments to which they were accredited. Morgan wasn't sure what his opinion was on it – considering the dismal human rights records of most of the world's countries, including sometimes his own – but, he gave the man credit for having the compassion and sheer gall to push such a new and strange agenda in Washington, a town that lived on precedent. This emphasis was unprecedented.

He took his time answering. He'd learned during his time in the military that it was never a good idea to respond too quickly to a question.

"Mr. Chairman," he said finally. "I will make it my

main issue to engage the government of Naganda at every opportunity on this important issue, while at the same time not forgetting my most important mission – the protection of American citizens and their interests."

The chairman smiled. Morgan felt relieved. He'd given the answer that was expected. In short, he'd said nothing, but it had sounded profound.

The chairman asked one or two more perfunctory questions, and then turned the floor over to the ranking member of the committee, a dour looking republican from California with a bad comb over vainly attempting to cover the broad bald spot on his florid skull. He also went on at length about his contributions to America's security, and his support of robust diplomacy, although he didn't mention any former military service. He then halfheartedly praised the president and his administration for the emphasis placed on support for American business abroad. "Tell me, Mr. Morgan, if confirmed as ambassador to Naganda, what will you do to improve the business climate there for American companies?"

This was not a question that Morgan had anticipated, nor had he been really prepared for it. Oh, he'd been briefed on Naganda's economy – what there was of it. Basically agricultural, with eighty percent of the population living in rural areas, the country grew cotton, maize, tapioca, and peanuts primarily. There was gold, titanium, and alluvial diamonds as well. A jointly-owned British-American firm controlled the titanium mining, and a few rogue Americans occasionally participated in the largely unregulated diamond market, but other than that, there were no significant American commercial interests in Naganda.

Morgan reasoned, though, that he would have to give the senator a satisfactory answer to his question. He'd always had the ability to think on his feet, although it had gotten him into trouble on more than one occasion. But, he'd been chosen to be ambassador, a job that surely required the ability to handle unexpected situations.

"Senator," he said. "I take the duty to support American industry seriously, and I assure you that, if confirmed, that will be a high priority for me in Naganda."

Again, a profound sounding answer completely devoid of substance. He heard quiet murmurs of approval from behind him. The senator from California smiled thinly and yielded to the gentleman sitting on the chairman's right, a democrat from New York. Younger looking than any of the others on the panel, he continuously ran his hand through his thick brown hair, smiling at nothing in particular.

"Mr. Morgan," he said. "What are your views on the chances for democratic reform in Naganda?"

About as much chance as a snowball rolling through hell and not losing weight, Morgan thought. Of course, he would *never* say that aloud – not here. "Senator, that is difficult to assess. If I am confirmed, however, I will continue my predecessor's efforts to help the Nagandan government move to greater transparency and a more representative government."

His predecessor had, in fact, done little beyond occasionally mentioning to the foreign minister when they met that Washington would like to see democratic elections in Naganda. The foreign minister would reply that Nagandans would like to see democratic elections in Naganda, and that would end their conversation. He had no doubt that his efforts would be similar. His answer, though, seemed to satisfy the senator, who yielded to the last member of the committee, a firebrand republican from Georgia who, despite being on the foreign relations committee, felt the United States gave too much money to foreigners, gave in too much to foreign interests, and that it should tend more to its own business 'back home.'

Morgan had been warned about him, and the fact that he would be likely to ask an unanticipated question; a question designed to throw him off guard or to embarrass the administration, or both. He could feel a knot in his stomach as he looked up at the man's vulpine features. The beady blue eyes, thin lips, and narrow nose, all set in a narrow-faced head that, with his receding hairline, all combined to add to his menacing look.

Unlike the other three, he didn't bother making a speech about his great achievements, nor did he mention the administration. He steepled his fingers and rested his pointed chin on them, glaring down at Morgan.

"Mr. Morgan, the former ruler of Naganda, Joshua

Saidu, was little more than a tin pot dictator, bereft of a scintilla of intelligence or compassion for his people," he said in a voice dripping with scorn. "According to the intelligence and news reports I've seen, he was more interested in dallying with underage girls than leading his country." He stopped and took a sip from the glass at his elbow. "But, having said all that – he was nonetheless recognized as the legitimate head of state, recognized by us and other governments. Now, we have this upstart army captain ousting him from power and taking over in what can only be described as an extralegal usurpation of power. Can you explain to me why we are granting recognition to this illegal leader and his cabal? Doesn't this fly in the face of our calls for more democracy on the African continent?"

Morgan felt his cheeks flame. He was glad that his dark complexion hid what was a blush of anger. He was too close to his goal to screw it up by engaging in an argument with a member of the committee that could sink his career by voting against his confirmation. It galled him that he, in fact, partially agreed with the man. By recognizing the coup in Naganda, the U.S. had undercut its own message about the need to foster democracy in Africa. He knew that he was treading on dangerous ground, and no matter what he said he was likely to offend powerful interests, either in the senate or the administration.

Joshua Saidu, the deposed Nagandan leader, *had* been a despot. He wasn't a violent man, but he was vainglorious and wasteful, spending the country's meager income on trips to Europe, fancy parties and parades, a sumptuous palace for him and his many wives, and empty displays of pomp and ceremony. He'd been the country's leader since it gained independence from Great Britain, and in the ten years since independence he had taken what had once been one of the Queen's most productive colonies and reduced it to begging the international community for food to feed its starving people. A member of the majority Ganda tribe, the group for which the country was named, Saidu had paid little attention to his own tribe, and none at all to the Buntu and Chiveru, the other two ethnic groups that accounted for fifteen and five percent of the population respectively. In January, 1978, Musa Gweru, a captain in the Nagandan army, and a member of the Buntu tribe, had assembled the Buntu soldiers in his unit and marched on the capital, Mabuntu to protest the treatment accorded Buntu by the army high command and to demand a pay increase. At the sight of armed soldiers outside his residence, Saidu had fled out the back entrance and sought refuge in the Nigerian embassy. The Nigerian ambassador had negotiated between Saidu and Gweru, resulting in Saidu stepping down and turning the reins of power over to the young captain. After two days of silence, Gweru finally announced the formation of the Provisional State Ruling Council, or PSRC, which was comprised of fellow junior officers of the army, from all three tribes. Nigeria and the other countries of Africa granted immediate recognition to the PSRC government. The UN issued a statement decrying the extra-legal transfer of power, but, since the PSRC did not recall the Nagandan UN representative, reluctantly recognized the change. The European, Asian, and Latin American countries quickly followed the UN example. After a week of dithering and making public statements against change of government by coup d'état, the United States, accompanied by Australia, Canada and Great Britain granted recognition to the Gweru-led government.

He concentrated on his briefing cards, shuffling them as if looking for the answer to the senator's question, but knowing that nothing in the notes he'd been given addressed this potentially explosive issue. Finally, after allowing his breathing to ease, he looked up, straight into the senator's eyes.

"You make a valid point, senator," he said. "I can only say that the decision to recognize Captain Gweru's takeover was made after careful consideration at the highest levels of government. If we're to encourage more transparency and accountability in Africa at large, and Naganda specifically, we have little choice but to work with what exists on the ground. It is my hope that, if confirmed, I will be able to exert some influence on the current government of Naganda to move as rapidly as possible to a more representative form of government."

He let his breath out. He hadn't heard any gasps of surprise from behind him, so he was fairly confident that he hadn't inadvertently said anything that would paint the administration or the State Department into a corner. Whether or not the senator bought his response was another matter entirely. The man's glare changed into a leering smile. That, thought Morgan, couldn't be good.

"So," the senator said after a pregnant pause. "You plan to *encourage* Captain Gweru and the junta to relinquish power? That might take a powerful lot of arm twisting, Mr. Morgan – are you sure you're up to it?"

Morgan didn't need talking points to respond to that question. It was directed squarely at his ability to get the job done. He fixed the senator with a cold gaze.

"Senator, I *am* capable of twisting arms when necessary," he said. "But, in order to twist a man's arm I must first take his hand."

The senator from Georgia's eyes went round with surprise. *"Ah ha,"* Morgan thought. *"Bet you weren't expecting that answer."* He continued to lock gazes with the man. It was important, he knew, not to look as if you were cowed – impressed, and respectful, but not fearful. He'd learned that during his years in the army, especially his time in Special Forces in Vietnam during some of the most ferocious fighting of that war. Finally, the senator broke the gaze, and smiled.

"Well said, Mr. Morgan. Well said. You know, I think you just might be the man for this job. Mr. Chairman, I relinquish the rest of my time."

Morgan let out a slow sigh of relief. While he wasn't sure exactly what was going on, he had the feeling that he'd just passed some crucial test. He turned his gaze to the chairman, who was smiling down at him.

"Thank you for appearing before us today, Mr. Morgan," he said. "On behalf of the committee I also want to thank you for your candid answers to our questions. I wish you the best of luck in your future . . . endeavors. Ladies and gentlemen, this hearing is now closed, and thank you all for coming."

Jonathan Appleby leaned in close to Morgan and in a voice that was barely above a whisper, said, "Good work, David. You showed the bastards what you're made of. I know you're unfamiliar with the workings of this place, but I can tell you that your confirmation is a shoe-in. Now, get up there and shake hands with the committee, and then get out of here and get yourself a stiff drink and some rest – you earned it."

Morgan shook hands with Appleby and Clerk, thanking them for coming, and then rose and walked up to the curved dais to shake hands with the members of the committee, starting with the chairman and ranking member, and then with the other two. The smiles seemed genuine and the handshakes were firm – each of them congratulating him and thanking him for his service. In a few short minutes the atmosphere in the room, so tense until now, had warmed to a comfortable level.

After greeting the committee, Morgan turned to the audience, heading straight for Alison, Lee, and Rachel. Lee shook his hand and clapped him on the shoulder.

"You aced it, David," he said. "No doubt about that."

Alison and Rachel hugged him.

"It was like an inquisition," Alison whispered into

his ear. "But, you were so calm and cool."

"Cool as a cucumber," Rachel quipped.

Symington pushed between Alison and Rachel, holding out his hand. "I must agree," he said. "You did a great job. Now, you need to go unwind. We'll see you in the office tomorrow morning."

Morgan was still in a semi-daze. It had, he knew, all been theater, with the members of the committee reading their lines – from a script that hadn't been shared with him – and him responding mostly adlib. He thanked everyone for coming and started for the door. A stiff drink and a nap was the only thing he wanted. It hadn't been all that different from the times he'd come back from an extended patrol in Cambodia during the war. He'd maintained his cool, calm demeanor throughout the operation, much as he'd done while on a combat patrol. Now that it was over, he was on the verge of collapse, and for that, he needed to be alone.

Charles Ray

Chapter Two.

June 21-22, 1978, Francis Scott Key Hotel and Africa Bureau,
Department of State, Washington, DC

Morgan took a taxi straight from the Dirksen Senate Office Building to the Francis Scott Key Hotel on Twentieth Street, not far from the Department of State building.

Before entering the hotel, he walked down to a small liquor store near E Street and Twenty-First Avenue and bought a half-pint bottle of vodka and a large bottle of lime juice. Back in this room, he looked at his watch. It was 3:50 in the afternoon. He'd eaten a light lunch before the hearing, and it was far too early for supper, even though his stomach felt empty. He knew it wasn't wise to drink on an empty stomach, but the tension of the hearing needed relief.

In his room, he took off his jacket, tie, and shirt, and kicked off his shoes. He then poured a third of a glass of vodka and filled it the rest of the way with the lime juice. He took down half the glass in the first swallow. The bite of the vodka and the slight bittersweet taste of the lime juice felt warm sliding down his throat.

After emptying the glass, he decided the vodka concoction would be better with ice, so, a bit unsteady on his feet he padded outside and down the hall to the ice machine in the alcove near the stairs and filled the room's ice bucket. Returning to the room, he made another, going a bit easier on the vodka. He might as well have skipped that part of the ritual. After four of the even weakened drinks, his tension daze had been replaced by a warm haze – the earlier episode at the hearing just a fuzzy thought in his mind. Deep in the rearmost recesses of his brain was a voice telling him he should get up, get dressed and go out for supper. That voice, though, eventually faded.

He woke up the next morning at 5:30, lying on top of the bed spread, still in his pants and undershirt, with a mouth that felt like it was filled with cotton wool and the feeling of a ten-piece orchestra playing in his skull.

Cursing himself for his over indulgence, he eased out of bed, disrobed, and limped to the tiny shower stall. He stood under the nozzle, and turned it on full force, and as cold as possible, shivering as the needles of water pummeled his aching head. When his headache had subsided to a manageable level, he turned the hot water handle until it was just short of scalding, and scrubbed until he tingled all over. Finally, feeling half alive, he got out and toweled off.

After relieving himself, he brushed his teeth, rinsing twice with the astringent mouthwash in the tiny plastic bottle on the sink, and then carefully shaved off the morning stubble, nicking himself twice in the process.

He pulled on his gray pants and tucked a light blue shirt into them, and then fumbled several times knotting his best red tie. When the tie was finally firmly seated around his neck – a bit too tight, but he decided that he deserved to suffer after so foolishly getting so drunk, so he just flexed his neck muscles until it no longer felt like he was being garroted. He then put on his black jacket and went downstairs to the hotel dining room for breakfast.

His stomach almost rebelled at the greasy smell of the limp, undercooked bacon on the buffet line, but he knew he'd need to get something solid into his stomach or he'd get sick by mid-morning. He put two slices of the bacon on the plate, adding two biscuits, a small pile of hash brown potatoes, and scrambled eggs. On the way to an empty table in the corner, he grabbed a bottle of Tabasco sauce.

Sitting at the table, ignoring the scattering of other diners, he poured a third of the spicy sauce over the eggs. The first few bites almost didn't stay down, but as he ate, his stomach began to settle. By the time he'd finished, washing it down with two cups of hot, black coffee, he almost felt human again.

He debated going back to his room, but decided he might as well face the day. It was 7:45 when he emerged from the hotel, and the weather was already warm and humid, signaling a hot July to come. He walked south on Twentieth Street toward E Street, and then west to Twenty-First. A block south he turned west onto D Street to the employee entrance of Main State, joining a line of employees entering past the guard who eyed each individual's entry badge. Inside the D Street lobby, he turned toward the left and took the elevator up to the fifth floor, emerging in corridor 9. He then walked over to corridor 5 and walked the width of the building toward the front and corridor 1 where the Naganda country directorate and desk officers were located.

The Naganda desk officer, a young FS-04 on his third tour, his first in Washington, was waiting for him in the reception area. Morgan had to search his memory for the young man's name, thanks to the effects of half a bottle of vodka, but it finally came – Gregory Wells. A native of Kentucky, Wells had served two years in the Peace Corps before joining the Foreign Service, so he was somewhat older than most of the other desk officers who had joined right out of college. He stood when Morgan entered.

"Mr. Ambassador," he said in a soft southern accent. "I hope you had a good night's rest."

"If you only knew," Morgan thought, but he simply smiled, nodded, and said, "Yes, I did. What's on my agenda for the morning?"

Wells motioned toward a tiny cubicle of an office behind the secretary's desk that had been set aside for

Morgan's use while he was preparing for his confirmation hearings. "I have a schedule for you on your desk. Would you like a cup of coffee before we get started?"

"No, I've had my quota for the day," Morgan said, shaking his head. "Let's get to it."

Wells stepped aside to allow Morgan to enter the office first. When Morgan had settled himself behind the gray, government-issue desk, Wells sat in the stiff back chair in front of it. He reached over and picked up a single sheet of paper.

"I've kept your schedule light today to give you a chance to fully decompress after yesterday's hearing. The main items are the selection of your secretary and DCM."

Morgan knew he wanted as his personal secretary – Mary Sung, his secretary when he was deputy chief of mission in Dagastan. He'd been given a list of three candidates to be his DCM, or deputy chief of mission. There were two men and a woman. He'd interviewed all three, and while all were imminently qualified, he was wavering between two, a senior political officer who had served in Kenya and Nigeria, and the woman, a consular officer who had not only served in Rhodesia, Guinea, and Madagascar, but in Colombia and Thailand, and a tour in the Department's Bureau of Consular Affairs. Ed Harris, the country director, had been pushing him to select the political officer, but the woman, a Kansan named Susan Pinchon, had impressed him during the interview with her poise and calm demeanor. The political officer, a New Yorker who had graduated from Fletcher School of Diplomacy, while qualified, had struck him as a bit too stiff and formal – and, a bit full of himself. He knew that his choice wouldn't go over well in the directorate, but as ambassador, it was his decision - and his alone - to make.

"I've decided that I want Mary Sung as my secretary," he said. "She's currently working in Personnel. I've spoken to her, and she's willing to take the job. If possible, I'd like her to arrive at post at the same time as I do, or as close as possible."

"That won't be a problem, sir," Wells said. "I'll get the paperwork started this morning. In fact, it might even be a good idea if she gets there before you do. She can help prepare for your arrival."

Morgan liked the young desk officer. He had a knack of seeing what needed to be done, and wasn't shy about making suggestions. Happily, he was newly assigned to a two-year tour, so Morgan would have him backstopping the embassy for most of his own tour.

"Good idea, make it so. Now, the DCM – I think I want Pinchon. She really impressed me during the interview, and I think she and I can work well together."

Wells frowned, but nodded. "Very well, sir . . . I, uh, well, there's been something of a hitch regarding the deputy position."

Something was troubling Wells. Morgan felt a flash of anger – not at the desk officer, but, if someone else in the directorate was trying to undercut him on this issue, there would be hell to pay.

"Don't tell me there's a problem with her being assigned?"

"No, sir, not at all – uh, well, as you know, the country director and the DAS Symington preferred Wilmington, but they both recognize that this is your choice to make. No, it's the current deputy. He's asking to have his tour curtailed immediately, so your new deputy will have to report for duty shortly after your own arrival. Having the number one and two positions changing at the same time could prove a little unsettling for the embassy staff."

Morgan had a hunch that he knew why the current deputy had asked for a reassignment, and if it was accurate, it was just as well. The relationship between an ambassador and a deputy chief of mission has to be based on trust and mutual respect. He didn't want, though, to bother Wells with his speculation. "We'll just have to deal with it," he said. "I've faced similar situations when I was in the army, when the top leadership of my unit changed *en masse*. With a little effort, we can make it work. Get in touch with Pinchon and let her know she'll have to move her travel plans to the front burner."

Wells smiled. "Will do, sir. Anything else?"

"Yes, get in touch with Lee Kennedy in DSS, and Alison Chambers in INR. I want to talk to them. Oh, and, if possible, I'd like to talk to both of them at the same time."

"Of course," Wells said. "May I ask why? Just in case they ask."

"Not now. They're old friends, so if you tell them I want to talk to them about something important, they won't ask questions. I'd like to talk to them first before I tell you what it's about. It's a sensitive matter, you understand. It'll all be clear when the time comes."

The nice thing about being an ambassador, more accurately in Morgan's case, an ambassador-designate, was that junior ranks were conditioned to do what you asked, and if you chose not to explain why, to salute and execute. In some ways it was like the military – without the discipline and military bearing. Morgan mentally cautioned himself not to begin taking it all too seriously.

"Yes, sir," Wells said. "I'll see if they're available this morning."

He put the single sheet neatly back in the center of the otherwise empty desk and left.

Morgan sat back in the chair, looking up at the low ceiling of the cramped little office. He wanted very much to go back to his hotel room and crawl under the sheet for ten or twelve hours. Even though his headache was gone, his mouth still felt dry and his eyeballs itched. He could, he knew, just close his eyes and take a nap here in his little temporary private office, but sleeping at his place of work was something he found it uncomfortable to even think about. He fought the urge to close his eyes, by blinking rapidly until the items in the room had a blurry haze surrounding them.

He didn't notice the door opening at first, and when he did he was startled to see the broad-shouldered, dark figure of Carlton Raine standing there, framed by the lights in the reception area. He hadn't seen the CIA agent since leaving Dagastan.

"Man," Raine said. "You look like something the dog drug in. Did you tie one on yesterday after your hearing?"

Morgan stood and, smiling, extended a hand, which Raine grasped firmly. He was glad to see the man who had saved his life when he and his security officer were ambushed in Dagastan.

"More like one tied me on," he said. "I forgot to count drinks – and, because of that I forgot to eat."

Raine made a face. "Eew! Booze on an empty stomach – that's a lethal combination."

"Tell me about it. Hey, what are you doing here? Have you been reassigned from the garden spot of the world?"

"As a matter of fact, I have," Raine said, smiling broadly. "Two weeks ago in fact. I'm now the chief of station at the embassy in Mabuntu."

It took a few seconds for Morgan's brain to process that information. When it did, he smiled.

"We'll be working together again. Now, that's good news. Have you been there yet?"

"Yeah, I've been there a week. I just came back to Langley for a few days of briefings and went straight out. I wanted to get back for your confirmation hearing, but I missed my connecting flight in Amsterdam and didn't get in until late last night."

Morgan motioned to a chair, and then sat back down. "Okay, I'm glad you're here. Can you fill me in," he said. "What's going on out there?"

Raine leaned forward, placing his elbows on the edge of the desk. "Well, now, I'm pretty good at what I do, but I've only been in country for a week, so I'm still in the process of catching up," he said. "If you have a few minutes, though, I'll tell you what I know."

Chapter Three

As Morgan settled back in his chair, Carlton Raine began to demonstrate that he was, in fact, very good at his job.

"I suppose you've heard the dirt on this guy, Joshua Saidu, the former head honcho in Naganda," he said. Morgan nodded and made a sour face. "Yeah, he's that bad, and more. Rumor has it that he kept a stable of underage girls in the basement of his mansion to satisfy his twisted desires. That, though, wasn't the reason the army guys moved on him."

"I understand the coup was really accidental," Morgan said. "Gweru and his men were really in the capital to complain about pay and living conditions, and Saidu bolted."

Raine smiled and nodded. "You've been doing your homework. That's precisely what happened."

"Well, if they didn't want to take over the country, why didn't they just press their case with the second in command?"

"First, Saidu didn't really *have* a second in command," Raine said. "The man didn't believe in sharing anything. He used the National Security Service under the control of Julius Bongo, who was also chief of staff of the army, to keep the military under control. That was as close to a number two as you can get. Bongo feared that if he moved against the young officers after Saidu flew the coop, he might suffer for all that he'd done to them before, so he also went into hiding. The senior officers of the military decided to back the young Turks, figuring that if things went wrong, the young guys would take the fall, and they could move in. The international community's recognition of the junta caught them off guard, and as often happens in these little jerk water countries, these guys liked being in charge."

"Afflicted with the Big Man Syndrome, eh?"

"Big time. The top leaders in the junta convoy to work at State House every morning in high-speed convoys of Land Rovers and pickups with guys carrying machine guns and RPGs all over the place, and they strut around with armed bodyguards like Roman legions."

In Morgan's mind, images similar to Dagastan after the coup formed. When those on the bottom took over, he knew, they tended to emulate the ones who had previously been on top.

"Has the situation improved any?"

"I don't know what it was like before, but I doubt it," Raine said. "The poor are still scratching for a living. Oh, the army has it better, now that one of their own is in charge – at least, that part of the army that's loyal to Gweru. He put his uncle, Gideon Banda, in charge of the Nagandan National Security Service, and made him chief of staff of the army. But, the double-N, double-S, as the security service is affectionately known, is still as ruthless as ever, and anyone in the army who steps out of line, is still likely to disappear."

"I take it you're declared to the security service," Morgan said, referring to the agency's normal practice of having its senior man in an embassy known to the country's top spies. "With the head of security also being in charge of the military that must cause some jurisdictional disputes with our defense attaché."

Raine chuckled. "It could, but our attaché, a sharp army colonel named Liam Brennan, is a savvy guy, and pretty easy to work with – at least, that's been my observation during the week I was there. They don't have much of an army – about six battalions – so he spends most of his time keeping an eye on the Soviets. The GRU has about five guys under cover in their embassy."

"Shit, and here I'd thought by going to Africa I'd get away from our Russian friends."

"Oh, it gets better," Raine said. "We got a ton of Chinese Communists prowling around as well. I can promise you, your tour will not be boring."

"What can you tell me about the foreign

community in Naganda?"

"Not a lot. You have a few Brits who stayed on after independence, mostly in the capital, and a large Lebanese community that has been there for a century or more. Out in the countryside there are American missionaries, and some of them have been there since the 1800s, too. The Chinese are doing *aid* projects, which means the Chinese community is growing. That's about it, except for the diplomatic community, and that's about what you'd expect – a lot of guys running around interviewing each other for their dispatches back to the home office, and bored wives with nothing to do but play bridge and drink."

In a mere week's time, Raine had catalogued Naganda, and Morgan knew that he was only scratching the surface. As one of the first blacks to be recruited by the agency for field duty, he'd had to be better than good to succeed. It helped that he was just naturally good at the business – he could be charming and affable one minute, and a cold-faced killing machine the next, and he had an encyclopedic memory. He was also a good judge of people, and if he thought well of the defense attaché, Morgan knew that his intelligence team was first rate.

"I guess," he said. "That just leaves the embassy family. What's your take on *our* people?"

Raine frowned, and the muscles in his jaw tightened. "Most are pretty good. The DCM's a racist prick, but I hear he's asking to be curtailed. You're lucky to lose him. You have a pretty good political chief, except he's a bit full of himself. I already mentioned Brennan, the DATT. Unfortunately, I didn't get a chance to get to know most of the others. All in all, though, I'd say you're inheriting an outfit that you can whip into shape."

"I just hope I don't have to whip too hard." They shared a laugh.

There was a polite rap on the door, and Wells opened it and stuck his head in. "Lee Kennedy and Alison Chambers are here to see you," he said.

"Hey, Blood," Morgan said, using Raine's nickname, a label he'd achieved because of some of the dangerous field missions he'd been on. "I have to meet with these people. Let's get together for a drink before you head back."

Charles Ray

Chapter Four

As Lee Kennedy and Alison Chambers entered the office, Morgan introduced them briefly to Carlton Raine. The three exchanged perfunctory handshakes, and Raine strode purposefully away.

"Who is he?" Kennedy asked.

Morgan explained his relationship with Raine and his new assignment.

"He certainly looks like someone who can take care of himself," Chambers said.

"You don't know the half of it," Morgan said, chuckling. "Remind me to tell you about it someday." He motioned them to chairs. "For now, though, I have an important issue to discuss with the two of you."

He settled himself behind the desk, forming a steeple with his fingers and resting his chin on the points of his stiffened digits.

"You sound serious," Kennedy said. "There's no

problem is there?"

Morgan laughed again. "No, no problem. But, I am serious, though. I'm going to make the two of you a proposal – a request, really – and, I want you to give it some very serious thought before you make up your minds."

They looked at each other, their brows furrowed and confusion in their expressions.

"Okay, already," Chambers said. "You have our attention. What's this mysterious proposal?"

"Well, you – especially you Alison – know that Naganda is a country in turmoil. I was just told this morning that the current DCM is curtailing, so there'll be a wholesale change in post leadership. I'm going to have my hands full getting things under control, so I'll need people I can trust, and people with a proven track record of accomplishment to help me do it."

"So, you want our help in picking people for your staff?" Kennedy asked.

"Not exactly," Morgan said. "What I want is for the two of you to be part of my staff."

Their mouths gaped open. They locked gazes again.

"Uh, well, I can see Lee here being your RSO," Chambers said. "But, I'm not Foreign Service. There are no jobs in an embassy for me."

"Besides," Kennedy added. "We just got married, and as much as I'd love working for you, I'm not sure I want to be separated from Alison so early in our relationship."

She laid a hand on his arm, smiling lovingly at him. "You wouldn't be separated. I can take leave without pay." She turned to Morgan. "It would be a two year tour for him, right?"

Morgan nodded. "Yes, unless I could talk him into extending a year, so I'd have him for my entire tour."

"I don't want you to have to put your career on hold for me," Kennedy said with an insistent tone in his voice.

"But, Lee, darling, I -"

"She wouldn't have to put her career on hold," Morgan interrupted. "In addition to needing a reliable security officer, I'm going to need someone I can turn to for political advice. I've been told that I can hire spouses for jobs in the embassy, and since you already have top security clearance, I think I could hire you as my special advisor."

"It sounds intriguing," she said. "But, what about Rachel? There is no high school for diplomatic kids in Naganda."

Morgan had thought about that, and he'd done his homework.

"You might consider enrolling her in one of the international schools in Europe," he said. "They offer excellent education, and I think she'd love it. I've heard of the *Ecole Internationale* in Geneva. It's a top school.

She'd get a great preparation for college."

Kennedy smiled and bobbed his head up and down. "And, my Rachel, sixteen going on thirty, would love it, I'm pretty sure of that. Of course, I do need to discuss it with her first."

"Of course," Morgan said. "Take a few days to mull it over, and get back to me."

Kennedy turned to Alison. "You really want to do this, don't you?"

"Of course I do, but we have to think about what's best for Rachel as well."

"I am thinking about that," he said. "But, I tell you, she'll love it – she really will."

"You want to do it, too, don't you?"

"You bet your ass I do. I've been here in DC too long. I need to get back into the field. Rachel's a Foreign Service brat, she's flexible and strong. I just *know* she'll agree."

"Okay, but do me a favor – ask her first. She's a young woman now. Treat her like one. If we're going to do this, we're doing it as a family."

"Yes, ma'am," he said, smiling. "You're the boss."

"And, don't you forget it, mister." She turned to Morgan. "We'll call you later today after Lee's had a chance to talk with Rachel." She winked at Kennedy. "But, I think you just got yourself a new RSO and special advisor."

Chapter Five

June 30, 1978
Mabuntu, Naganda

Senator Appleby had called it correctly. The Foreign Relations Committee had approved Morgan's nomination and it had been quickly passed by the full senate on a voice vote. He was sworn in by the State Department's director of protocol two days later, and a day later was on a plane, by way of Amsterdam, to Naganda. He hated flying – always had. At six feet tall, he never fit comfortably in the economy class seats. But, as an ambassador on the way to post for the first time, he was authorized to fly in business class. That meant more leg room, seats that reclined far enough to allow him to sleep, though fitfully, free-flowing drinks, and a choice of food served on real china rather than plastic plates.

His flight from Dulles International Airport near Washington had landed in Amsterdam's Schipol Airport at 6:00 pm, and he had eleven hours to kill before his 5:00 am departure to Mabuntu, so he'd put his carry-on bag in a locker, gone through the immigration checkpoint, and taken a taxi from the airport to Amsterdam's famous red light district. He'd visited before, and the sex shops, peep shows, brothels, and prostitutes on display in red-lit windows didn't really do anything for him. But, there was little else to do in the city after dark, but drink, dine, or chase after whores. He found after walking for a block through the infamous city center that he didn't have the desire for drinking or whoring, and he'd eaten on the plane, so he wasn't hungry, so he hailed a taxi and went back to the airport, where he walked through the airport's hundreds of shops selling everything from Dutch cheese to French perfume to pornographic pictures for an hour, and then retrieved his bag and spent the three hours before boarding sleeping fitfully on one of the padded chairs in the departure area.

As a business class passenger, he was among the first to board. His seat was near the front of the business class area, where he could see the even more sumptuous accommodations in first class. The stewardess, a buxom brunette with the name 'Monika' on the gold wing-shaped name tag over her left breast, served him a vodka tonic and a view of her cleavage as soon as he'd settled into his seat. The business class section only had four passengers, Morgan and three balding businessmen who immediately went to sleep as soon as the plane took off. The flight attendant, who introduced herself to Morgan as Monika Loewenthal, asked him if he wanted anything to eat. He passed on the food, but ordered another vodka tonic – and got another lingering view down the front of her blouse and a beaming smile.

By the end of the nine-hour flight, Morgan had eaten one meal, drunk four vodka tonics, and exchanged addresses and phone numbers with Monika, who informed him that she flew the Amsterdam-Mabuntu flight three times a week and usually overnighted in Mabuntu on the third flight. Unfortunately, this was just the second flight – the third would be on Sunday, July 3d. Morgan asked her to call him when she came in. He expected to be relatively settled in his new residence by then, and wanted her to have dinner with him. Smiling enigmatically, she assured him that she would.

As the pilot started the descent into the airport at Mabuntu, the other passengers in business class woke up, and Monika was busy preparing the cabin for landing. She gave Morgan's arm a gentle squeeze as he got off the plane. There was promise in the warm, lingering gaze she gave him.

The warmth of Monika's gaze was blasted away as soon as he stepped through the aircraft door and onto the wheeled landing ladder. The hot, humid air slammed against him like a two-hundred pound linebacker. A sour, fetid smell that he couldn't identify mixed in with the biting odor of aviation fuel, almost making him gag. He wrinkled his nose and breathed slowly. It didn't help much. He noticed that most of the passengers didn't seem to notice either the heat or the odor – no doubt frequent visitors. The few first time arrivals were evident from their expressions, ranging from dismay to disgust, and the fact that many of

them had put their hands over their noses. After the
heat and smell, the next thing Morgan noticed was the
noise. Not just the usual engine noise of an airport,
but the incessant squawk of human voices. Vendors,
airport workers – even other passengers – all talking
nonstop, and at the top of their voices.

At the bottom of the ladder, a skinny black man in
an ill-fitting blue uniform motioned him toward a one-
story building with a corrugated tin roof and green
mold on its concrete walls. A door on the right had a
crudely lettered sign over it that said, 'Immigration and
Customs.' The passengers were all headed that way, so
Morgan turned and followed.

Inside the cramped room that housed Nagandan
Immigration and Customs, the heat and odor was even
more oppressive and the noise of people shouting into
each other's faces threatened to give Morgan a
headache. The crowd seemed to be milling about as
people crowded forward toward the three booths
housing bored looking men in khaki uniforms. Morgan
looked around in confusion. He'd been told that there
would be someone from the embassy and the foreign
ministry to meet him, but in the crush of the crowd he
saw no one who seemed to fit that description. He
shrugged and inserted himself into a knot of people
edging toward the booth on the far right of the room,
when he felt a tug at his sleeve.

He turned to see a tall, medium brown skinned
man with a severely receding hairline and upper front
teeth that pushed against his thick lips standing there
smiling at him. The man's dark blue cotton suit was

stained at the arm pits and neck from sweat. Morgan was wearing a tan, summer weight jacket over khaki pants and was already sweating. How anyone could wear a dark suit in this climate he didn't understand.

"Ambassador Morgan, sah?" the man asked.

"Yes," Morgan said. "That's me."

The man smiled broadly, showing crooked and stained teeth.

"Oh, very good, sah. I'm Cedric Mboko from the foreign ministry. May I have your passport and luggage claim checks please?"

Morgan handed over the requested documents. Mboko motioned him to follow, and then began not so gently shoving people aside as they made their way around the edge of the crowd and to the booth on the right. Mboko showed Morgan's black diplomatic passport and his own ID to the immigration officer who frowned and waved them through. They entered a darkened room with platforms to either side; behind which stood more bored looking men in khaki uniforms. Mboko nodded at them, and they ignored him.

Pushing through a set of double doors, they emerged into the large entrance hall of the airport, an area that was more crowded, noisier, and smellier than anything Morgan had experienced to that point. He looked around at the packed, milling crowd, still breathing shallowly to minimize the odorous assault on his olfactory system. Off to the right, he saw a group of smiling white faces, standing out like neon signs in the sea of black faces. He smiled when he recognized Susan Pinchon, a broad shouldered woman who was only an inch shorter than his own six feet, her dark brown hair pulled back in a severe bun. The system had worked at light speed to get her orders published, and her transfer not only approved but implemented. With her were two white men, both shorter than she was. Then, an oval brown face emerged from behind one of the men – Mary Sung. She bounced up and down on her short, bowed legs, waving at Morgan. He waved back.

"Ah," Mboko said. "I see the people from your embassy over there. There is also Mr. Kabo, the America's desk officer."

Morgan saw a very dark man, about Mary Sung's height, dressed in a dark, three-piece suit, his bald head gleaming under the harsh sunlight filtering through the flyspecked glass of the large front windows, standing just to the right of the group of embassy people. So, he thought, this is my welcome party from the government – a flunky and the desk officer – this is getting off to a rollicking start.

As they approached the group, Susan Pinchon stepped forward, holding out a hand, which Morgan grasped. Her handshake was warm, firm, and dry, and she looked at him with a welcoming gaze, a slight smile on her unadorned lips.

"Welcome to Naganda, Mr. Ambassador," she said in a deep, husky voice. "Let me introduce you to your welcoming party." She moved over toward the small, dark man. "This is Mr. Jonathan Kabo, director of the foreign ministry's Americas section."

The man proffered his small dark hand. His grip was weak, almost effeminate, and his palms were sweaty.

"Your Excellency," he said in a cultured British accent. "On behalf of His Excellency, Foreign Minister Gabriel Simbawashe, I would like to welcome you to the Republic of Naganda."

Morgan resisted wiping his hand after releasing the man's grasp. "Thank you Mr. Kabo," he said. "It is an honor to be in your country."

"You are no doubt tired after such a long flight from America," Kabo said. "I will greet you more appropriately tomorrow morning at my office in the ministry. You will want to retire to your residence to rest up. Cedric will take care of the immigration formalities and your luggage."

Having made what Morgan took to be a set speech, Kabo stepped back, fixing Mboko with an icy stare.

"Now, Mr. Ambassador, allow me to introduce the staff," Pinchon said. She turned to the small group standing expectantly by. "This is Thomas Breedlove, the embassy political counselor." A tall, angular man with his blond hair combed straight back on an oval, high browed head, stepped forward and shook Morgan's hand. He had a firm, dry grip, but his blue eyes held no sign of welcome. "This gentleman is

Colonel Liam Brennan, the defense attaché." Brennan, a broad-shouldered man with sandy brown hair cut short in military style, and twinkling brown eyes, grasped Morgan's hand in an almost crushing grip. "And, you know Mary Sung, of course." Morgan took Sung's small hand with both of his. She smiled up at him.

"Nice to see you again, Mary," he said.

"You too . . . Mr. Ambassador," she said. Her eyes glistened.

"It's nice to meet all of you," Morgan said. "Thank you for coming to meet me."

Pinchon laid a hand on his arm. "You'll want to go to the residence, of course," she said. "Your car and driver are waiting outside. I'll ride with you." She turned to the others. "I'll see the rest of you back at the embassy."

Morgan noticed a tightening of Breedlove's jaw, and a flicker of emotion in his icy blue eyes.

"Oh shit," He thought. *"I haven't even unpacked, and already I sense dissension in the ranks."*

This, though, wasn't the time or place to deal with it. Besides, his body was silently screaming for a cold drink and a long nap after nearly a full day of travel.

"Okay," he said. "I guess I'll see all of you at the embassy tomorrow."

He let Pinchon lead him through the milling crowd

of people there to meet passengers or who were trying to sell trinkets to passengers and those meeting passengers alike.

Inside the terminal, the heat, humidity and odor of oil, sweat, and the spices, flowers and fruit the vendors were hawking had been oppressive. When they exited the double glass doors into the glare of the West African afternoon sun, the heat and humidity soared, instantly soaking Morgan in a coating of uncomfortable sweat that caused his jacket to stick to his underarms and his pants to bunch up at his crotch. The smell at least was bearable thanks to a warm breeze coming from the west. It was, though, just as noisy – a cacophony of voices coming at him from all sides. Morgan clutched his briefcase to his side. In it he carried his Letters of Credence and Commission, which had to be presented to the head of state.

Pinchon made her way expertly through the press of bodies, most of whom only stared in awe at the tall, dark brown man following the tall white woman. They made their way to the curb, an uneven slab of cracked gray concrete that was the same color as the terminal building, without the coating of gray-green mold. Sickly looking green shoots sprouted up from the cracks. Here and there, in little depressions in the sidewalk and the macadam street beyond, were red-orange puddles with grayish scum floating on them.

If the scene inside the terminal could be called chaotic, outside on the bumpy street that had more potholes than macadam, with all manner of vehicles from army trucks to rickety looking jitneys overloaded with passengers carrying everything from children to chickens vying for space, horns blowing and drivers yelling at each other, was beyond chaos. In addition to the vehicles, all being driven at high speed as drivers jockeyed for position, pedestrians, including small children, darted across the street, narrowly missing being crushed by the oncoming vehicles.

They walked along the sidewalk. A line of the colorful jitneys, pickups and jeeps with gaudily painted platforms erected behind the driver's seat, were parked in front of the terminal. Finally, they came to a shiny black 1975 Lincoln Continental Sedan with two metal poles affixed to the front bumper on either side of the rectangular headlights. A tall, well-built black man, who looked like he could be a defensive guard for a professional football team, stood near the front. He was dressed in dark blue trousers that stretched over his muscular thighs, and a white shirt whose sleeves looked like his biceps and chest muscles would burst it at the seams. Square of jaw, with a prominent forehead and close cropped black hair, he had widely spaced eyes that, as Morgan got closer he could see were bloodshot and the whites were yellowish – a sure sign that the man had at some point in his life had malaria, like more than half the population of Naganda.

As Morgan and Pinchon approached, the man snapped to attention. His fleshy lips were stretched in a welcoming smile.

"Mr. Ambassador," she said. "May I introduce you

to George Toko? He's your driver. George has been the ambassador's driver since the embassy first opened, and he's one of the best drivers in Naganda."

"I am best driver in all of West Africa, mama," Toko said simply. "Welcome to Naganda, pa."

Morgan looked at his deputy with a quizzical expression. "Mama? Pa?"

She laughed. "It's an expression of respect here," she said. "People often address their superiors in that manner. I'll admit it takes some getting used to, especially considering that George is ten years older than me. You'll learn not to flinch when you hear it."

"Mr. Ambassador, sah," Toko said. "I'm ready to take you to your residence." He stepped around and opened the rear right passenger door, and stood at attention.

Morgan shrugged. He was being bombarded with unfamiliar cultural norms along with everything else. As he'd learned in the army, though, it was best to relax and let things flow. He got in, placing his briefcase on the floor. Toko closed the door and ran around to open the other passenger door. Pinchon went around and got in next to him. When his passengers were seated, Toko reached in and took a small American flag from the front passenger seat and affixed it to the left pole, and then got behind the wheel and expertly wheeled away from the curb.

As the car began moving, Morgan felt a blast of cold air, and he noticed that the interior of the vehicle had a slight pine smell. He took a deep breath.

Unlike many former British colonies, Naganda had switched the driving pattern upon gaining independence, and drove on the right side of the road, so that its traffic would accord with its neighbors.

Pinchon laughed again. "In your car, in the office, and in your residence are the only places you can get away from the heat and smell. Again, though, you start not to notice it too much after a few days."

Morgan nodded and sat back in the seat, letting his head nestle in the headrest. He also noticed that it was quieter inside the car. He hoped the same would be true of his office and residence. The constant noise could really be distracting, and he didn't think he'd ever become truly accustomed to it. Through the lightly tinted windows of the Lincoln he took in the scenery they passed. The traffic, once they left the airport, was even more chaotic, and included carts drawn by donkeys along with the motorized vehicles. Traffic policemen in dark blue uniforms stood at most of the intersections vainly trying to establish order, but no one paid them any attention. The pedestrian traffic was also heavier, with men carrying heavy loads on their backs or atop their heads, and many women in gaily colored wrap around dresses and headscarves, with even heavier loads on their heads, many also with infants strapped to their waists or backs.

The architecture along the road from the airport was a mixture of colonial buildings, most of gray stone or brick covered in gray-green mold, and huts with thatch or corrugated tin roofs. Many of the huts had little gardens beside them being tended by young girls wearing only skirts, their dark, bare breasts, glistening with sweat, swinging as they worked.

After twenty minutes driving the road angled upward and the buildings thinned out. A few thatch huts stood in the middle of fields with limp, brownish green plants dotting them. Most of the huts had cook fires outside, being tended by young girls or elderly looking women, all with their upper bodies bare. In one vacant field, a group of boys were playing soccer on the uneven ground. They stopped and stared as the black limo passed. Naked infants played in the dirt surrounding the huts. Chickens and sickly looking yellow dogs picked in the piles of garbage that dotted the roadside, scattering as the car neared, only to return to their foraging as soon as it passed.

As the road got steeper, it also wound like a serpent through thick broad leaf trees that formed a canopy over it, plunging it into dark shade.

They came out of the trees near the top of a hill. Ahead, Morgan saw a tall stone wall, topped by concertina wire. Toko turned right onto a gravel surfaced road that led toward a massive iron gate. As they approached, the gate swung inward and a guard, dressed in dark blue, stepped out and stood to the side. A soldier wearing a green field uniform, with an AK-47 over his shoulder stepped out and stood to the other side. As they passed, both men saluted. Morgan's military instincts kicked in. He returned the salutes. Both men smiled broadly. Pinchon smiled and nodded.

Then Morgan turned his attention to the view through the car's front window. They were approaching a sprawling white stone building that looked like several cubes had been randomly set on the hillside and stitched together. The roof was green corrugated iron. The grounds around the building were a profusion of trees and tropical plants, none that Morgan recognized.

Toko expertly wheeled the car around, stopping in front of a large, covered porch with a tile floor. He got out and opened the door for Morgan. Pinchon got out of the other side.

"Welcome to Signal Hill," she said.

"That's a strange name for an ambassador's residence," Morgan said.

"That's the name of this area. This house was the home of the colonial governor. He had a cannon up here that was used to signal whenever the colony had problems or came under attack – or so I'm told. It just seemed right that we keep the tradition by calling the residence by the same name."

More culture to absorb, Morgan thought. It did have a nice ring to it, though.

The massive front door of the residence swung open, and two men and a woman emerged. One man was dressed in the same outfit as Toko, but wearing a white apron around his waist. The other man wore a set of blue overalls. The woman wore a black dress with a starched white collar. They beamed broad smiles of welcome, but remained silent.

Morgan shot a querying look at Pinchon.

"This is your residential staff," she said. She motioned them forward. "This is the new ambassador. Sir, this is Matthew John Nkomo, your cook." The man with the apron bowed. "Mariama Bandu is your housekeeper." The woman curtsied. "And, last but not least, your gardener, William Toko. William is George's younger brother." The gardener bowed.

"Welcome, sah," they said in unison.

"You can sign the new work contracts with them when you come into the embassy next week." Pinchon said. "For now, they're being paid by the embassy admin section. You'll find an information packet in your master bedroom. It has the embassy main switch, my personal number, and other information about Naganda. Unless you wish, we'll leave you to decompress for the weekend and George will pick you up to come into the embassy Monday morning."

"That sounds fine to me," Morgan said. "I am a little bushed from the flight. But, before you go back to the embassy, could I have a private word with you."

"Yes, sir." She turned to Toko. "I'll be a few minutes, George."

The household staff stood aside as Morgan and Pinchon entered. Inside, the place was cool, and the dark wood floors gleamed. He'd been shown photographs of the furniture, and everything was just as the pictures had shown. Later, he would put in some private art work, as well as the official artwork provided by the Arts in Embassy program of the State Department's Foreign Buildings Office. At first glance, though, the place looked fine as it was.

They walked through the entrance foyer and into a cavernous room that had small groupings of settees and chairs with small occasional tables placed around the walls. Off to the right, he knew, was the official dining room and kitchen. To the left were his study, and the bedrooms – the master bedroom, which was his personal living space, and three guest bedrooms.

"Where can we have some privacy?" he asked.

"The study is the first room on the left," she said. "That's where you'll usually do your pull-asides during receptions."

"Sah, would you and madam like a cup of tea or something light to eat?" Nkomo asked.

"I think tea would be fine," Morgan said. "I ate on the plane, so I'm fine until supper."

The cook darted off to the right. Morgan followed Pinchon to the left and into the first door on the left. The study was small, only in comparison to the reception area. He'd seen general's offices that were smaller. It had dark curtains over the window, and thick carpet on the floor. The dark, wood panel walls were as polished as the floor outside. A large oak desk sat on the left, and behind it was a high-back leather chair. Across from the desk were a small sofa, two occasional chairs, and an oval coffee table. Pinchon left the door open. Morgan motioned her to the sofa. He sat on one of the chairs facing her. Almost immediately, Nkomo entered carrying a large, round silver tray containing a silver urn, two teacups with saucers, a sugar bowl and a small container of milk. The cups, saucers and containers were of translucent china and were embossed with the Great Seal of the United States. Nkomo put the tray on the coffee table and quietly withdrew, pulling the door shut as he left.

"What did you want to discus, sir?" Pinchon asked.

"First, when we're in private, can the sir," he said. "I'm David, or Dave, and you're Susan. You and I have to work closely together and trust each other. I find that too much formality can inhibit progress."

"Okay, David it is."

"Good. Now, the other thing," he said. "At the airport, I sensed a little tension between you and Breedlove. What's that all about?"

Her face hardened momentarily, then she took a deep breath. "I'd hoped you wouldn't notice that. It's nothing I can't handle, but I suppose you do need to know. Tom is old school Foreign Service, and considers himself something of an Africa expert. He resents working for a woman – feels that the DCM job is beyond my capability merely because of my gender. He also doesn't think someone without years of experience on the continent should be in a leadership position here."

"I suppose that will include me as well."

Her eyes went wide. "Oh my goodness – how stupid of me not to have thought of that. Now that you mention it though, I suppose that's so. Do you think it'll be a problem?"

"Like you, I don't think it's something I can't handle. I had similar situations when I was in the army. Of course, it's ultimately up to him. If he produces, I really don't care much what he thinks. We'll just have to see. You know, though, that you can come to me if you have a problem you can't deal with on your own."

Her expression softened. "Thanks, David. That's good to know. But, I think I can handle Tom. I grew up with four brothers, two older and two younger. I managed them, and they were a lot tougher than he would ever hope to be."

Chapter Six

Morgan had been even more exhausted than he thought. On Friday, after Susan Pinchon had left the residence, he drank his tea, took a long hot shower, and lay down across the big king sized bed in the master bedroom, and didn't wake up until after seven on Saturday morning.

He spent the rest of the weekend exploring the house and grounds and getting to know the staff – and, more importantly, letting them get to know him. He learned that all three had served every ambassador since the embassy was first opened. None of them were married, and were intensely dedicated to their jobs. After the shock of his arrival, the residence in just two days had become a kind of refuge, a place where he knew he'd be able to get away when the press of his diplomatic business became too much.

Susan Pinchon and George Toko were at the residence at 7:30 Monday morning to take him for his first day in the embassy.

"I hope you had a restful weekend," Pinchon said as the limo exited the compound gate.

"Yes, I did," Morgan replied. "I hadn't realized how tired I was until I lay down on the bed. But, now I'm ready to slay dragons."

"Well, the first dragon we have for you is His Excellency Gideon Simbawashe, the esteemed foreign minister. Jonathan Kabo called me late Friday, and said Simbawashe wants to see you this morning. We'll stop at Jonathan's office first, and then he'll escort us up to the minister's office. By the way, I hope you don't think it presumptuous of me to include myself in your meeting."

"Not at all. I would have insisted you come if you hadn't. I want you to know everything I know. After all, when I'm absent, you have to act in my stead. Will we be going to the embassy first, or the ministry?"

"We'll go straight to the ministry."

Morgan didn't have a lot of experience in such matters, but he didn't recall the foreign minister meeting his ambassador so early after his arrival when he served as the number two in Dagastan. Then again, he wasn't as familiar yet with African customs as he hoped eventually to become.

He decided that trying to figure things out in the absence of more in depth knowledge was a waste of his mental energy, so he just sat back to enjoy the ride and take in the scenery. He also was cataloguing landmarks as they drove. Another habit from his army days – he liked to be aware of the terrain in which he operated.

Like many West Africans, Nagandans are early risers. Once they were through the wooded area and into the settlements on the outskirts of Mabuntu, they encountered women on their way to market with goods for sale or on their way to gather wood, young boys driving scrawny cattle in search of grazing ground, children fortunate enough to have parents who could afford the fees on their way to school, and the noisy traffic that darted to and fro seeking a way around the many barriers that appeared often without warning in the roadway.

About halfway back toward the airport, Toko took a sharp left onto a street that was a bit better kept up than the rest of the routes, and entered the city proper. An armed soldier at the intersection watched them idly, but kept his AK-47 cradled across his chest.

The city streets were if anything even more crowded than the country roads, with a large number of military vehicles mixed in with the civilian traffic.

They passed the sprawling City Market, a large normally vacant field which in the early morning every day was covered with rows and piles of everything one could imagine, including used clothing, freshly butchered meat, fruits and vegetables, carved wooden furniture, and metal toys made from beer cans that had been cut opened and flattened. Early morning shoppers weaved in and out among the wildly gesticulating and shouting merchants, and mangy dogs sniffed around the perimeter seeking the rare tossed-away treat.

Beyond the open market were buildings left over from the colonial era. Shops, workshops, restaurants and office buildings lined the bumpy street. Most of the shops, selling clothing and sundry items, were owned by Lebanese, a non-African community that had been present in Naganda from the time it was colonized by the English in the mid-1700s. Most of the buildings were constructed of gray stone. A tall red-brick two-story building near the center of the city was the exception. The Nagandan Central Bank, formerly the British Bank of Commerce, was the only building that didn't look faded and worn. Most of Naganda's government buildings, including State House, where the head of state's offices were located, and the foreign ministry, were located on the north end of town, separated from the rest of the city by barricades across the street, which were manned by scowling young soldiers brandishing AK-47s and RPGs.

At the sight of the red, white, and blue national standard flying on the Lincoln's bumper, the soldiers flung aside the barricade and let Morgan's vehicle pass. The foreign ministry was located not far from where they entered the restricted area. A four-story gray stone building, it sat inside a walled compound guarded by more green-clad soldiers. Toko drove into the compound, following the curved drive around and underneath a *porte cochere* at the front entrance. An elderly man opened the entrance door as Morgan got out of the car. He held the door for Morgan and Pinchon to enter, and motioned them to a desk opposite the door. He then closed the door and rushed behind the desk, pushing a dusty ledger toward them.

"Please, sah," he said. "You and madam sign visitor book. Someone will be down to escort you."

Brushing at the dust, Morgan entered his name and organization on the first blank page. Pinchon signed underneath him. They looked around for a place to sit. There were two scuffed leather sofas across the room, but they were, like the ledger, covered in dust. They decided to stand.

After about five minutes, Cedric Mboko came through a set of double doors to the left of the reception desk. He smiled broadly as he approached, his hand extended. "Excellence, Ma'am," he said. "Mr. Kabo is expecting you. If you will please, follow me."

After perfunctory handshakes, he spun on his heels and started at a brisk pace toward the door. They had to hustle to keep up with him. Through the door, they entered a dusty, dimly lit corridor that stretched off to the right and left. Doors lined the wall to their front, most of them closed. Except for the sound of their footfalls, though, the corridor was silent. They passed an elevator with metal grate doors that had a crudely lettered 'Out of Service' sign wired to the grate, and came to an opening in the wall with wooden steps leading upward.

"I must apologize," Mboko said. "The elevator never works, and Mr. Kabo's office is on the third floor. The minister's office is on the fourth floor."

Pinchon looked at Morgan and shrugged.

"My once a week visits here are my main exercise," she said wryly.

By the time they'd reached the third floor in the dusty stairwell Morgan felt a coating of grit on his face and hands. He knew the grit would be embedded deeply in the fabric of his clothing as well, and wondered about the quality of local dry cleaning. At the third floor, Mboko pushed open a door, leading them into a corridor that was better illuminated than the ground floor had been. He walked to the left and to the end of the corridor, stopping and knocking on the door.

There was a muffled 'come in.' Mboko pushed open the door, and stepped aside to let Morgan and Pinchon enter. It was a small room with a large woman sitting behind a small desk, two stiff-back wooden chairs, and a small sofa at an angle in front of the desk.

"The American ambassador to see Mr. Kabo," Mboko said.

Without acknowledging them, the woman rose and entered a door to her right. After a moment, she came back out.

"He'll be with you momentarily," she said and resumed her seat behind the desk, again ignoring them.

Morgan looked at the dust-laden sofa, and decided to sit on one of the chairs. Piinchon smiled and copied him. Mboko frowned, and took out a white handkerchief and dusted off one of the cushions on the sofa and sat. They sat in companionable silence for the next ten minutes. Morgan was accustomed to waiting, and he was pleased to note that she also didn't seem discomfited by the delay. Mboko, though, continually fidgeted, looking at the gold Rolex on his thin wrist from time to time and then glancing at the door to his boss's office.

Finally, the door swung open, and Kabo stood there in his dark suit, the dark stains still apparent at the armpits.

"Mr. Ambassador, Miss Pinchon, please, do come in," as if they'd just arrived, rather than being left cooling their heels for ten minutes.

Kabo's office was spartanly furnished. A simple gray metal desk, behind which sat a scuffed, leather-backed chair. Two similar chairs sat in front of the desk, and a plain wooden chair sat off to the side. On the wall behind his desk was a large framed photo of a youngish looking man in the green field uniform of the Nagandan army. The man's face was dark brown, with broad brows, and an unsmiling expression. The walls were otherwise bare. A three-shelf bookcase sat in the corner. It contained several dusty green notebooks. Morgan couldn't read the penciled labels. Kabo motioned them to the chairs in front of his desk and sat in his own chair. Mboko took the plain chair. On Kabo's desk was a single sheet of paper. He fussed with it, aligning it precisely with the desk's edge.

After aligning the paper to his satisfaction, Kabo

looked up at Morgan. "I hope, excellency that you had a restful weekend."

"I did," Morgan said. "But, now I'm anxious to get to work."

"Ah, yes, but you understand that until you have presented your credentials to His Excellency, the head of state, you are forbidden to participate in public events? Speaking of which, you did remember to bring your letter of credence and other documents?"

Morgan removed the documents from his briefcase and passed them to Kabo, who spent several minutes reading them. He then nodded.

"Excellent," he said. "Everything appears to be in order. Your diplomatic identification card will be issued within the next three days, and we will schedule the ceremony for presentation of your credentials as soon as possible." He pushed the documents aside and stood. "Now, if you will come with me, we'll go to the foreign minister's office."

Morgan, Pinchon, and Mboko followed him to the stairwell. While Morgan and Pinchon followed Kabo upstairs, Mboko went down. "I'll meet the two of you in the lobby when you're finished," he said over his shoulder as he went around the corner.

On the top floor, they came out of the stairwell into a broad corridor that, instead of uneven wood slats like the others, was covered in a thick, red, yellow and green carpet. At the end of the carpet, a large Nagandan flag, with its red, yellow, and green stripes, hung from a brass pole. They walked toward the flag, ending their journey in front of double wooden doors in dark mahogany. Kabo rapped lightly on the doors, and then pushed them open. He stepped aside and motioned Morgan and Pinchon in.

The foreign minister's reception area was as large as Kabo's entire office, reception area included. The secretary, a young, medium brown-skinned woman with her hair done in tight braids on her oval head, a bit too much lipstick on her thick lips, and her ample breasts nearly spilling out of the plunging neckline of the bright green dress she wore, sat behind a large dark brown wooden desk with brass fittings. She looked up and welcomed them with a broad smile.

"Ah, excellencies, please be seated." She pointed to a large, four-cushion leather sofa to the left of the door. "His excellency the minister will be with you shortly."

She then stood and disappeared through a door to her right, reappearing a moment later.

"May I offer you coffee or tea?" she asked.

Morgan declined. Not knowing how long the minister might keep him waiting, he didn't want to risk having to go to the toilet – in fact, considering the condition of the building that he'd seen so far he didn't want to risk having to use their facilities under any circumstances. Pinchon also declined, but Kabo asked for a cup of tea. The secretary turned to a cabinet behind her desk and poured dark, steaming liquid into a fine porcelain cup. She put the cup on a tray, added small containers of milk and sugar, and gave it to Kabo. He poured most of the milk and four teaspoons of sugar into the tea, put the tray on the coffee table at his right and, loudly slurping, began drinking.

After three or four minutes, the small door opened. A large man, his shoulders almost as wide as the door opening, and his head less than an inch from the top of the door, dressed in a dark blue, finely tailored suit, pearl gray shirt, and red tie, stood there. He had a square head, thick, tightly curled hair, black, but flecked at the temples with gray, a thick beard and mustache, a wide nose, thick lips, and close-set eyes with yellowed whites and bloodshot. He looked like someone Morgan wouldn't want to meet in a dark alley.

"Mr. Ambassador," he said in a booming voice. "Please, come in."

With Pinchon and Kabo trailing, Morgan followed the man into his office.

It was even more sumptuous than the secretary's office. The desk, made of some deep black wood, was six feet wide and four feet deep. He had a set of pens that Morgan was sure were gold, prominently displayed in the center. His chair was high-backed, carved of the same wood as the desk, with velvet pads on the armrests and seat. Two smaller versions of his chair sat in front of the desk. To the left were another version of the chair, and two small sofas covered in the same velvet fabric as his chair. A black wood oval coffee table sat in front of the sofas. On it was a silver tray containing a plate of cookies, a silver urn, and four porcelain cups. To the side were containers of sugar and milk. Silver spoons lay next to the four cups.

"Excellency, may I present the American ambassador, David Morgan. You know, of course, Miss Pinchon," Kabo said. "Ambassador . . . Miss Pinchon, His Excellency Gabriel Simbawashe, foreign minister of the Republic of Naganda."

Simbawashe's huge hand swallowed Morgan's as they shook. He motioned him to one of the sofas nearest the large chair. He then shook Pinchon's hand, taking hers in both of his and leering down at her. She sat next to Morgan on the sofa.

Simbawashe then sat, and for a long interval merely looked at Morgan, his square, dark face expressionless. Morgan looked back at him, equally without expression. Finally, Simbawashe smiled as if the two of them had shared some secret information.

"Ambassador Morgan," he said. Welcome to Naganda. I trust my staff has been taking good care of you?"

Morgan nodded. "Yes, Mr. Kabo and his man . . . Cedric . . . met me at the airport. I have no complaints."

He knew at this point that he should be making small talk about how happy he was to be in Naganda, how beautiful the country was, and other mindless, meaningless junk. But, he hadn't decided whether or not he was pleased, and so far, what he'd seen of the country had been anything but beautiful. Besides, he wasn't very good at idle chitchat. Simbawashe didn't seem to notice.

"Very good – I'm happy to hear that." The big head slowly bobbed up and down. "We will try to arrange your first meeting with the head of state as soon as possible. In the meantime, I trust you will honor protocol and avoid public appearances or public statements."

"I understand," Morgan said. "I have quite enough work inside the embassy itself to keep me busy for a while."

Simbawashe leaned forward, raising a large dark hand, his index finger pointing at the ceiling. "There is one other thing, ambassador," he said. "Your predecessor had an unfortunate habit of occasionally making public statements critical of our government – comments on how we should be doing things. We consider this to be unwarranted involvement in our domestic affairs, and would hope you'll not fall prey to the same disease."

Morgan had no doubt that at some point he would make a statement – either public or directly to the government – that would piss them off. That was part of his job description as American ambassador. He wasn't sure, though, whether he should make an issue of it before he'd even presented his credentials.

"Mr. Minister," he said. "When I was a little boy growing up in Maryland, my grandmother always told me that I should never try to teach a dog how to suck eggs. I've always followed her advice."

The minister's brow furrowed. "I, uh, do not understand what you mean, ambassador," he said. Then he scowled. "Is this some kind of American insult?"

Morgan laughed softly. "Not all, minister. It's an old folk saying that roughly means you shouldn't try to teach people things that they know better than you do. I have no desire or intention to tell you how to run your government. That's something for Nagandans to decide."

Simbawashe looked confused. Morgan knew he was trying to decipher the meaning of what he'd just said. *"Good luck with that,"* he thought. He'd managed to leave the door open to multiple interpretations of his response. The only part that was, to him, unambiguous, was the part about not telling the locals how to run their government. He would comment when he thought it necessary to advance U.S. interests, but, he was only a temporary visitor, and had always felt that outsiders stepped over the line when they tried to tell other people how to run things.

Finally, Simbawashe smiled – if only faintly. "Very well, then," he said. "I look forward to working with you."

Charles Ray

Chapter Seven

Morgan and Pinchon were at the embassy by 9:30. A five story building located on Independence Boulevard near the center of town, the Embassy of the United States of America was one of the first foreign diplomatic establishments opened in newly independent Naganda. Constructed of granite taken from a quarry in the country's interior, the once white building had grayed with age, and it was decided not to repaint it. The American flag flew from a diagonal pole over the front entrance. Two of the embassy guards stood to either side of the door. A Nagandan soldier stood on the sidewalk to the right, his dark brown eyes scanning the sidewalk in both directions, his dark face emotionless.

She escorted him through the front entrance, and introduced him to the young Marine corporal standing duty at Post One. They then proceeded to perhaps the only elevator in Mabuntu that worked. With the sound of cables creaking, the elevator took them to the fourth floor, where Mary Sung waited with a cup of coffee in hand and a smile on her face.

"Welcome again, Mr. Ambassador," she said, handing Morgan the coffee. "I made it just like you like it."

He took a sip. She had indeed – just as she'd done for him in Dagastan. "Thanks, Mary. This is delicious."

"Let's get you settled in your office, Mr. Ambassador," Pinchon said. "I assume you'll want to start getting filled in on what's happening?"

"I have a read packet on your desk," Mary Sung said.

"Great," Morgan said. "Give me a few minutes to scan that, and then I'll want to start speaking with the staff. I will, of course, visit each of them in their individual offices, but in the interest of time, maybe I'll do the first meetings in my office."

"Sure thing," Sung said. "Just tell me who and when you want them."

"Let me introduce you to my secretary," Pinchon said. She pointed to a short, chubby redhead who was standing aside from them with an expectant look on her freckled face. "This is Peggy Marks."

The redhead reached out a pudgy hand. "Please to meet you, Mr. Ambassador," she said. "Welcome to Naganda."

Her grip was firm and dry, and her smile was genuine. Morgan breathed a sigh of relief. At least the front office seemed in order. I thanked them all and went into his office, the second door along the wall on the right, the first being the door to his deputy's office. It was spacious, although not nearly as large as the foreign minister's office. A large executive desk on the right, with the American flag on his right and the blue, starred, ambassador flag on his left, on brass stands behind him, a tall, glass-fronted bookcase containing a few reference books, and a nice leather backed chair. An old manual typewriter sat on a table to his right. Directly in front of his door were a leather sofa and two leather cushioned chairs grouped around a rectangular coffee table. The walls were bare, but as soon as his stuff arrived, he'd decorate them with his commission and a few personal photos. After the oppressive heat outside, the cool air made it possible for him to ignore the persistent hum of the air conditioning system.

He removed his jacket and hung it on a rack in the right rear corner, and sat behind his desk. For a moment, he just leaned back in the chair, looking up at the beige ceiling, letting it all soak in.

Then, he took a deep breath and opened the large brown folder in the center of his desk. Sung had been thorough. On top of the stack of papers he slid out of the folder was a roster of the embassy staff, by section and job title. He had no doubt she'd also done research into the strengths and weaknesses of each of them. He'd ask her about that later. Next was the embassy phone list, both a full letter-sized sheet and a small laminated card for his wallet with key numbers. He put these two to the side for further study.

The rest of the documents consisted of a list of pending issues, the embassy reporting schedule, and housekeeping documents, such as an application for the embassy commissary association, an application for his embassy access badge, a country information sheet, and the notification that his household effects and unaccompanied baggage had been shipped and would arrive within the month.

He was reading the country information sheet to see if it contained anything he hadn't already been told during his briefings in Washington when Mary Sung walked in.

"Mr. Ambassador, Maya Livingstone, the Peace Corps country director would like to speak with you. I'd ordinarily have her pretty low on the list of people for you to see, but she says she's leaving for an up-country trip today and might not be back for a few days."

Morgan hadn't thought about prioritizing his meetings, although Carlton Raine was uppermost on his mind. Other than a contractor from the Office for Foreign Disaster Assistance, or OFDA, who handled distribution of the food aid from the U.S. Government, Raine, and the defense attaché, the Peace Corps country director was the only other non-State Department member of his country team. With ten Peace Corps volunteers scattered about the countryside, he imagined she spent a lot of time on the road, so it would not be convenient to put off meeting her.

"Go ahead and send her in, Mary," he said. "I might as well get started meeting my team."

Maya Livingstone was young, tall, with an attractive round face and eyes that were light brown – almost golden – and that always seemed to be smiling. She had skin the color of coffee with a heavy infusion of cream, and wore her hair braided in the local style. She also dressed in the local style, with a colorful yellow and green one-piece dress wrapped around her body, accenting her slightly thick waist and ample hips. Morgan rose to greet her as she entered.

"Miss Livingstone, thanks for dropping in to see me."

Her grip was warm and strong, and she looked him directly in the eye.

"My pleasure, Mr. Ambassador," she said in a cultured southern accent. "Sorry for barging into your schedule like this, but I'm on my way to visit volunteers upcountry, and might not be back for a couple of days. Oh, and please, call me Maya."

He ushered her to the sofa in the corner, and then took the chair facing her.

"Not a problem . . . Maya," Morgan said. "I know your time is short, so why don't we skipped the pleasantries and formalities, and you tell me about yourself and your program?"

The eldest daughter of a Baptist preacher, Maya was a native of Atlanta, Georgia. She had received her B.A. in English Literature from Spelman College, a private college for black women in Atlanta, and had applied for a job with the Peace Corps immediately after graduation. After doing several jobs at headquarters for three years, she'd been assigned to Naganda as country director, with ten volunteers under her supervision.

The program in Naganda was pretty typical, though small. The ten volunteers were scattered about the country, mostly working in isolated rural villages on such projects as water sanitation, rudimentary health care, and English teaching. The teaching projects were quite popular, because, despite being a British colony for over 100 years, students in the rural areas only got the most basic English language instruction, and seldom heard it spoken in their homes. As a consequence, rural people were at a disadvantage in the capital where English was not only the official government language, but the language of commerce as well.

"Volunteers are here for an eighteen month tour," she said. "And, they seldom get into the city – maybe once every six to eight weeks. There's hardly any electricity in most villages, and no phone service, so they're pretty cut off from civilization – if you call what we have here in Mabuntu civilization. Anyway, I try to get around to each one of them at least once a month."

"That must keep you pretty busy," Morgan said. She smiled in agreement. "Look, I'd like to visit some of your projects after I've settled in. Could that be arranged?"

"I suppose it could. Let me take a look at what we're doing and see what we can set up. I do know the villagers would be ecstatic at a visit from the American ambassador."

They shook hands again, and Morgan wished her a safe trip. When she'd gone, he asked Mary Sung to have Carlton Raine come down.

The agency man, dressed in a dusty green safari outfit, the pants with extra pockets on the legs, showed up in his door minutes later.

"You wanted to see me, boss?" he asked cheerfully.

"Yeah, Blood," Morgan said. "Come on in and park it."

Raine sat on the sofa, his long legs stretched out to the side of the coffee table, and his arm draped over the arm.

"How'd your meeting with his nibs the foreign minister go?" he asked after Morgan had seated himself in the chair opposite.

Morgan gave him a summary. Raine doubled over laughing when he got to the part about 'dogs sucking eggs.' "I think he's probably still trying to figure that one out," Morgan said. "Now, though, tell me what I *really* need to know about this place."

"Same old Dave Morgan – can the small talk, and

get right down to business. Okay, Mr. Ambassador, I'll give you the basic lecture. Take careful notes, because there'll be a test later."

Raine gave him brief biographical sketches of Musa Gweru, the head of Naganda's military junta, and Gideon Banda, his uncle, and head of intelligence and military services. Gweru, he said, had not previously shown any inclination to politics, and had probably been pressured by his army colleagues to be the coup leader for that reason. His uncle, on the other hand, was reputed to have ambitions, but hadn't been able to amass enough of a following. Joshua Saidu, the ousted leader, was living in exile in his mansion on the outskirts of the capital. Gweru had decided not to take any kind of punitive action against the former despot, Raine said, which had earned him points with the international community, but was likely to come back to bite him in the ass, because Saidu and some of his supporters, most notably former military chief Julius Bongo, were rumored to be working with the Chinese to make a comeback. The Chinese, Raine pointed out, were a factor that had to be watched carefully. Latecomers in this part of Africa, they were alternating between supporting wars of national revolution, and enticing local leaders with no-strings-attached aid projects and loans. Raine hadn't been able to get a specific handle on what the Chinese were up to in Naganda. Like his military counterpart, the defense attaché, his orders from Washington were to focus on the Soviets. The Russians in Naganda had been supporters of the Saidu regime, but had gone along with the rest of the international community and given tepid support to Gweru's junta. Some of his sources, though, were telling Raine that the true beneficiary of Soviet support was Gweru's uncle.

"You've learned a lot in a short time," Morgan said. "But, what does it all mean?"

"I wish the hell I knew. As if the political situation's not convoluted enough, there are reports that some geologist from England thinks there are oil deposits in Chiveru land. Some engineers from Petrolux Petroleum were here in Mabuntu last week, but have since disappeared, and I can't get a line on them."

Morgan recognized the company name. One of the largest oil companies in the U.S., with interests around the world, it had a reputation of moving into undeveloped areas ahead of the competition, getting sweetheart deals that effectively allowed it to monopolize the market, and raking in millions – little of which benefited the inhabitants of the area.

"That's all we need," Morgan said. "Russians and Chinese pulling the strings of the various factions, and a big oil company to further stir the pot. Keep me posted on what you find out."

"Happy to. If you want *everything*, you'll need to come up to my space on the fifth floor. There's stuff I can't bring down here."

"Sure thing. I'll have Mary work out a schedule."

"No need for that," Raine said. "You can come up anytime. If I'm not there, my analyst will be."

Morgan liked the way he and Raine had slipped easily back into the relationship they'd enjoyed in Dagastan. He promised to come up later to look at the station's read files, and Raine promised to show him the best and safest places in Mabuntu to eat and drink.

Morgan looked at his watch. It was nearly noon. His stomach was starting to growl. He mentioned it to Mary Sung, who suggested he eat at the embassy cafeteria in the basement. The food, she assured him, was passable, and it would give the embassy community, especially the embassy's Foreign Service National, or FSN employees, a chance to see the new ambassador.

Because his access badge hadn't been issued, she first escorted him to the security office on the first floor, near Post One, where his picture was taken, and a laminated badge attached to a chain, which allowed him to wear it around his neck, but easily remove it when necessary, was issued. She then escorted him to the basement which contained the medical unit, warehouse for office supplies, the copy room, and the cafeteria. The cafeteria was a large room in the rear that opened onto a sunken courtyard enclosed by the building on one side, and a ten foot high, razor wire topped metal fence on the other three. There were several tables with big beach umbrellas set on poles in the center dotted around the courtyard, and several groups of mostly FSNs were occupying them. Other local employees and some of the American staff were seated at tables inside.

The place had a sweetish smell, not at all unpleasant. Morgan asked Sung's recommendation on what to eat. She suggested the groundnut stew with rice. Groundnuts, or peanuts, are ground up into a liquid version of peanut butter and meat, in this case chicken, is cooked in the sauce along with local vegetables and peppers. This concoction is poured over a mound of rice. Morgan ordered the stew, with fried plantains and a syrupy orange soda. The first spoon of stew burned his mouth, but he withstood it, and subsequent spoonsful went down with ease. His experience with Thai peppers, when he visited Bangkok from Vietnam, had taught him to love them. It has also taught him not to try to ease the first burn by drinking liquid. Rather, a bit of plain rice will absorb the oils, and fairly quickly soothe the burning sensation.

After lunch, he and Sung took the stairs back to the fourth floor and his office. He had two more people that were on his 'must-see' list, the political counselor and the defense attaché, and he debated the order in which he should see them. He finally decided on talking to the attaché first. For one thing, he felt his meeting with Brennan would be more pleasant, and for another, he wanted to send a clear signal to Breedlove of where Morgan thought he ranked in the food chain.

He stuck his head out and asked Sung to call Colonel Brennan and see if he was available. The response came back quickly – 'he's on his way up.' The defense attaché office was on the first floor behind gray metal doors. A space that was, in its own way, as secure as the agency space on the fifth floor.

Five minutes later, Colonel Liam Brennan, in his green dress uniform complete with rows of colorful ribbons over his left breast, topped by the Combat Infantryman's Badge and a parachute badge, appeared in Morgan's door.

"Mr. Ambassador, you wanted to see me?" he asked, standing at ease in the door and waiting for Morgan to invite him to enter.

Morgan waved him in and pointed at the sofa. "Yes, Colonel Brennan," he said. "Just an informal chat to allow me to get to know you and your operation better. Please, have a seat."

Brennan sat, his knees together, and his back ramrod straight. The twinkle, though, was still in his eyes.

"When you appeared in your full uniform like that," Morgan said. "I was almost attempted to come to attention and salute." He smiled to show that he was mainly joking – but, only partially. He still at times reverted to his military background.

Brennan laughed. "I'm all decked out today because I have to attend a passing out ceremony of new recruits at Nagandan army HQ. Sorry I didn't wear it for your arrival, but I'd been upcountry in an area where it's not a good idea to go in uniform, and didn't have time to change and get to the airport."

Morgan was tempted to ask why there were areas that an American military uniform wasn't a good idea, but decided to save that discussion for another time when he could more fully delve into it. For now, he just wanted to take the man's measure, and at the same time, let himself be seen as the man in charge of the embassy. He didn't think the latter would be a problem for an army officer who was fully indoctrinated in the concept of chain of command.

"No problem," he said. "I know how that can be sometimes. I don't want to take too much of your time, so why don't you tell me a bit about yourself and what your office is doing here."

Brennan relaxed, and leaned forward, his hands on his knees. "Well, there's not much to tell about me," he said. "I'm from Texas originally – a little ranch near Laredo. When I graduated from high school, I decided I wanted to see the world beyond Texas, so I enlisted. That was twenty-two years ago. After four years enlisted service, I attended officer candidate school at Fort Benning – that's in Georgia – and after getting my commission, I was assigned to the Twenty-Fourth Infantry Division in Germany. I spent two years in Augsburg, and was posted back to Benning, where I served for four years as a tactical officer in jump school. Then, I did three years with the Eighty-Second Airborne Division at Fort Bragg, North Carolina. In '66, I was assigned to the First Cav in Vietnam. I came back and did the infantry career course, and back to Vietnam where I was assigned to the First Infantry Division just in time for the Tet Offensive of '68. After serving in the Big Red One, I went to Command and General Staff College at Fort Leavenworth, Kansas, and then applied for attaché duty. I've been doing that ever since. This is my third tour. My other assignments were Kenya and Mozambique." He paused, his smile broadening. "This, though, is one of the strangest attaché assignments anyone could have. The Nagandans don't have much of an army to speak of, just about six battalions, mostly infantry, and they have no external enemies to deal with. My main objective here is to keep an eye on Ivan. The Soviets have been really active in the region lately, and Washington wants to know what they're up to."

"What are the Russians doing with an army as small as this one?" Morgan asked.

"That's the really strange thing – nothing really. Most of their contact is with the politicians. Lately, though, they seem to be paying more attention to the Chicoms. In the last year, the Chinese presence here has ticked up significantly."

"What's here that would interest the Chinese?"

"The same things they're interested in all over Africa – resources. Naganda has diamonds, gold, and titanium. We – Americans and Brits, that is – control the titanium through British-American Rutile, but our Chinese friends have been pushing for a share of the pie. They're also doing aid projects, roads and buildings, mostly in and around the capital. Like the Russians, they seem mostly interested in the politicians. Since Gweru and his boys took over, both have been courting them heavily."

Morgan made a mental note to do more research on Naganda's resource situation, and get a handle on whoever was playing in that field. BAR, as the rutile mining operation was known, topped his list of outside interests to look into as soon as he could legitimately work outside the embassy.

"That's all very interesting," he said. "I imagine it keeps you pretty busy. I'd like a more detailed briefing in the coming days." Then, he asked the question that had to be dealt with. "How are your relations with the station?"

"Not bad. We coordinate closely, and keep in our respective lanes. The new guy, Raine, is easy to work with, and unlike his predecessor, he keeps me fully informed of what he's doing."

Morgan wasn't surprised. He knew Raine, and had judged Brennan to be equally professional. It seemed that his intelligence team, at least, was humming smoothly. He thanked Brennan for his time and promised to come down to the attaché offices to meet the rest of the staff and get a fuller briefing as soon as it was convenient.

Next on his list was the political counselor, Thomas Breedlove. He didn't want to judge the man too harshly just on the basis of the brief observation at the airport, but he also trusted his ability to read people, and Breedlove struck him as a potential problem. It would be a challenge to keep that potential from becoming a reality. He asked his secretary to have Breedlove come to his office.

Charles Ray

Chapter Eight

Breedlove appeared in his office, his coat free of wrinkles and his tie perfectly knotted. Without waiting for Morgan to invite him in, he walked in and sat on the sofa.

"Mr. Ambassador," he said in an East Coast accent. "Again, welcome to Naganda. I imagine you've been busy getting read in?"

"Yeah, I've been getting information through a fire hose." Morgan wanted to put the man at ease. It would be easier to learn what he needed to know about him if he was relaxed and not on guard. "Why don't you open your spigot and tell me about yourself, and some of the key issues you're working on."

Morgan sat relaxed in the chair facing Breedlove, a half smile on his face.

The political counselor sat upright, facing Morgan with a face devoid of emotion, except for something in his eyes that Morgan was having difficulty reading.

"I'm from a small suburb of Boston," he said. "I graduated from Yale in 1963, and immediately joined the Foreign Service through the examination process. I've served only in Africa, with two tours in the Department, there in the Bureau of African Affairs. As to the issues we're working on, we are of course monitoring the human rights situation, and trying to assess the direction Gweru's government will go in the future."

Morgan felt heat in his cheeks. Breedlove was doing what many of his ilk did, those who had served exclusively in one area of the world, and spoke of it in brief uninformative terms, either assuming their listener knew what they were talking about, or were deliberately being obtuse. Either motive angered him. But, he wasn't quite ready to respond to the man in anger. He would give him ample opportunity to clean up his act, or else he'd give him enough rope for a good old fashioned hanging.

"What parts of Africa have you served in?" he asked.

"I've done political jobs in Accra, Nairobi, Addis, Maputo, Durban, Joburg, and Pretoria."

He'd done it again – instead of saying Ghana, Kenya, Ethiopia, Mozambique, and three cities in South Africa, he'd used the city names, and in the case of Addis Ababa and Johannesburg, the slang versions popular with the Africa hands. Morgan decided to show him that, despite having never served on the continent before, he had done his homework.

"Looks like you've pretty much covered the continent," he said. "How do you compare a place like Ethiopia with South Africa?"

"Well, frankly, South Africa is the better administered of the two – apartheid notwithstanding. If the Afrikaners ever learn to share power with the blacks, that country will be a powerhouse on the continent."

A neutral answer at best. In Morgan's view, the efficiency of South Africa was akin to the efficiency of Nazi Germany as long as the white minority kept the black majority under the iron rule of segregation. That, though, was an issue for someone else to deal with – his objective was to get a handle on Naganda.

"How about giving me a bit more detail on the issues you're reporting on here."

Breedlove looked puzzled. He studied his carefully manicured fingernails for a few seconds before answering. "Uh, well," he said. "I recently completed an analysis of Naganda's UN voting record, contrasting the current regime with the last – especially with regards to their support for our positions."

Now, it was Morgan who looked puzzled. While such a report might be of interest to some policy wonk in Washington who studied such things, he failed to see how it contributed to their understanding of the country's current situation, or how it advanced U.S. national security interests.

"What was Washington's reaction to that report?"

he asked.

"There's been no reaction," Breedlove said. His look of puzzlement turned to one of distaste. "The cable's been held up by the DCM. *She* seems to think I should spend more time looking into what the Chinese are up to here."

From what he'd heard so far, Morgan agreed. His opinion of Susan Pinchon went up a notch.

"That would seem to make sense to me," he said. "Especially given the Chinese-Soviet competition for dominance of the Communist world."

"But, there's nothing in Naganda for them to compete over."

The man was either monumentally arrogant, or monumentally stupid, Morgan thought. The two old adversaries didn't need a lot over which to compete, but Naganda had an abundant supply of titanium, which was important not only to the American and British defense sectors, but the Russians and Chinese, and probably a few other countries as well. Morgan decided to be charitable, and attribute Breedlove's ignorance to the tunnel vision that narrow specialists develop – able to see only their area of expertise to the exclusion of the rest of the universe.

"Nonetheless," he said. "I think it would be worth looking into. You might be surprised at what you find if you start turning over rocks."

"Well, if you insist." Breedlove's tone was petulant and condescending at the same time. "But, I think it would be best if I sent my completed cables directly to you, rather than routing them through the DCM."

It wasn't lost on Morgan that Breedlove refused to refer to Susan Pinchon by name as was the Foreign Service custom. Whatever it was about her that bugged him was really deep seated. That, though, wasn't of concern – not initially at least. For how, what Morgan had to do was establish his way of doing things, and in no uncertain terms.

"All paperwork coming from the staff to me *will* go through the DCM," he said coldly. "And, that includes reporting cables."

"But, she doesn't know all that much about the politics of Africa," Breedlove protested.

"I think you're mistaken in that. Furthermore, Susan is the manager of the embassy and the country team, and I for one trust her judgment."

Breedlove opened his mouth as if to speak, but then he snapped it shut, and closed his eyes.

He opened his eyes and mouth at the same time. "Very well, Mr. Ambassador," he said. "It will be as you wish."

Chapter Nine

Ten days after his arrival in Naganda, Morgan's credential presentation ceremony was finally scheduled. Thursday morning, July 13, 10:30 a.m. the fancy parchment notice from the foreign ministry read.

Finally, he could come out of the isolation of an ambassador without recognition by the receiving state, and start getting to know the country.

The Embassy's July Fourth reception, because it included government officials and the foreign diplomatic community, was presided over by Susan Pinchon as charge d'affaires. Morgan stayed in the residence, fuming that the delay in presenting his credentials had prevented his participation. The embassy staff, however, had come to the residence after the official reception ended, and held a private ceremony to formally welcome him as their new soon-to-be official ambassador. He'd made a brief impromptu speech, recognizing all of them for their hard work and dedication, and ensuring them that he would continue to support their endeavors to advance U.S. interests, while at the same time helping the people of Naganda guide their country to greater democracy, respect for rule of law, and a better record on human rights. The senior local staff present all applauded at those words, while the American staff merely nodded in agreement, but looked skeptical.

Not that the time waiting had been wasted. He'd gotten to know most of the embassy staff, American and Nagandan alike, visiting them in their offices and workspaces – including visits to the mechanics in the embassy motor pool and the custodial staff in the broom closet in the basement they used as a break room when they weren't sweeping, wiping, or mopping the building. Both groups were ecstatic over his visits, having never been visited by anyone from the front office before.

His administrative officer, a dour native of Oregon named Albert Pembroke, gave him good news during their meeting. Lee Kennedy had been assigned as his regional security officer, and was scheduled to arrive with his wife and daughter on July 12. Morgan was amazed at the fact that the Department's personnel system could, when it wanted to, actually move expeditiously. Hector Gonzalez, originally from Las Vegas, was the embassy consular officer. A little on the chunky side, with a round face and a perpetual smile, at first glance people tended to under estimate him. Within five minutes of meeting him, though, Morgan learned that the former casino blackjack dealer had a master's degree in mathematics and spoke six languages. He could have, had he desired, chosen the political career track, but he told Morgan that he preferred dealing with people, and as a consular officer he had more opportunities to do that .

Morgan combined his arrival physical exam with his initial interview of the embassy nurse practitioner. Rebecca Storm was a tall, skinny redhead with a generous dusting of freckles on her oval face. The Oklahoman wore her hair pulled tightly upwards and shaped into a long tuft on the top of her head that looked like a thin bowling pin, or a handle projecting out of her skull. In addition to giving him a clean bill of health, she informed him that the embassy family was also in surprisingly good health – physically at least – although, she did worry a bit about Tom Breedlove, who she thought was too tightly wound. Morgan said he *did* seem to have a bad case of 'stick up the ass' disease, which sent the nurse into a fit of choking laughter. She informed him that she was glad to see that the new ambassador didn't have that illness.

His most interesting encounter, though, was with Richard Weir, the embassy's public affairs officer and spokesman. An officer of the International Communication Agency (ICA), which from 1953 to 1977 had been known as the U.S. Information Agency (USIA), Weir was from Monterey, California, and had graduated from the University of Southern California with a degree in mass communications. His job, in addition to acting as Morgan's spokesman with the media, was to disseminate accurate and unbiased information about U.S. policy and culture to local audiences. Outside the United States, ICA officers were identified as members of the U.S. Information Service, as it was becoming all too common for the initials of their parent agency to be jumbled and them suspected of actually being in the hire of another agency with similar initials.

Morgan met Weir in his office on the first floor of the embassy, which also doubled as a conference room for media encounters and cultural offerings. Although he was actually older than most of the other members of the country team, the former soccer player looked much younger, an appearance that was enhanced by his practice of wearing his dark brown hair cropped close in a military style.

"Glad you could come down and visit us in the bull pen, Mr. Ambassador," he said as Morgan walked into his office.

"Actually, I prefer meeting people in their own spaces," Morgan said. "I find I learn much more about them than I do when I summon them to my office. Now, tell me about yourself and what you do for me here in Naganda."

Because of the lack of power in communities outside the capital and the high illiteracy rate, most of ICA's programs were confined to the capital city. Weir had put together a traveling theater troupe – local performers with an occasional American visitor – to go around to the four provincial towns and some of the larger rural villages. Over time, this traveling theater had become quite popular, often the only outside entertainment many of the villagers had ever seen.

Weir traveled with them and had become a well-known and trusted figure in many places.

During a trip to several villages in Chiveru land, one of his local contacts had mentioned causally to him that there had been several white men in their territory of late. One, a British geologist, Weir had been aware of, although no one knew exactly his reason for the visit. The other, though, bothered him. According to his source, a woman from a small village, out gathering wood, saw a group of white men walking through the bush. She hid as they passed, and then fled back to her village to tell the headman. The men, she'd said, were carrying strange looking weapons, and seemed to be trying to avoid being seen. The headman had sent a group of village men to the area, but by the time they arrived, whoever the men were, they were long gone, only a few boot prints in the earth to mark their passing.

"What would a group of white men be doing that far out in the bush?" Morgan asked.

"That's what I've been asking myself ever since I heard it," Weir replied. "Chiveru land doesn't have any resources to speak of, other than wildlife and thick forests – hardly the type of thing that would attract an armed group."

"Have you heard of sightings in any other part of the country?"

Weir shook his head. "No, and only the one sighting in Chiveru. Given the political situation, though, it troubles me. There's talk in the villages that Joshua

Saidu is planning a move to depose Gweru and take back power. I worry that he might have hired white mercenaries to help him do that."

"Where on earth would Saidu get the money to afford mercenaries?"

"When Gweru took over, he not only didn't take any punitive action against Saidu, he didn't go after his assets or bank accounts," Weir said. "Rumor has it that Saidu has sixty to a hundred million dollars in a Swiss bank account. That'll buy a lot of guns, and shooters as well."

Morgan didn't want to think the country could be that close to civil war – which is what could happen if external forces got involved. There was, though, another possible reason for the white presence that had occurred to him.

"Is it possible that the second group was somehow connected with the British geologist? By the way, do you know what he was doing up there?"

"In answer to your first question, I suppose anything is possible. As to the second, my counterpart in the UK embassy doesn't even know. Apparently the guy was sponsored by private interests, not the British government."

Another enigma added to the list of things that Morgan would have to eventually deal with.

Chapter Ten

July 13, 1978, State House
Mabuntu, Naganda

Although the official notification had given 10:30 as the time for the credential presentation ceremony, Morgan's escort from the foreign ministry, accompanied by Jonathan Gandu, the chief of protocol for the junta, arrived at his residence at 7:30. The protocol chief, a smarmy looking, reddish brown skinned man with a protruding gut, and shiny, jet black hair that had clearly been dyed, informed Morgan that they had to go to State House early in order to rehearse the ceremony.

Inside the restricted area of the city, guarded by a platoon of Nagandan army troopers, State House was the former colonial governor's office. It was, in fact, a collection of buildings inside a compound surrounded by a high stone wall that had originally been pink, but was now a sickly salmon color, flecked with gray and green mold. The main building, in the center and approached by a cobblestone drive that circled at the entrance, was made of the same stone as the wall. There were several outbuildings. When they arrived, the foreign ministry convoy pulled in front of a small building to the right of the main building. Gandu hopped out of the ministry car and came back to Morgan's vehicle, which was one of three embassy cars carrying him, Susan Pinchon, the defense attaché, the political counselor, Mary Sung, Lee and Rachel Kennedy, and Alison Chambers. The latter three hadn't even had time to unpack, but Morgan insisted that he wanted them to be a part of his ceremony.

"Excellency," Gandu said. "We will wait in this building until his Excellency Captain Gweru is ready for you. We will also go over the details of the ceremony and do a rehearsal."

Morgan wondered what details could be so complicated that it required a rehearsal. He'd attended the ceremony for his ambassador in Dagastan, and there'd only been a few second's briefing just before it started. And, that had been in a Communist country with a Soviet tradition. Unfamiliar with British colonialism, he wondered what intricate customs the English had left in Naganda when they granted it independence. He held his tongue, though, and followed the unctuous little man into the building.

The first floor room took up the entire ground floor. To the left were several sofas set around a large elephant wood table upon which rested a silver tea pot, cups and saucers, milk and sugar containers, and a tray of golden cookies – or as the local called them, biscuits. The center and right was a large open space, covered in a dark brown carpet. Opposite the entrance were the Nagandan and American flags, the American flag on the right as Morgan faced it. He noticed lines of tape on the carpet in front of the flags.

Gandu motioned toward the sofas. "You may rest here until time," he said. "There are tea and biscuits." As Morgan turned to go, Gandu laid a hand on his arm. "But, first, Excellency, you and I must go over the details of the ceremony."

"What's to go over?" Morgan asked. "I hand my credentials to the head of state, he shakes my hand, I say how happy I am to be here, and it's done. Oh, by the way, you folks *did* remember to bring my credentials, didn't you? I left them at the foreign ministry."

"Don't fear, Excellency, your credentials are hear. As to the ceremony, I don't know what you're accustomed to in other places, but here in Naganda we have our own way of conducting such events. Now, if you'll please stand with your toes on the tape there." He pointed to the nearest line of tape.

Morgan complied, and found himself looking at a space between the two flags. On the floor in front of him were two other lines of tape, one almost directly in front and one to the right. He estimated the distance between these two and his own tape at about six feet. It seemed a great distance for what had to transpire, but he cautioned himself to remain calm and see what the ceremony involved.

"Will I be standing here when the head of state comes out, or what?" he asked.

"No, His Excellency will be standing there." He pointed to the tape in front of Morgan. "He will be accompanied by the foreign minister. You will enter the room, walk to your place – in the main reception hall there will be a discrete mark on the floor which you will not miss. You walk up, place your toes on the line and the ceremony will begin. First, you will be introduced by the foreign minister. Then, you will hand your credentials to the head of state. He will take them, hand them to the minister, and then shake your hand and welcome you to Naganda. You will make a brief set of remarks, and that concludes the first part of the ceremony."

Morgan knew that the presentation of credentials was in many countries followed by a brief chat between the new ambassador and the head of state. It was the ceremony, though, that gave him pause. If he followed Gandu's instructions when he handed over his credentials and again when he shook the man's hand, he'd be forced to bend at the waist or bow. He was not prepared to bow to a military dictator, but he kept his mouth shut.

"The second part," Gandu continued. "Will be in an area similar to the one here, with sofas – and a chair for Captain Gweru – and refreshments. You will have ten minutes to chat with His Excellency, after which you will take your leave, and the ceremony is concluded. Do you have any questions?"

He had many questions, but Morgan decided that Gandu wasn't the person to answer them. He shook his head.

"I guess the only thing left is to join the others and have a cup of tea until the ceremony," he said.

He walked over to the others and helped himself to a cup of tea. Gandu scurried off somewhere without a further word. As Morgan sipped tea, he ran the upcoming ceremony through his mind. The picture that was forming was, he was certain, quite different from what the Nagandans had in mind.

"I'd go easy on that tea if I were you," Mary Sung said. "I haven't seen a sign of a toilet anywhere around here."

Morgan smiled, and put his cup down. Leave it to his old secretary to be the one with the most situational awareness. He should have noticed that himself.

For two hours they sat, engaging in idle conversation. Rachel Kennedy was in awe of the things she'd seen since their arrival, and ecstatic at the prospect of leaving in late-August to attend school in Switzerland. Finally, Gandu came back, carrying a large red and gold folder, which he handed to Morgan.

"Your credentials are in the folder," he said. "You do remember the procedure we rehearsed, I trust?"

Morgan took the folder, and merely nodded, which seemed to satisfy Gandu. He turned and walked toward the exit, with Morgan and the others trailing behind him. Outside, they turned toward the main building. Two soldiers in the dark green dress uniform of the Nagandan army stood to either side of the main door. As Morgan approached, they snapped to attention and saluted.

Inside, four more soldiers, two on either side of the door, stood at rigid attention saluting. Once past them, Gandu motioned Morgan toward the front of the room where two men, one of them the foreign minister, awaited. He then shepherded the rest of Morgan's party off to the right where he left them standing. Morgan walked forward, part of his attention devoted to looking for the mark on the carpet, part on the slightly built, dark skinned man standing in front of him. Captain Musa Gweru was short even for a Nagandan, and looked younger than his thirty years. Slender, his dark green uniform almost sagged on his frame. His tightly curled hair was cropped close to his round skull. He had light brown eyes, bloodshot and with the yellowish cornea of someone who has had malaria. He locked gazes with Morgan as he approached - his face devoid of expression.

The foreign minister's round dark face, though, had an impatient look. He looked at the folder in Morgan's hand and raised his brows.

Morgan looked down at the line of tape on the carpet. He looked back up at Gweru. The captain started to raise his hand. Morgan realized that if he passed the folder from where he stood, he would have to bow, and he'd decided he was damn well not about to bow to a military dictator.

He took two small steps forward, and placed the folder on Gweru's outstretched left hand, and grasping the right hand in a firm grip he looked the man in the eyes. Gweru's eyes widened slightly, and as he returned Morgan's grip, he nodded.

"Welcome to Naganda, Mr. Ambassador," Gweru said.

Morgan stepped back to the tape.

"Excellency," he said. "I am honored to be here, and I look forward to working with you and your government to improve relations between our two countries and to aid the Nagandan people in realizing their goals and dreams."

He'd decided on this simple speech, rather than directly challenging the man on human rights and other issues from the start. It was still something of a challenge, though, if the frown on the foreign minister's face was any guide. So be it, Morgan thought. The man was probably already pissed that Morgan had not followed the instructions on passing the credentials, but he kept silent until Gweru nodded.

"Excellencies," the foreign minister said. "Shall we retire to the lounge area?"

He then led the way, with Gweru and Morgan walking side-by-side behind him, followed by Morgan's entourage, to the area of sofas and the high back chair. A tall very dark skinned man in blue knee pants and a white jacket stood at the side holding a tray containing a silver teapot.

When Gweru had taken his place in the high chair, Simbawashe sat to his left and Morgan to his right, on small sofas designed to seat two people. The others arranged themselves on the remaining sofas. The liveried servant poured tea, beginning with Gweru. When everyone had a coup of the steaming liquid, he withdrew.

Gweru lifted his cup. "Ambassador Morgan," he said in a voice that was surprisingly soft. "Again, allow me to welcome you to Naganda. I hope your arrival signals a new beginning in the relationship between your country and mine.

Morgan lifted his cup in response. "Excellency, I too hope that our countries will be able to forge a new and more mutually beneficial relationship. I certainly intend to do my part in achieving that. I hope that we will be able to deal with each other openly and honestly – addressing the negative issues in a spirit of openness."

Gweru laughed softly.

"I've been told that you were a soldier," he said. "I can see that you still retain the directness of a soldier."

Morgan saw warmth in the man's eyes – warmth, and something else that he couldn't define. Perhaps loneliness; he probably had no one he could talk candidly to, or who would speak openly to him. The burden of being a dictator.

"As an old soldier to a younger soldier," Morgan said. "I know you appreciate that focusing on the main mission is important."

"Yes, you are right. Tell me, did you serve in your country's war in Vietnam?"

Morgan nodded his assent, and Gweru immediately launched into a series of questions about his experiences in combat. The conversation had gone significantly past the time Morgan had been told was allotted. He noticed that the foreign minister was fidgeting, and out of the corner of his eye he saw Gandu near the main door pointing at his watch and making faces. Gweru, too, could see Gandu. He looked at Morgan, a faint smile on his face, and continued asking questions.

After nearly an hour of intensive questioning from Gweru about American military history and tactics, Morgan felt the urge to find a toilet to relieve his bladder. He'd been holding it in since leaving his residence that morning. He had the feeling that he was developing a good rapport with the junta leader, and he didn't want to jinx it by squirming in his chair trying to hold back the flow pushing against his crotch. He also didn't want to irreparably damage his relationship with the foreign ministry – that was the arm of the Nagandan government with which the embassy had the most active relations.

"Excellency," he said. "As a fellow soldier, I'm sure you're familiar with the quote attributed to the Duke of Wellington to young officers just before going to battle against Napoleon's forces, when he told them the most important thing was, take a piss whenever you have the opportunity."

"I believe I have heard such a saying," Gweru said. "What is its significance?"

"Well, sir, I've not been able to relieve myself since leaving my residence early this morning, if you take my meaning."

Gweru reared back in his chair, laughing loudly for the first time. He slapped his knee. "I do believe I understand you, sir. I have taken up far too much of your time. Do forgive me."

He stood. Everyone else followed suit. Gweru took Morgan's arm and guided him toward the door, pulling him out ahead of the others.

"Thank you, Excellency," Morgan said. "It has been a pleasure meeting you."

"Believe me, Mr. Ambassador," Gweru said quietly. "The pleasure has been mine. I hope that we'll have further opportunities to converse – under less restrictive circumstances."

He grasped Morgan's hand. Morgan felt, in addition to the man's calloused palm, the edges of a crumpled piece of paper. Gweru looked up at him with a conspiratorial expression. When he released the hand, Morgan discretely slipped the paper into his pocket. At the door, Gweru stopped to allow the foreign minister and Morgan's people to catch up with them.

They shook hands again. Morgan also shook hands with the foreign minister, whose grip was not as firm as it had been at their first meeting. The man had a strange expression on his face, but only mumbled congratulations to Morgan upon now being officially allowed to conduct public business.

Morgan waited until his car was outside the compound before taking the crumpled paper from his pocket and smoothing it out. On it was a telephone number. He didn't need anyone to explain whose number it was. He put it in the inside pocket of his jacket against the day when he would have to use it.

Charles Ray

Chapter Eleven

On the way back to the embassy, it started raining. Not just a normal rain, but a torrential downpour that rendered visibility to near zero and flooded the streets. Morgan's driver, George Toko, expertly navigated the big limo around the deepest of the filled potholes, and somehow managed not to hit the few foolhardy pedestrians who stayed outside in the rain.

"I thought the rainy season didn't start until the end of July," Morgan said.

"Normally, sah, that is so," Toko said. "But, these last few years, it's been coming at strange times. No worry, though, it only lasts for an hour or two."

It didn't last that long. Twenty-five minutes after the first drops fell, the rain stopped as suddenly as if someone had turned a tap on a faucet, and within five minutes, the few remaining clouds had disappeared. By the time they pulled up to the embassy, the heat of the July sun had evaporated all but the deepest of potholes and the dust was beginning to be stirred by passersby into a low lying yellow cloud that swirled around their knees.

Back in his office Morgan directed Mary Sung to work with the embassy protocol clerk and begin making appointments for courtesy calls on his diplomatic colleagues and the appropriate government ministers. He could have called on most of his fellow ambassadors even before presenting his credentials, but decided to do this necessary diplomatic chore as one project rather than split it up. He called Tom Breedlove and instructed him to work with other embassy sections to determine who else he should meet and then inform his secretary so she could make his schedule.

He spent the rest of the morning going through paperwork – the stack of telegrams that came in from Washington and other embassies overnight, internal embassy memos and notes, and a media summary prepared by the public affairs section. Naganda didn't have much in the way of domestic media beyond a radio station that broadcast intermittently and a weekly newspaper, both of which only served the capital, and the international media had only paid attention to the country for the first few weeks after the coup. Since then, Weir had told him, most international media covered the place by calling the embassy in search of quotes or leads on stories.

After lunch in the embassy cafeteria, he was back at his desk, neck deep in paperwork, when Mary Sung walked into his office. She closed the door.

"What's up, Mary?" he asked.

"Uh, there's a woman on the phone with a foreign accent – a Monika Loewenthal. She says she knows you."

It took a few moments for the name to register.

"That's right," he said. "I met her on the flight from Amsterdam. Go ahead and put her through."

She gave him a strange look, and then smiled as she left his office. Thank goodness for her discretion, he thought. He didn't particular want the rest of the embassy to be sticking its collective noses into his personal life.

When she came on the line, Monika Loewenthal informed Morgan that she was in Mabuntu overnight, having come in on the morning flight and scheduled to fly back to Amsterdam on the next day's late afternoon flight. She was staying at the Papa Loko Guest House, and was looking forward to having dinner with him. Morgan told her he'd be busy at the embassy until nearly five, but would swing by the guest house and pick her up shortly afterwards to take her to his official residence for a private dinner. After ringing off, he asked Sung to call the residence and let the staff know there would be two for dinner.

The rest of the day went by far too slowly for Morgan, but finally five o'clock came and he had Sung put away his papers, and headed to the guest house, which happened to be on the road to his residence anyway.

When they arrived at the residence, George asked

what time he should come back to pick up the lady. Monika squeezed Morgan's arm.

"I have a toothbrush in my purse," she whispered.

"Sounds like you had more than dinner in mind," Morgan whispered back.

"Let's call that dessert," she said, giving his arm another squeeze.

"Take the rest of the evening off, George," Morgan said. "And, pick us up Monday morning."

Chapter Twelve

Morgan awoke Monday with Monika's head nestled against his shoulder and her dark hair tickling his nose. The weekend had gone by in a delightful haze of talking and lovemaking. He'd given his household staff the weekend off and the two of them had cooked their own meals.

After breakfast, they showered together and dressed, and he dropped her at her hotel before going on to the embassy. He made a tentative lunch date with her, but warned her that his schedule could get hectic as he'd been warned that some of the government ministers had an annoying habit of agreeing to appointments thirty minutes before the scheduled time. She kissed him lightly on the cheek, causing George to chuckle softly, and said that she understood – promising to give him more warning before her next layover so that they could plan their time together better. Not, she reminded him, that their night hadn't been wonderful.

He was feeling a warm glow in his chest when he walked into the office. Mary Sung looked up at him and gave him a conspiratorial smile as he passed her desk.

He wasn't more than a few minutes into the morning paperwork when she walked in.

"Maya Livingstone is here to see you," she said. "And, she says it's urgent."

"By all means, send her in."

Maya Livingstone, dressed in a dusty brown safari suit, the pants stretched over her ample hips, and her brown boots covered in dried mud, had a worried look on her round, brown face when she entered Morgan's office. She was followed closely by a small woman with close-cropped blonde hair and a sun darkened face that had a dusting of dark red freckles on her nose and cheeks. She wore a pair of khaki pants that hung loosely on her small frame, and a faded yellow shirt that was two sizes too large. Her light blue eyes regarded Morgan with a mixture of fear and awe.

"Sorry for barging in on you like this, Mr. Ambassador," Livingstone said.

"No apologies necessary," Morgan said. He took her arm and guided her toward the sofa. The small woman followed. "Now, what's the problem?"

Livingstone inclined her head toward her companion. "Mr. Ambassador, this is Rebecca Taylor. She's a volunteer in the village of Ovimbi in Chiveru land." Taylor stuck out a hand that, when Morgan took it, disappeared into his. But, her grip was firm, and her palms were calloused from lots of heavy work.

"Please to meet you, sir," she said in a small voice.

Morgan motioned for them to sit. When Taylor sat on the sofa her feet barely reached the floor. Her small frame and voice made her look like a child in her early teens, but as he'd been shaking her hand, Morgan noticed the thin lines at the corners of her eyes that indicated she was older. He shot a questioning look at Livingstone.

"Becky, why don't you tell the ambassador what you told me," she said.

Before the woman could speak, Mary Sung entered carrying a tray with three mugs from which steam wafted. Morgan instantly recognized the scent – a hint of cinnamon. For certain special occasions, or when she sensed that someone was in need of special comforting, Sung added a dash of cinnamon to the coffee as it was brewing. This added a subtle sweet aroma to the woody aroma of the coffee, and just a hint of tangy cinnamon to the taste. She placed the three cups on the coffee table and silently withdrew.

"Why don't you try Mary's special blend before you get into your story," Morgan gently suggested.

Livingstone and Taylor picked up the white mugs, sniffing at them as they neared their faces. Taylor's face lit up like a kid at Christmas who has just discovered a brand-new red American Flyer bike under the tree. She held the mug beneath her nose, breathing deeply, for several seconds. Then, she took a sip – and then another. When she finally put her cup down, it was half empty. Sipping his own coffee, Morgan looked at her over the edge of his mug. He knew what was going through her mind. The same reaction he'd had the first time he'd tasted coffee brewed in this manner. He couldn't really explain it, but when pressed would say, it was like what heaven would taste like.

Taylor looked across the table at Morgan, and took a deep breath.

"My, that is a fantastic cup of coffee," she said. "They brew local coffee in Ovimbi, which is not too bad, but after drinking this, I'm spoiled for anything else."

"Mary's a wizard at this," Morgan said. "Now, why don't you tell me your story?"

"I'm running a pre- and post-natal care program for the women of Ovimbi Village," she said. "The infant mortality rate in this country is so high - it's really an important facet of their medical care that's missing.

Morgan tried not to look impatient. Like many people who care deeply about what they do, Rebecca Taylor just assumed that everyone else would be as interested as she was. He would let her get to the meat of her story in her own time.

"At any rate," she went on. "I work mostly in the main village. But, sometimes I travel to the outlying hamlets. A few days ago, just before Maya arrived, one of the women in a settlement just south of the main village reported that she'd seen white men moving through the bush when she was out gathering wood."

"Richard Weir, the PAO, told me a similar story a few days ago," Morgan said. "Did anyone in your village identify these men?"

"No," Taylor said, shaking her head. "In fact, at first, the men of the village refused to believe her. They don't get too many outsiders in that region, and they just put it down to a hysterical woman seeing hunters at a distance and making a mistake. But, this particular woman isn't given to hysteria, and she also refuses to be dismissed so casually. She nagged her husband until he got a couple of the other village men to go with him to investigate her sighting."

"What did they find?"

Taylor's face darkened and her eyes glistened with tears. "We don't know," she said. Her lips quivered. "The men didn't return by nightfall, so the next morning, the chief sent out another party to look for them. They were found very near where the woman had said she spotted the white men – all dead from gunshot wounds."

Charles Ray

Chapter Thirteen

After Livingstone and Taylor left, Morgan went down to the embassy cafeteria for lunch. He spent more time talking to the various members of the embassy staff who were surprised to see him in the facility again than eating, but was happy to be able to make face-to-face contact with so many of those under his leadership in the non-threatening environment the cafeteria afforded.

Back in his office, he pondered what he'd heard from the two Peace Corps people, which tended to validate what Weir had told him. There was a group of strange white men wandering around the countryside – mainly in Chiveru land – which had to spell trouble. Taking a yellow legal pad from his desk, he began making notes. The problem was that he really knew so little. Little about the strange group, and even less about what it portended for Naganda and for him as the American representative. At the bottom of the page, he wrote a reminder to check with Carlton Raine to see if any of the man's sources could shed light on the situation.

As he was about to tear the sheet off and have Sung file it in a special folder there was a tap on his door. He looked up to see Liam Brennan standing in the door, his expression unreadable.

"Colonel, come in," he said. "What's up?"

Without waiting to be seated on the sofa, the defense attaché walked over and sat on the straight back chair at the side of Morgan's desk.

"Ambassador, I've picked up some information I think you'll want to hear," Brennan said. "Some of it's potentially bad news, and some of it doesn't make a whole hell of a lot of sense."

"Maybe you should give me the bad news first," Morgan said.

Brennan laughed gruffly. "I've been having meeting privately with some of the more junior officers in the Nagandan military – I just happen to speak both Ganda and Buntu, thanks to a cousin whose parents were missionaries out here before independence. He was born here, and spoke the main dialects like a native. As a teenager, he worked at the airport. His job was to ride his bike down the runway before planes landed or took off, driving livestock out of the way. Spent most of his time with the locals growing up, so he was more native than American really. After independence, his dad retired and they came back to Texas. He loved teaching, and taught me to speak both languages, which was a treat to a kid living in the ass end of Texas. Anyway, that's just to give you the background on how I'm able to get to know people here. What I'm hearing from some of the younger officers, Ganda and Bantu, is that some of the senior Ganda officers are still loyal to Joshua Saidu, and they're planning a countercoup to put him back in office."

Pulling his legal pad back, Morgan began making notes.

"You think the rumors have any credibility?" he asked.

"Afraid so. I've heard it from too many different sources. The young guys are really worried. Hell, they have it good under Gweru, and don't want to go back to the bad old days."

Bad news just kept piling up. First, the story of a strange group of whites wandering around, and now the possibility of more internal strife, with soldier pitted against soldier, and the civilians of Naganda caught in the middle. Morgan told Brennan what Weir and Taylor had told him.

"Do you think this strange group is related to the coup rumors?" he asked.

"Damned if I know." The colonel rubbed his jaw. "I suppose it could be, but this is the first I've heard of the presence of another force. I'll start asking around. If there is an attempted move on Gweru, it won't be as peaceful as his takeover – it'll be pretty damned bloody."

"We need as much advance warning as we can get," Morgan said. "With Peace Corps volunteers in the countryside, not to mention the missionaries, we'll need to be able to move them to safety."

"Shit, if we have to do a NEO, we'll be up the creek. With no seaport, we'd have to either have the Air Force fly in, or figure a way to make it out overland."

Morgan wasn't elated at the thought of having to do a noncombatant evacuation operation, or NEO, under any circumstances, but certainly not so early in his tour. He was just getting to know the country, but he was familiar with the region from map study, and he knew that getting several hundred Americans out of a landlocked West African country would pose a challenge to the U.S. military. In addition, he knew that if the Americans started leaving, the rest of the foreign community would want to pull out as well, and there would be general panic among the locals. The military term 'cluster fuck' came to mind.

"Let's hope it doesn't come to that," he said. "If we can learn who's behind it, maybe you can use your contacts and language ability to talk them out of it. Now, what's the rest of your news?"

"I got a strange report from the DATT in Conakry. A Panamanian registry freighter docked at Conakry, and offloaded three large crates. He happened to be at the docks at the time and noticed that the crates had Chinese markings on them, so he followed up on where they were going. They were loaded on barges, one crate per barge, and taken inland. As far as he can tell, they crossed the border and were heading this way."

"Did he find out what was in the crates?" Morgan asked.

"No – he asked at the port, but all the officials there claimed ignorance. Whatever it was, though, it was damned heavy. The barges sank almost to the gunwales when the crates were put on board."

"Maybe it was industrial equipment for the rutile mining operation."

Brennan shook his head. "I don't think so," he said. "BAR gets most of its mining equipment from England or Denmark, and it comes through Dakar or Douala. I've never known them to order Chinese equipment."

Morgan made another note.

"Did your guy get the measurements of the crates?" He was certain that he had. Defense attachés are trained information gatherers.

"Yeah, and he's asked the folks back in DC to try and figure out what might have been in those crates."

"What do you think?" Morgan asked. "If it's not mining equipment, what other heavy equipment would be coming into Naganda – especially from China?"

"I'm at a loss. I mean, it could be a lot of things, machinery or vehicles maybe. It'll help if I can get a lead on who it's being shipped to. The only thing I'm pretty sure of is that it can't be good."

Of course, Morgan thought. So far, he'd only experienced a few *good* things – actually, only one, Monika Loewenthal. It was beginning to look like his tour of duty in Naganda was going to make Dagastan look like a picnic.

"Keep me posted on what you find," he said. "While you're at it, check with Raine and his folks. Maybe they'll have some insights."

"That was my next stop," Brennan said.

Chapter Fourteen

July 18, 1978, African Affairs Bureau,
Department of State, Washington, DC

Three men sat at one end of the long table in the fifth floor conference room belonging to the State Department's Bureau of African Affairs. Jason Symington, the bureau's deputy assistant secretary responsible for West Africa had called the emergency meeting and sat at the head of the table. To his right was Edward Harris, country director for Naganda, Sierra Leone, and Mali, and to his left was Gregory Wells who had been recently assigned as the Nagandan desk officer. On the table in front of Symington was a dispatch from the embassy in Mabuntu. He looked at the three green sheets as if they were poisonous snakes.

"Greg," he said, fixing the young officer with an icy stare. "What do you make of this cable from Mabuntu?"

The cable, which had come in during the night, was a report of the information David Morgan had received from Richard Weir, Rebecca Taylor, and Colonel Brennan. In dry prose it laid out the events as they'd been related to Morgan, and ended with a comment: 'The embassy is unable to determine what these events portend, and will continue to reach out to all of our contacts for further details. We believe, however, that it is likely that they are related, and if so, that it means we are likely to see further instability in Naganda.'

"Ambassador Morgan has information from a number of different sources – all reliable," Wells said. "I think -"

"None of this comes from the political counselor at post," Harris said, cutting Wells off. "I suggest we call Tom Breedlove and get his read on this."

"I did that first thing this morning," Wells said. "He said that none of his sources have told him anything about white mercenaries in Naganda, and he's heard nothing about villagers being killed."

"Well, there you have it," Wells said. "I'm not sure we should put too much credence in information that the political section hasn't gathered."

"With all due respect, Ed, I disagree. We know we can trust the defense attaché, and Dick Weir's got a good track record for having good contacts within the local community. In addition, the Peace Corps volunteer independently confirmed what Dick heard from his contact."

Harris glared at the young officer. His cheeks flamed red.

"Are you questioning my judgment?"

Wells leaned back as if struck.

"N-no – I just think we'd be wrong to . . . dismiss this information . . . out of hand."

Symington looked from one man to the other, a wolfish smile on his face. He tended to agree with the younger officer, but kept his silence. He enjoyed seeing the two of them spar with each other. It surprised him that an officer as junior as Wells would even consider disagreeing with his superior. Wells would either rise high in the service, or flame out by the end of his current tour.

"There's a reason we have political officers at our embassies," Harris said. "And, that's to make sense of political events. Employees in the other specialties should stick to their job descriptions."

"I understand your point, sir, but the situation in Naganda is far too fluid and unpredictable to rely solely on traditional methods. Besides, Ambassador Morgan trusts the information."

"Ha, Morgan's no Africa expert," Harris said. "I'm not even convinced he's fully qualified for the job."

Now it was Wells who had the red face. He'd only met with Morgan briefly, but he was impressed by the man, and not a small bit discomfited to listen to him being maligned by another senior officer. He wanted to tell Harris to go to hell – that he was totally wrong about David Morgan. But, the man wrote his performance evaluation, and he also wanted nothing more than a career as a diplomat. A negative performance review in his current job would be tantamount to a career death sentence. His jaw hurt from clenching his teeth to keep from blurting out some unfortunate remark.

Symington could see the younger man's discomfort, and though he enjoyed the spectacle, those above him would be wanting answers to the 'Naganda problem,' so he'd have to forego further enjoyment.

"Now, now, Ed," he said. "I think young Greg here has a good point. Morgan has information from independent sources, and I don't think we can dismiss the defense attaché's information out of hand. It all seems to hang together."

Harris stared openmouthed at *his* superior. Wells continued to clench his teeth, now to avoid smiling. He'd just witnessed his boss get an effective ass chewing and it made him feel good to see the pompous dickhead put in his place.

"B-but, Jason, you *know* Morgan's not an Africa hand. Sure, he was a DCM, and I suppose he had a good record in his other bureau, but he didn't grow up in the Africa bureau like you and I did."

Symington slowly shook his head. "Sorry, Ed," he said. "But, personally, I think far too much is made of this growing up in a bureau nonsense. The world's getting too complicated and interconnected for someone who only knows one region to be really successful. We're going to need people like Morgan, and it's time we faced up to it."

Harris sank into his chair like a deflated air bag. "Okay, so what should we do?"

Symington looked at Wells. "What do you suggest, Greg?" he asked.

"I think we need to get INR to pull out all the stops to get information on that shipment through Conakry," Wells said. "For now, we should also instruct the embassy to approach the government about the report of villagers being killed."

"What if the government is involved in it?" Harris asked. "If we tell them what we know about the mercenaries, that blows the whole thing."

"We don't have to tell them all the details," Wells said. "Just that we'd heard that villagers had been killed, and we're registering concern on human rights grounds – see how they react."

Symington nodded approvingly. The young desk officer had potential – maybe he would rise high after all.

"I like it," he said. "Draft the instructions and get them up to me within the hour. I need to brief the assistant secretary before he goes to the secretary's morning brief."

Charles Ray

Chapter Fifteen

July 19, 1978, State House,
Mabuntu, Naganda

Morgan had received instructions from the State Department in the overnight cable traffic to contact the government of Naganda at the highest level to register concern over the reported killing of villagers in Chiveru land, as he'd anticipated they would. He'd been following the advice given him by an old sergeant major when he was a young captain doing his first combat tour – never carry out an order you haven't told your commander to give you.

He'd been surprised when his request for an urgent meeting with Gweru had been immediately agreed to. He and Susan Pinchon were scheduled to meet with the junta chief at 9:30 am. They arrived at State House at 9:15.

He expected to see someone from the foreign

ministry, but was met instead by Gandu, the State House protocol chief. He led them to one of the small buildings adjacent to the large ceremonial structure, showed them to a small room with a large high backed chair opposite the door and smaller chairs lining the walls on either side. A long, low table sat between the rows of chairs. Silver tea urns, cups, sugar and cream were spaced evenly on the table.

While they waited, Morgan poured tea for himself and Pinchon, and sat back enjoying the rich flavor of English tea – without the heavy infusion of sugar and cream in the English style that was preferred by the locals.

"So, how do you think Gweru will react to your message?" Pinchon asked.

"I wish I knew." Morgan's plan was to deliver the message he'd been instructed to deliver, but at the same time, he wanted to feel Gweru out a bit more, and see if he could find out if the man knew of the rumors of a possible move against him. He'd be walking a fine line, very close to violating his instructions, but he'd decided it was worth the risk.

They'd almost finished their tea, when the door opened, and Gweru, dressed in a Nagandan field uniform without any decorations or rank insignia, walked in. He was followed closely by a man in full dress uniform, complete with a number of colorful decorations, who was an older, taller, and much heavier version of himself. Gweru smiled shyly when he saw Morgan, walking forward quickly with his dark brown hand outstretched. The older man glared at Morgan and Pinchon with eyes so bloodshot the yellowing of his corneas wasn't noticeable.

"Ambassador Morgan," Gweru said. "I am happy that we have a second chance to meet. Miss Pinchon, I welcome you also." He'd grasped Morgan's hands warmly. As he released Morgan's hand, he turned and gestured at the other man. "May I present the Supreme Commander of the Armed Forces and Chief of Intelligence and Security General Gideon Banda?"

Banda's expression showed no welcome, and his handshake, when Morgan grasped his hand, was limp. He snatched his hand back as soon as Morgan had released it. The man ignored Pinchon's extended hand, merely bowing curtly and walking to the first chair to the right of the high chair.

Gweru winced at the man, but said nothing. He motioned Morgan to the first chair to his left and Pinchon took the one on Morgan's left.

When they were seated, Gweru leaned forward and poured a cup of tea. Banda followed suit.

"Thank you for agreeing to seem me at such short notice," Morgan said. His intention had been to take some time warming the man up, but the scowl on Banda's face made him want to get his business over with as quickly as possible.

Gweru nodded, with a hint of a smile. "I have been looking forward to taking further with you," he said. "I suppose, though, knowing how you Americans like to get right down to business, you'll want to talk first about why you asked to see me?"

Morgan plunged right in. He told Gweru about the report he'd received about villagers being gunned down near Ovimbi Village, and expressed the U.S. Government's concern that this might be viewed as a violation of human rights. He then asked if any military or police unit might have been in the area around the time of the alleged incident. This hadn't been in his instructions, but he felt it necessary to ask. Gweru's eyes widened as he asked the question, and he shot a questioning look at Banda, who was looking furious.

"Are you insinuating that Nagandan military or police units might have done this?" Banda glared at Morgan. Flecks of spittle flew from between his thick lips. "How dare you."

"Methinks thou doest protest too much," Morgan thought. "Not at all, general," he said gently. "I merely wondered if any of your security forces were aware of the incident."

"Of course not," Banda said. "I have heard nothing of it either. I wonder if whoever told you this might not be . . . mistaken."

A subtle way of calling not only his source, but Morgan himself, a liar, but Morgan refused to let the man bait him.

"I trust the source of the information. Actually, I have the information from two sources independently, so that tends to corroborate it in my book."

"Yes, I can see how that would be," Gweru said. "Uncle . . . er, General Banda, do we have any units near this Ovimbi?"

Uncle, Morgan thought – yes, he remembered reading that Gideon Banda was an uncle on Gweru's maternal side. There didn't, though, appear to be all that much affection between them.

"No, excellency," Banda said. "You know how the Chiveru can be. They don't like to have army units on their land, and they handle what few crimes occur through their tribal courts."

"So, you can't really say that the incident didn't happen," Morgan said.

Banda sputtered and opened his mouth to speak. Gweru cut him off with a sharp motion of his hand. "He has a point, general. But, Ambassador Morgan, I can assure you that none of my soldiers would do such a thing, and very few of our police have weapons – just the central security service. Are you sure the victims were shot?"

"I didn't see it for myself, of course, but I trust the source. Bullet wounds are hard to mistake. Would there be any other armed people in that region?"

Gweru shook his head. "The Chiveru are traditionalists. Even in this day and age, they insist on hunting with spear and bow, or with handmade traps. I doubt if there is a gun among them. In addition, they're the most peaceful of this country's tribes –

there is seldom violence in their land."

Morgan had toyed with the idea of telling Gweru about the reports of white men in the area. He hadn't discussed it with Pinchon, knowing she'd advise against it. He looked from Gweru to Banda. Gweru looked a bit confused, and Banda still looked furious, but neither of them looked as if they were being dishonest. They *didn't* know about the killings.

"I've also heard rumors, unconfirmed at this point, of a group of armed men in the vicinity of the village where these killings took place. Would you know anything about that?"

The looks of shock on both men's faces were, Morgan was sure, genuine.

"Where did you hear this?" Banda asked in a demanding tone.

"Sorry, but I'm not at liberty to divulge my sources." Morgan smiled slightly as he shook his head. "But, like the source who told me about the killings, I trust these sources."

"Did your, uh, sources identify these men?" Gweru stared at Morgan. "Or, can you share that information?"

There was only so much Morgan was prepared to share until he knew the man better, and he wasn't prepared to *ever* be too open with Banda. He considered himself a good judge of character, and Gweru impressed him as a basically decent individual. Banda, on the other hand, reeked of evil and greed. He looked to Morgan like a man who would sell his mother's soul for personal gain.

"I'm afraid the sources could only tell me that there were armed men in Chiveru territory," he said. "They couldn't tell me how many, or with what specific types of arms."

That much was true. He'd left out the part about the men being white.

"That is too bad," Gweru said. "It would be helpful to know who they are."

"Yes, I'm aware of that." Morgan decided to try one more tack. "Is it possible that the former ruler might have brought in a force to try and take power back?"

He felt Pinchon stiffen. He knew what she must be thinking. Not only had he exceeded his instructions, but he was dangerously close to divulging classified information. Looking at Gweru and Banda, though, he saw that the information had struck a nerve. Both men looked nervous.

"I . . . suppose . . . it is possible that he would do that," Gweru said.

"I told you, you should have gotten rid of him," Banda said.

"And, I told *you*, uncle, that we've had enough violence." Gweru's voice had a steely tone. "We have to find a way for all the people of Naganda to live together in peace."

"Yes, but -"

"- No, we will not talk further of this, uncle." Gweru faced Morgan. "I appreciate you sharing this information with me, Excellency. If you should learn more that you can share, please call me anytime. In the meantime, we will check into this incident in Ovimbi. If there is a foreign force in Naganda, it will be dealt with, I assure you of that."

As he finished speaking, he turned and glared at Banda. The general shrank back in his chair, a strange look on his face.

"Yes . . . Excellency," he said. "I will have some of my agents go to Ovimbi immediately. We will get to the bottom of this."

When Banda looked at Morgan, though, there was only blazing hate in his bloodshot eyes. Morgan felt a tingling in his spine. Banda wasn't one he'd want to meet in a dark alley.

On the ride back to the embassy, Pinchon, still stiff backed, sat in silence. When Morgan could take it no longer, he laid a hand on her arm.

"I know what you're thinking," he said. "But, I felt it was necessary."

"I suppose it was," she said after a moment of hesitation. "I just hope you know what you're doing. You're playing with fire, you know."

He knew – he knew all too well.

Chapter Sixteen

After returning to the embassy, Morgan had Breedlove send Dewey Feinstein, a junior officer assigned to the political section, to his office, where he and Pinchon sat down with him and drafted a cable to Washington describing his meeting with Gweru.

He played down the discussion about the presence of white mercenaries in Naganda, simply having Feinstein write that he'd asked if Gweru or Banda thought there might be armed men present in Chiveru territory, and that they'd both answered in the negative. He knew that even this might raise eyebrows in Washington, and even earn him a peevish note back from the country director, but he believed in being honest, and felt that Washington should know this. If they couldn't deal with bad news, it was more their problem than his.

Morgan watched as the young officer filled a yellow pad with notes. He hadn't asked one question as mainly Morgan, with Pinchon occasionally pitching in, recounted Morgan's version of their meeting. Finally,

Morgan felt enough had been said. He wanted, though, to check Feinstein's comprehension.

"Okay, Dewey," he said. "You think you have all that?"

Scratching at the beginning fuzz of a beard on his rounded chin, Feinstein looked at Morgan with uncertainty in his dark brown eyes.

"Well, sir, I was wondering whether it's wise to add the part about the mercenaries to the cable – considering that the Department's instructions didn't mention them," he said.

Morgan was impressed that he'd caught that. "I imagine that'll cause a bit of consternation," he said. "But, we *did* discuss it; although we said nothing about them being mercenaries – just armed men – so, it wouldn't be honest not to let Washington know that."

"You're not worried that they'll be upset?"

"No, son, I'm not worried," Morgan said. "They pay me to make decisions, not to wait for instructions. It was my decision that it was important to discuss that specific issue with Gweru, and I'm prepared to stand by it."

Feinstein smiled and held the pad against his chest. "Very well, sir," he said. "I'll have a draft ready for you to read in about an hour. I assume you'll want Tom to clear it first?"

Morgan hadn't really thought about the political

counselor. He should have included him in the meeting, but it had slipped his mind. While Breedlove hadn't impressed him so far, he didn't want to completely write him off without giving him more of a chance. "Yes," he said. "By all means have him clear it. If he brings up the armed men, though, be sure you tell him that I want that to be in the cable."

When Feinstein had gone, Pinchon looked at Morgan with a sad, half-smile on her face.

"You know Tom will want to take that part out," she said. "He's definitely the 'don't make waves' type, and will insist on reporting only on the issues we were instructed to discuss with the government."

"He can insist all he wants. The cables still go out with my name at the bottom," Morgan said. "Which means *I* have the final say."

She was chuckling when she left his office.

Pinchon had been right. Almost as soon as she was out of sight, the phone rang. It was Breedlove, complaining about the mention of the armed men in the cable. When Morgan said, bluntly, that it was to be left in, he made a second half-hearted attempt to talk him out of it, and then gave up, saying the finished cable would be on his desk for his approval within the hour.

While waiting for the cable, Morgan went through the rest of the papers on his desk – more of the same as always – making notes on some with follow up questions, appending instructions on others, and marking a large number for the 'round file,' meaning they were to be destroyed.

He was just about to knock off for an early lunch when Mary Sung came in.

"Sir, there's a local downstairs who says he needs to speak with you, and that it's urgent."

Morgan looked up at her, smiling. "If it's a visa issue, have him talk to the consular chief. If it's about money we owe him, send him to admin. For anything else, turn him over to Lee Kennedy."

"Lee's with him now," she said. "He got on the phone when I tried passing the guy off to someone else, and said he thinks you should talk to him."

Morgan rubbed his chin. If his RSO thought he should see the visitor, it must be important. Morgan trusted Lee Kennedy almost as much as he trusted Carlton Raine.

"Okay," he said. "But, call Alison and have her sit in on the meeting. For that matter, ask Susan to be here as well."

Pinchon was in his office immediately, followed closely by Alison Chambers, who was getting settled into her job as his special assistant. There hadn't been room in the executive suite for her, and he didn't think she'd be comfortable in the political section, so she'd been given an office near the defense attaché section. Mary Sung rearranged the chairs, bringing in two extra chairs, so the visitor could be put on the sofa with the others facing him in a semi-circle. She then went to the little kitchenette behind her desk to make a fresh pot of tea.

Fifteen minutes later, Lee Kennedy appeared in Morgan's doorway. Behind him was a tall, dignified looking man with skin the color of mahogany, a high, broad forehead, and dark brown eyes that seemed to bore right through whatever he was looking at. He had a white skullcap perched atop his close-cropped hair, and wore a flowing white robe that fell to mid-calf. On his feet he wore a pair of scuffed, brown leather sandals. Morgan stood to welcome him.

"Mr. Ambassador," Kennedy said. "May I present al-haji Ali Kabbah.? Mr. Kabbah, this is Ambassador David Morgan."

The man's hand, when Morgan grasped it, was warm – the palms smooth. His grip was firm, and he made direct eye contact with Morgan. After releasing Morgan's grip, he put his hand to his chest and inclined his head slightly. Morgan copied the gesture.

"al-haji Kabbah," Morgan said. "*As-Salaam Alaikum* – welcome to my embassy."

The man smiled. "*Wa Alaikum As-Salaam* – and, upon you be peace. I'm surprised that you are familiar with the proper Islamic greeting, Mr. Ambassador."

"In my last posting there were Muslims," Morgan said. He saw no need to explain further. He motioned toward the sofa. "Won't you please be seated? Can I offer you a cup of tea?"

"Thank you. A cup of tea would be nice," Kabbah

said after he was seated. Morgan poured for him. Again, Kabbah smiled. The gesture of respect didn't go unnoticed.

After everyone had a cup of tea, David lifted his cup. "Again, welcome to my embassy," he said. He waited for Kabbah to lift his cup and take a sip, before drinking. Then he put the cup down.

"I thank you for taking the time to see me," Kabbah said in a deep voice with an upper class English accent. "I know you are a very busy man. But, I have a matter to discuss that I think you might find important.

Morgan inclined his head, signaling the man to continue.

"I suppose I should first properly identify and introduce myself. I am recently retired from the United Nations. I served that august body for many years. I was hired as a junior staff member of the High Commissioner for Refugees when I finished my studies at Cambridge. I was, by the way, one of the first people from Naganda, and the first member of the Chiveru tribe, to study abroad, and was the first Nagandan to hold a UN job. I rose to the level of division director before retirement."

"Your people must be very proud of you," Morgan said.

"Some are . . . some, not so much." Kabbah chuckled. "Not many of our people have had much exposure to the outside world – least of all our military people. Captain Gweru attended military training in England, and I believe he might even have had some training in your country, but few others in the Nagandan army have ever been outside the country. His uncle, Gideon Banda, for instance – he is ostensibly head of the army, and except for brief trips to neighboring countries, he's never been anywhere even in Africa. I returned here after retiring from the UN, in the hope that I'd be able to introduce the modern world to Naganda – starting, of course, with my own people, the Chiveru."

"Have you had any success?"

Kabbah shook his head. He picked up his cup and sipped at the tea, looking sadly at Morgan over the rim.

"Very little, I'm afraid," he said. "You must understand, the people of Naganda have little reason to trust outsiders. When the English came in 1822, the native peoples welcomed them with open arms – thinking these strange white men with their weapons that spit fire only came to trade. Instead, they were put under the yoke of colonialism for the over a century. Since independence, our former masters have done little for us. Oh, they offer places in their schools for a few of those who qualify, but little in the way of assistance to build the necessary infrastructure comes from them." Morgan opened his mouth to speak, but Kabbah held up a hand. "I know what you're going to say, ambassador – and, you're right. We Nagandans need to take responsibility for our own development. I understand that, but it's difficult to explain that concept to someone who has only known a state of subordination and dependence."

Morgan noticed that Chambers was leaning forward. "You have something to say, Ms. Chambers? Ms. Alison Chambers is my special advisor, al-haji." he said. "In fact, I've been remiss in not introducing my staff. You know Mr. Kennedy, my security officer, of course, and Ms. Chambers." He inclined his head toward Pinchon. "And, Ms. Susan Pinchon is my deputy chief of mission."

Kabbah acknowledged each with a nod and a smile, and then, he surprised Morgan by extending his hand to each of the women, placing it over his breast after shaking each. "It is a pleasure to meet you," he said. He looked at Morgan. "Ah, ambassador, you seemed surprised by my shaking hands with women. You must understand – Islam in Naganda, and in much of West Africa, with the possible exception of Nigeria, is much more liberal than in other parts of the Muslim world. We have people who follow most of the major religions in all tribes. While most Chiveru are Muslim, we also have Christians – as do the Ganda and Buntu. Nagandans are forty percent Muslim, sixty percent Christian, and one hundred percent traditional. Here, for example, interfaith marriages are not at all uncommon. My late wife, for instance, was raised in a Baptist mission, and followed that faith even though she married me – a Muslim."

"So, there is no conflict between faiths here?" Chambers asked.

"None at all," he said. "Typically, in mixed marriages, the children will follow different faiths when they grow up. The boys mostly adopt Christianity because most of the lucrative trades in Naganda are dominated by Christians thanks to our colonial masters, while the girls follow Islam for the security it gives them when they marry."

"The rest of the world could take a lesson from Naganda on that," Chambers said. "We're seeing more and more Christian-Muslim and Jewish-Muslim conflict in other regions every day."

"For Nagandans, the central focus is the immediate family, followed by the clan lineage," he said. "Our conflicts tend to be over resources rather than belief systems. And, that is why I've come to you. I fear that we have a conflict brewing, and it is over control of a potentially lucrative resource."

"I was under the impression that the gold and diamonds in Naganda were under government control," Morgan said.

"They are, and little of the income from either filter down to the average person," Kabbah said. "Oh, the villagers get some income from working the alluvial deposits, but the majority of the money goes into the pockets of the diamond dealers and corrupt government ministers. My people have long come to terms with that situation, though. No, the problem is a new resource, which unfortunately happens to be in Chiveru Land. You might have heard that a British geologist was in our land recently?"

Morgan nodded. "Yes, but we don't know why he was here."

"He was doing a geological survey of the country on behalf of an international oil company. There have long been rumors that parts of West Africa contain large pools of oil under the earth. Unfortunately, he found that in Naganda, we *do* have oil."

"Surely, that's good news," Chambers said. "Assuming that the government will equitably share the revenue, it should help build the necessary infrastructure."

"That, dear lady, is a dangerous assumption. Like the gold and diamonds, most of the income will go into the treasury of the foreign oil company. What's left will be siphoned off by ministers and other officials." He took another sip of tea. "That, in itself, would probably not be a disaster. Just business as usual. But, the problem is that the geologist only found oil in one region of the country – in Chiveru Land. We've maintained peace mainly because each tribe has been left in control of its traditional territory. Only in Mabuntu do the tribes really intermingle. Now, though, there's likely to be a mad scramble by Ganda and Buntu to grab tracts of land in Chiveru Land, and that could lead to intertribal conflict."

"Have you spoken to anyone in the government about this?" Pinchon asked.

"I asked to meet with Captain Gweru," he said. "But, I was shunted off to his uncle, Gideon Banda. He claimed to have no knowledge of an oil survey and basically gave me the cold shoulder."

"Do you think he was telling the truth?" Morgan asked.

Kabbah laughed. "The man was lying through his tobacco stained teeth," he said. "During my years with the UN, I've been lied to by experts, and Banda's hardly an expert. I can always tell when he's lying."

"How is that?"

"His lips were moving," he said. "Whenever the man's lips move, he's lying."

"I sympathize with you," Morgan said. "But, I'm not sure there's anything we can do to help you."

"I was hoping that you'd agree to meet with the paramount chief of the Chiveru, Idoma Changa," Kabbah said. "Here what he has to say."

"I've heard that Chief Changa never leaves his headquarters compound," Lee Kennedy said.

"That is correct."

"That would mean the ambassador would have to travel there. I'm not sure that's a good idea at the moment."

"I assure you, Mr. Kennedy, the ambassador would be perfectly safe. Chiveru are not only the most peaceful of Naganda's people, but they take care of visitors. They wouldn't allow anything to happen to him during his visit."

Morgan could see that Kennedy was on the verge of blurting out something about the armed men in Chiveru Land. "Let me think about, al-haji," he said. "We'll get back to you once we've had time to discuss it."

Chapter Seventeen

After Kabbah left, Morgan reassured Kennedy by saying that he wasn't planning to travel to visit Changa, but he didn't want to be rude to their guest. He then spent the rest of the day finishing the pile of paper on his desk. He left the embassy early to prepare to attend a reception at the French embassy.

He wasn't sure of the reason for the reception, since the French had already celebrated their national day on July 14, but as the American ambassador, he was expected to put in an appearance at all of the official functions held by the other countries. His absence might send the wrong signals to others in the diplomatic community.

According to the invitation, the reception was to start at 6:00 pm, so Morgan scheduled his departure from the residence to allow his arrival at the precise hour. He'd expected to be among the first to arrive, but was surprised when he walked into the large reception hall of the French ambassador's residence and found a large crowd already hovering around a large table of hors d'ouevres, most with a fluted champagne glass in his or her free hand. Many were fellow diplomats, but there were also several locals, including military officers in full dress uniform.

Andre LeFarge, the French ambassador, was standing in the center of the room, talking to a large, buxom blonde woman. When he saw Morgan, he broke off his conversation and rushed over to welcome him.

"David, *mon ami,* I am so happy that you were able to accept my invitation," he said, grasping Morgan's hand warmly. A slender man, with rounded shoulders and a slight paunch, he had a large hooked nose in a narrow face, with small blue eyes set wide to either side. His forehead was high and topped by a brown widow's peak. While he had the habit of looking at people down his long nose, Morgan had found him to actually be quite the opposite of what he'd thought the French to be – he was warm and friendly, and had an almost American sense of humor. "I am so glad you're here. I was getting quite bored with the rest of the party."

"Thanks for inviting me, Andre," Morgan said. "By the way, what's the occasion?"

"*Mon ami Americain,* we French do not need to have a reason for a party." He patted Morgan's bicep. "But, *actuellement,* it was an excuse to introduce you to the community at large, and perhaps have an informal chat. I didn't bill it as such, so everyone, especially you, would be at ease. This is okay, *n'cest pa?*"

"I suppose so." Morgan shrugged. "I could use a

little relaxation. It's been a hectic week so far."

"Is that so? Maybe later you can tell me about your week. For now, though, you must have some champagne and caviar."

He took Morgan's arm and guided him to the table, which was laden with cheese, fruit, and several silver bowls of black caviar. Snapping his fingers, LeFarge ordered the livered waiter to pour Morgan a glass of champagne, and another for him. When the glasses were filled, LeFarge lifted his glass, clinking it against Morgan's.

"To *liberte, egalite, et fraternite*," he said, and took a long swallow.

Morgan smiled and took a sip. He wasn't a particular fan of champagne, but had to admit that the dry, slightly sweet taste was refreshing.

"Here, here, Andre," a voice from behind Morgan said. "Are you monopolizing our new arrival already?"

Morgan turned to face Richard Barton-Ketterling, the British ambassador. As tall and broad-shouldered as Morgan, he looked more like the member of the Queen's Royal Guards he had once been than a diplomat. His thin brown hair was cropped close to his round skull, and he looked at the world warily with light brown eyes that were almost amber.

"Richard, glad to see you," Morgan said, shaking the man's hand.

"I was not monopolizing him," LeFarge said. "Merely

welcoming him to our little *soiree*."

"And, you weren't asking him what his thoughts are on our little country, I suppose?"

"Oh, Richard, what kind of diplomat would I be if I did not, eh? Of course, you interrupted us before I could."

The two men turned their gaze on Morgan.

"In that case," Barton-Ketterling said. "I came just in time, for I too would be interested in your observations."

Morgan wasn't in the least surprised. Contrary to what many people believe, diplomats seldom attend or host parties simply for amusement. A lot of what they report back to their capitals comes from idle chitchat at such functions. He knew that he too would be listening carefully to every conversation – occasionally asking questions to elicit more information.

"I haven't really made up my mind about the place," he said. "I get the sense, though, that all is not well in paradise."

"Can you be a bit more specific?" LeFarge asked. "What troubles you?"

"Nothing really specific – more a gut feeling – and, I'm not sure it would be appropriate to discuss it here." He looked around at the crowd. No one appeared to be paying them any special attention, but he knew that the ears of those nearest were tuned in to their conversation.

LeFarge leaned close. "I see," he said in a low voice, which Morgan knew was sure to draw even more attention. The ambassadors of the U.S., Britain, and France in a huddle had to cause people to wonder. "Perhaps later the three of us could retire to my study for a . . . more private chat?"

That would give him a chance as well to pump the two of them for information. "Of course," he said.

"For now, though, you must enjoy the party," LeFarge said. "So, circulate – make yourself known. There are many others here who want the pleasure of speaking with the American ambassador."

Morgan laughed. That was true. People, who, if he was an ordinary citizen, would never bother speaking to him, sought him out, wanted to know what he thought about all manner of things. He put his champagne glass on the table, piled some caviar on top of a small, round wheat cracker, ate it, took a deep breath and started circulating.

He hadn't gone three steps before the rush started. First, the Nigerian ambassador collared him, complaining about the lack of U.S. support to his government in settling its northern Muslim problem, to which Morgan replied that the United States tried not to get involved in another nation's internal affairs, and that if the central government paid more attention to its citizens it might get closer to an internal solution. The Nigerian took a few seconds to process Morgan's answer, and then walked off in a huff.

This didn't, however, deter others from blocking his

passage through the room to ask questions, his opinion, or express their displeasure with one or another American policy – the United National senior representative wanted to know the U.S. position on establishing an International Criminal Court to try suspected war criminals, a question that Morgan hadn't previously encountered, and one he ducked by saying that this wasn't an area he'd dealt with, and that the American representative to the UN was the one to address it, which earned him a stern look from the UN official, a normally cheerful Dutchman.

Morgan was beginning to think that the only people at the party not upset with him over U.S. policy, or his refusal to engage in debate about it, were LeFarge and Barton-Ketterling. And, he wasn't completely sure about the two of them – there were things he couldn't share with even them, which could make for a somewhat lopsided conversation. Everyone wanted *his* opinion, or so they said. But, what they really wanted was the American representative's opinion, which would be dutifully reported to their respective masters as the *American* opinion, each striving to demonstrate his (or in the case of the Swedish and Norwegian ambassadors, her) ability to elicit information from the Americans. Not that he faulted them. He was doing the same – except that he always attributed the source and made it clear that this might not represent the views of the source's government. Diplomats are supposed to only give their government's official line on issues, but Morgan knew that some had a tendency to insert their personal views into their private conversations – it's human nature to try and demonstrate your superiority, but it meant that conversations at receptions always had to be taken with a healthy dose of skepticism.

Looking for a brief respite from the unending inquisition, Morgan found a quiet space in the corner of the room near a tall potted palm. He grabbed a vodka tonic from the bar and tried to conceal himself behind the tree without looking as if he was hiding – by standing with the fronds of the palm draped across his shoulder and facing diagonally across to the other corner, occasionally taking sips from his glass.

It worked for all of three minutes.

"Ah, Comrade Ambassador Morgan," a gruff voice said from his right. "I hef been vanting to talk vit you all evening."

Morgan swiveled his head, looking over the palm frond into the round, florid face of Ivan Nabakov, the ambassador of the USSR. A native of St. Petersburg and a member of the Soviet Communist Party since he was in high school, Nabakov looked the part of a *nomenklatura* or party *apparatchik,* from his ill-fitting brown suit to the spots of red on his cheeks or burst veins in his nose. His English, unlike the soviet authorities Morgan had encountered in Dagastan, was atrocious – his accent so heavy one had to lean forward to understand him, which then subjected the listener to a blast from his breath that smelled like stale vodka and old fish eggs. Morgan had been avoiding the man from his arrival in Naganda.

"Ambassador Nabakov," he said. "How are you this

fine evening?"

Morgan leaned back to try and get out of the path of the noxious fumes emanating from the man's mouth, which only caused Nabakov to lean in closer.

"You did not pay a courtesy call on me after you arrived," Nabakov said. His fleshy lips pouted, and specks of spittle dripped over the stubble on his chin. "I have been wanting to discuss the situation in this country with you."

A child of the Cold War, Morgan reflexively distrusted Russians, and had deliberately avoided the man. He realized, though, that he would have to deal with him at some point, so it might as well be here at the reception, where he could always use the presence of others to break off the conversation if it ventured into subjects he didn't wish to discuss with the representative of America's number-one enemy. Enemy to his country though he might be, nonetheless, Morgan had no wish to alienate him, turning him into a personal enemy.

"Yes," he said. "My sincere apologies for that, but, I've been quite busy adjusting to a new environment and a demanding job. I'm still in the process of understanding the situation in Naganda, so I'm afraid I don't have any concrete impressions or opinions as yet."

Nabakov nodded and smiled. "Of that, I have no doubt," he said. "You Americans are often slow to understand the intricacies of foreign environments. I have heard it is because of the size of your country.

Hah! The Soviet Union is much larger, and we have many different nationalities within our borders, and yet, we seem to have better understanding of local conditions when we are in foreign countries than you do. I do not seek your views, comrade – I wish to share my views with you, to help you understand better what is happening here."

Morgan hadn't been expecting that. He would have thought the man would want to pump him for information – instead, he came bearing gifts. *"Well,* Morgan thought, *I'll have to be on my guard. I smell a Trojan horse here."* He returned Nabakov's smile. "Of course, Ambassador Nabakov," he said. "I'd appreciate your views. As one of the most senior ambassadors here, I know you're quite knowledgeable."

Nabakov looked around, his eyes narrowing. A middle eastern looking man in a well-tailored suit was passing, and Nabakov watched him until he was several feet away, and then he leaned in closer to Morgan, speaking in a voice that was barely above a whisper. "You are no doubt concerned about the rivalry between the various Nagandan factions," he said. "This, my friend, is a mistake. They will always be at each other's throats, and there is nothing we can do about it. What you need to pay attention to is the hand from the outside that is stirring the pot."

"I don't know much about Naganda yet, but I wonder what about the country could possibly interest outsiders?" Morgan wondered if Nabakov knew about the presence of the mercenaries. In fact, he wondered if the Russian might not be involved in that presence.

While he was reluctant to discuss the subject with his British and French allies, and would tread carefully when he did, he had *no* intention of discussing it with the Russian.

"There is more to this country than you Americans understand," Nabakov said. He took out a silk handkerchief and noisily blew his nose, then crumpled the cloth and stuffed it back into his jacket pocket. "While there is nothing here of strategic interest to the Soviet Union, beyond the solidarity of those fighting Western Imperialism, there is another country with its eyes on the region. You Americans are always acting frightened of us, but you need to be more wary of the dragon."

Morgan's eyebrows lifted. "Dragon – what dragon have we to fear?"

"Do you not know that the dragon refers to our Communist brethren to the east?" Morgan still looked puzzled. Nabakov looked exasperated. "You Americans are so ignorant of the world. I am talking about the Chinese. They have been moving into Africa like the hordes of Genghis Khan – like locusts – and, they will devour everything in their path. It is they who you should be concerned about."

This was the first Morgan had heard about the Chinese. He knew the Peoples' Republic had an embassy in Naganda, and that there were a number of Chinese merchants in the country, but he had yet to meet the Chinese ambassador, who he'd noticed was absent from the reception, and had heard no one mention anything they were involved in.

"What could there possibly be of interest here to the Chinese?" he asked.

"That, my friend, is the question. With the Chinese, who knows? I only know that they are up to something, and that it means nothing good for either of our countries. I caution you to beware of them."

With that, and one last noxious breath into Morgan's face, Nabakov spun on his heel and walked away.

One more fly in the ointment, Morgan thought. He made a mental note to ask Raine to take a look at Chinese activity. For that matter, he'd also assign Alison Chambers to look into it. If the Chinese had their fingers in the pot, things could get roiled up. The Russian was clearly concerned. But, for all Morgan knew, it could be because the Chinese were interfering with whatever nefarious actions the Russians were undertaking. Things were getting interesting, and not in a good way. He now had to worry about the Russian bear and the Chinese dragon.

Charles Ray

Chapter Eighteen

After the Russian had left him, Morgan spent the next hour eating, drinking, and making small talk with a succession of diplomats, local officials, and the odd lot who end up on diplomatic invitation lists, about a variety of things – thankfully, no one else brought up the Chinese, mercenaries, or probed too deeply about his thoughts on the problems of Naganda. As the crowd wound down, Andre LeFarge invited him and Barton-Ketterling to his private study, leaving the French deputy to host the few guest remaining. They had whiskey and cigars and shared information on the local situation until well after midnight. Morgan had too many whiskeys, which, on top of the champagne gave him one hell of a hangover the next morning.

He managed to recover by late afternoon, and left the embassy early, ate a light supper and turned in early, making Friday a bearable day.

On Saturday, he spent the day lounging around the residence, and had dinner with Chambers, Kennedy, and Rachel in their residence on the other side of town, forcing himself to limit his alcoholic intake to avoid Sunday being a repeat of Thursday. He didn't even bother getting out of his pajamas all day Sunday, basically sitting around listening to classical music on the residence's music system. He gave his cook and housekeeper the day off, and prepared his own meals.

When he arrived at the embassy at 7:30 Monday morning, he felt like a new man – ready to face whatever challenges Naganda wanted to throw at him.

Once he'd had his second cup of coffee and gone through the overnight cable traffic, he had Mary Sung call Alison Chambers to his office. She arrived within three minutes.

"Mr. Ambassador, you wanted to see me?" she asked as she walked in. "What's on the agenda for today?"

Morgan walked across and closed the door. "How about we can the 'Mr. Ambassador' stuff when we're alone, Alison," he said. "I'm must Dave." She nodded. "Now, I never got a chance to discuss with you my conversation with the Russian ambassador last week."

"I'll bet that was fun," she said, chuckling.

He told her what the man had said about the Chinese. "I want you to look under every rock you can find," he said. "See if you can find out what the Chinese are up to."

"Wouldn't the guys upstairs be better suited for that job?"

"I have them looking too," he said. "But, the more eyes on it, the more likely we are to learn something."

She laughed again. "You would have done well in INR – or even as a spook. You have a natural inclination for ferreting out information."

"I learned it in the army. Now, you get out there and start shaking the trees – see what falls out."

"You do know that Tom Breedlove is going to have puppies when he gets wind of this."

"Yeah," Morgan said. "I guess I'll have to find something interesting for him to do to make it up. Unfortunately, he hasn't shown me he's really a team player, and frankly, I don't really trust him."

"I don't think he's a bad guy," she said. "He's just a careerist who's mainly interested in his next promotion."

"You might be right. I'll give him the benefit of the doubt, but I can't give him forever. If he wants to be on my team, he'll have to prove it to me. Now, get out of here, so I can get some work done."

After she'd gone, he went over more paperwork, but his mind was no longer on it. He was about to forget it all and spend some time walking around the embassy, poking into offices and closets to see what people were doing, when Sung walked in.

"Mr. Ambassador, there's a gentleman here to see you. An American businessman named Benjamin Holder," she said.

"Did you suggest that he talk to Breedlove?"

"Yes, but he insists on speaking with you."

Morgan's inclination was to be just as insistent that the man go through the proper channels, but one of his jobs as ambassador was to support American business. He would, though, have Breedlove sit in on the meeting. That would give him another opportunity to assess the political counselor.

"Okay, but have Tom Breedlove come up and join us," he said.

Benjamin Holder, when Sung admitted him and Breedlove to Morgan's office, didn't look to happy at having been kept waiting. He was dressed in a dark blue suit, totally unsuited to the hot climate, showing darker circles at the armpits from sweat. His hair was combed straight back to cover the bald spot that started at the center of his skull.

"Ambassador Morgan," he said. "Thank you for seeing me."

"My pleasure," Morgan said. "Have you met Thomas Breedlove, my political-economic counselor? He'll be sitting in the meeting with us."

"I'd really rather our meeting be private, ambassador," Holder said.

"Of course you would, but that's not the way I do things." "I understand," Morgan said. "But, Mr. Breedlove handles all matters relating to American business. This way, I don't have to repeat what you tell

me."

Holder still didn't look happy, but Morgan's tone left no room for debate. That and the six-inch height advantage he had on the man helped.

"Very well, if you insist," Holder said.

Morgan led him to the sofa. He took the chair to the right, leaving the left-hand chair for Breedlove, who sat and crossed his legs, a note pad on his knee and his pen poised above it. Morgan smiled. He was at least playing his role properly.

"Now, Mr. Holder," Morgan said. "What can we do for you?"

Holder took business cards from his coat pocket, handing one to Morgan and another to Breedlove. The card identified him as the Vice President for International Operations of Petrolux, headquartered in Houston, Texas. Petrolux was the company that Morgan had heard had people in Naganda for a while. Morgan wondered why the man had waited so long to contact the embassy.

"My company has been looking to expand oil exploration operations in West Africa for some time," Holder said. "There's a strong possibility that Naganda has a significant deposit of oil, and we think we could get in ahead of the competition."

"Where in Naganda is this oil?" Breedlove asked.

"Uh, I'm not too familiar with the country," Holder said. He looked down at his hands as he spoke.

Morgan knew he was lying.

"Would it be in Chiveru Land?" Morgan asked. "The area where a certain British geologist did a survey recently?"

Holder looked momentarily surprised, but recovered quickly. He regarded Morgan through half-closed eyes.

"I see you're already well informed," he said. "I guess I might as well admit it. Yes, as a matter of fact, the Chiveru are sitting on billions of barrels of oil, and Petrolux is determined to get it out of the ground."

"I thought Petrolux had given up on Africa after losing out to Shell-BP and the other developers in Nigeria back in 1956," Breedlove said. "You guys came in dead last in the bidding."

Holder's cheeks flamed red. Morgan suppressed a smile. Breedlove might *be* a careerist, but he knew his stuff. Maybe, Morgan thought, there was hope for him yet.

Holder cleared his throat. "It's true we didn't do so well in Nigeria. We were late to the game, and the other producers had already staked the best claims and bought off all the key officials. Here in Naganda, though, we're ahead of the curve."

"Then, what do you need from us?" Morgan asked.

"Ahem, well, while we have the advantage at the moment of sole possession of the location of the oil deposits here, once word gets out, there'll be a scramble to influence the government. We'd like your assistance in that regard."

"We'll always assist American companies in legitimate ventures," Morgan said. "You must remember, though, that if other American companies are involved, we must treat each equally."

"Yes, yes," Holder said. "I understand that. We're okay with that as long as you don't disclose proprietary information. But, if you'll help us with the government, that's the really important thing."

Morgan looked at Breedlove. The political counselor gave an almost imperceptible nod of assent.

"We'll be happy to assist where we can," Morgan said. "If you'll just provide Mr. Breedlove here with the details of your project, we'll see what we can do to convince the government to work with you."

Holder looked hesitant.

"Mr. Breedlove and his staff are the experts in this," Morgan continued. "I assure you, you're in good hands."

"It's not that," Holder said. "There is one small wrinkle that complicates the deal."

Morgan and Breedlove shared a look. *"Of course,"* Morgan thought. *"There's always a wrinkle."* "And, what is that?" he asked Holder.

"The main pool of oil, according to the limey geologist we hired, is under the village of Ovimbi. In order to exploit it, the village will need to be relocated."

Chapter Nineteen

After Holder's departure, Morgan called Breedlove back to his office. Breedlove called Feinstein to escort Holder to the political section.

"I'm not sure Mr. Holder was completely open with us," he said. "When you talk to him, see if you can pry more information about Petrolux's venture."

Breedlove looked at his notes. "Other than the problem of relocating an entire village," he said. "It seems like a pretty straight forward case of business advocacy. I'm familiar with Petrolux, and they're a legitimate company."

Morgan couldn't believe what he was hearing. The man was tone deaf. How could he so casually dismiss the prospect of moving hundreds of people from their traditional homes?

"I don't think moving people from their homes qualifies as a straight forward situation," Morgan said. "The Chiveru have armed men in their territory, which has them upset enough. If the government moves in and strong arms them of their land, it could lead to intertribal strife."

"That's a problem the government would have to deal with, but our first obligation is to the American company. We should, of course, point it out when we talk to the government, and let them make their own decision, shouldn't we?"

Morgan thought it over for a few seconds. Basically, Breedlove was correct – it should be up to the Nagandan government – but, the embassy's involvement in such a decision just didn't sit right with him. He couldn't quite pinpoint the source of his unease, other than the feeling that Holder hadn't impressed him as completely honest in his presentation. There were just too many unanswered questions.

"Dig into it anyway," he said. "I'm not making a firm decision on what we'll do until I know more."

With a skeptical expression on his face, Breedlove acquiesced and said he'd get back to Morgan as soon as he'd done his research.

Morgan waited until he was sure Breedlove was back in his office before having Sung call Alison Chambers and ask her to come to see him. He still didn't trust Breedlove totally, but he wanted to avoid provoking a confrontation between him and Chambers. A few minutes later, Chambers appeared in front of his desk.

"You wanted to see me, Dave?"

"Yeah, have a seat. I have some more work for you." He then filled her in on his conversation with Holder, and his reservations about him and his company.

"The man can't seriously be considering asking the government to relocate an entire village?" she said when he'd finished.

"That's one of the few things he said that I believe. I don't think he gives a damn about the disruption it might cause either. I need you to get everything you can on Petrolux - and Mr. Holder in particular. I have a bad feeling about this."

"His company hired the British geologist to survey the country?" Morgan nodded. "What about the armed white men in Chiveru Land? Do you think Petrolux might also be behind them?"

Morgan felt like kicking himself. He hadn't even thought about the possibility.

"Why would they be?"

"Think about," Chambers said. "If they're anxious to have control of the oil there, they'd want to keep others out, right? What better way than have a bunch of thugs with guns?"

"Shit, I hadn't thought of it in that way. Find out if they've ever used mercenaries in the past. One other thing, Alison – I need to get a feel for how this might go down if Petrolux convinces the government to go along. What's the potential for violence? Who in the government would be involved? With the coup rumors, and the Chinese-Russian puzzle, I'd like to know if we have another possible crisis looming."

"Will do," she said. "Dave, there is one other thing." She looked hesitant.

"Not another problem I hope."

"Sort of," she said. "I know Lee's against you going to Chiveru Land right now – and, I sensed that you were cool to the idea as well – but, I think you should consider taking Kabbah up on the proposal to meet with Idoma Changa."

"I promised Lee I wouldn't do that. Why would you suggest that I piss off my RSO right now?"

"If you think he'll be pissed at you, think of how he'll feel when he learns that I proposed you do it? But, think about it – if you want to know how this Petrolux deal will impact the Chiveru, what better way than to talk to them directly?"

Morgan rested his chin on his steepled hands. She was right of course. He could sit here in his air conditioned embassy office and issue instructions, read dispatches, and hold meetings, but if he really wanted to know what was happening on the ground, he needed to walk that ground. Rather than academically studying what life was like for Naganda's minority tribe, he could find out from the people themselves. Soldier or diplomat, the principle was the same – you had to put boots on the ground to really know the situation.

"I suppose you have a point," he said. "I guess I need to get out of the capital at some point anyway – might as well make that first trip to the area where everything seems to be happening."

"I'd like to go along with you," she said.

That brought him up short. It was one thing to put himself at risk. Putting members of his staff – other than his security people, who got paid to take risks – was an entirely different matter. There was no doubt that having Chambers along to get her expert opinion on what they saw and heard would be valuable, but it would be hard enough getting Kennedy to agree to *him* going. The RSO would insist on going along too, and if Chambers went, not only would she be at risk, but Kennedy's daughter, Rachel, would be left alone.

"I'm not sure that's a good idea. Lee will be upset enough at me for going. If I try to take you along, he might just ask to be curtailed. Besides, you know he'll want to go along, and one of you has to stay here and take care of Rachel."

"Damn, I hadn't thought of that. You think you could talk him into not going?"

He laughed. "Do *you* think he could be talked out of going?"

"Shit," she said. "I guess I'm stuck babysitting."

Chapter Twenty

July 27, 1978,
Chiveru Land, Naganda

It took nearly an hour of arguing – sometimes heated – for Morgan to convince Lee Kennedy that the trip to Chiveru Land was worth the risk, and then another two days to make the arrangements, which included contacting Ali Kabbah, giving him time to contact the Chiveru chief and make an appointment, and then arranging the vehicles.

Tucked in the northeast corner of the country, Chiveru Land had no paved roads, and many of the dirt tracks were impassable during the rainy season. As it turned out, Chief Changa's headquarters was in the village of Ovimbi, which was located on a broad plateau that drained well, so the dirt roads, though bumpy, allowed the embassy's Land Rover to navigate the four-hour drive from the capital fairly easily.

Kennedy, after checking the security situation, had decided a single vehicle would be sufficient. George Toko drove, with Kennedy riding shotgun, his hand never far from the Colt Commander .38 Super he wore in a hip holster. Morgan and Kabbah rode in the back. Their bags were stowed in the cargo area behind the rear seats. Morgan would have felt more comfortable if he'd also been armed, but decided it would be inappropriate for the American ambassador to visit the senior official in Chiveru Land packing heat.

The rainy season had gotten well underway, and they were caught in a deluge as they left the capital, which turned the road into a sea of mud. Toko's driving skills, and the Land Rover's construction, made for a bumpy ride, but they managed. The rain, as usual, stopped after an hour, and within another hour the mud had dried to be replaced by yellow-brown dust that seeped through every crevice in the vehicle, getting in their hair, eyes, noses, and mouths, and coating every exposed surface. Morgan noticed that Kennedy looked as uncomfortable as he felt, but Toko and Kabbah seemed to take it all in stride.

The farther away from Mabuntu they drove the more rudimentary the road became. They passed through a succession of villages – circular mud huts covered with palm frond roofs, usually in ragged lines on either side of the road, with bare breasted women tending cook fires, carrying wood or large earthen jugs on their heads, with babies strapped to their backs or their over-sized hips, and naked children playing in the dirt. Here and there, men worked in the fields near the huts, or sat around on logs and benches drinking the potent beer the locals favored. Toko expertly avoided the chickens, dogs, and the occasional cow that constantly wandered on or crossed the road, sending the chickens scrambling in a cloud of dust as he leaned on the horn to warn them off.

They'd left the embassy at ten in the morning, stopped at the halfway point and had groundnut stew and rice, washed down with tepid cokes, at a ramshackle hut in a nondescript village, with over a dozen village urchins crowded around gawking at the two foreigners, remarking that one was almost black like them, while the other was a red white man, referring to Kennedy's complexion after only a few days exposure to the infrequent sunny days. Kennedy took it all in good humor, making faces at the young boys who ventured too close and laughing along with them as they rolled in the dirt in response to his expressions.

They pulled into Ovimbi at half past two, coming to a halt in a cloud of dust in front of the largest structure in the place, located in the center of a semi-circular grid of beaten dirt paths that were lined with a combination of mud huts with thatched roofs, and clapboard shacks with rusty corrugated iron roofs. Behind the building, the white dome of a mosque could be seen against the deep green of the surrounding forest, and directly in front of it, surrounded by huts, was a small whitewashed building with a cross over the front door – symbols of two religions that in other parts of the world were in competition, existing in apparent harmony. The ever present crowd of village boys met them at the edge of the village and ran along with the vehicle until they were about fifty yards from the large building, stopping at some invisible line in the dirt and standing there, their mouths agape. Two elderly men, bald on top, with hair on the sides and back of their heads like white tufts of cotton, stood to either side of the door to the building. They wore multi-colored robes that came to mid-thigh, and short blue pants, the faded fabric of which was just half an inch below the hem of the robes.

Kabbah emerged from the vehicle and bowed slightly at the two men. They inclined their heads toward him. He exchanged a greeting with them in the local language, and then launched into a longer speech, none of which Morgan or Kennedy understood. When he finished his speech, one of the old men said something and then went inside the building.

"He is informing the paramount chief that there are visitors," Kabbah said to Morgan. "We must wait here until the chief recognizes our presence and summons us."

"Are these the chief's guards?" Morgan asked.

Kabbah laughed. "Oh, no," he said. "They are part of the village council. They serve as the principal counselors to the chief. In his village, the chief has no need of guards – no one would dare harm him here. To do so would be to court the wrath of the ancestors, and condemn the violator to eternal banishment."

"Man, if we could get people in other places to go along with that custom, my job would be a heck of a lot easier," Kennedy said.

"You've heard the saying, 'it takes a village to raise a child'?" Kabbah asked. Kennedy nodded his assent. "Well, it takes a village, or in this case, a tribe, to have such customs. We have people who violate the rules, but very rarely, because one of the worst punishments that can be inflicted upon someone is to be shunned by everyone else – to become in effect a non-person. In your society, everyone is already alone, so such a punishment wouldn't work."

"Do the other tribes have similar customs?" Morgan asked.

"Similar, but at the same time, different," Kabbah responded. "Among the Chiveru, the custom applies to everyone in the territory or village, regardless of where they come from. The Ganda and Buntu have rules against harming each other, but those rules do not apply to outsiders."

"So, if a Ganda or Buntu does harm to a member of another tribe, there is no punishment?"

"We have national laws against it, thanks to the British, but English law does not usually penetrate to the countryside."

"Why not?" Kennedy asked. "They colonized the whole country, didn't they?"

"They controlled the country," Kabbah said. "But, Englishmen seldom ventured outside Mabuntu. They left control of the rural areas in the hands of traditional chiefs. So, in Naganda we have two sets of laws – English-based law in the capital, and traditional tribal law everywhere else. Each tribe has slightly different laws, which is why we tend to stay in our own areas."

"There's no movement across tribal lines?" Morgan asked in amazement.

"Oh, there's movement – always has been. Enterprising tradesmen who run the commerce between and among the tribes, some of them settle in an area they particularly like, and adopt that tribe's ways; there's even marriage across tribal lines, just as there is marriage across religious lines. But, when someone, and it's usually a man, decides to relocate to another tribe's area, he is welcome as long as he abides by that tribe's customs."

"So, people aren't tied to a particular area?"

"Please do not misunderstand me," Kabbah said. "There *has* always been movement across tribal boundaries, but only of a small percentage of the population. Women, for instance, seldom leave the place of their birth, and the vast majority of our people are buried not far from where they were born. We Nagandans, especially the Chiveru people, view the land as sacred. It contains the spirit of our ancestors with whom we hope someday to reunite. In any society you will have the few outliers, the explorers and adventurers, even in your American society. When I worked in the UN headquarters in New York, I had a chance to travel to many parts of America, and I met many people who, like Nagandans, would not conceive of leaving the place of their birth."

That, Morgan knew to be true. He'd seen studies indicated that nearly half the working population of the United States never used vacation days and probably far fewer than half the population even had a passport, or had traveled outside their home states. People, it seemed, were more alike than they knew. He'd even met employees in the Department of State, the government agency responsible for foreign affairs, who had never even been to Canada or Mexico, or even as far away as Florida. He'd met one man, a clerk in the department's publication office, who'd bragged that he'd only been in one foreign country once in his life – and that was to walk across the bridge at Niagara Falls in to Canada for a grand total of one hour, and he'd been happy to get back into the good old U.S.A. which he planned never to leave again.

The elderly man returned and said something to Kabbah. He placed his hand over his chest, which the old man reciprocated, then he turned to Morgan.

"We can go in to see the paramount chief now," Kabbah said.

"Will we have to remove our shoes?" Morgan asked.

"No, that is only required in the mosque."

The old man pushed the door open and stepped aside to allow them to enter. Kabbah led the way, followed by Morgan and then Kennedy. Inside the door they found themselves in a small alcove facing a brightly decorated tapestry hanging from the wooden rafters. Candles in wooden sconces were set high in the walls, their flames flickering slightly from a stray breeze. But, even with the candles, the temperature in the alcove was several degrees cooler than it had been outside. When the door thudded close behind them, the sounds from outside were cut off completely.

Kabbah parted the tapestry in the center and motioned them through.

The room beyond was even cooler than the alcove. A large open space with rough wooden columns down the sides supporting the roof beams which were covered with golden thatch, its walls were decorated with shields, spears, and monkey-pod wood carvings of animals and people. The floor was covered with a dark blue velvety fabric with a pattern similar to the tapestry at the entrance. Monkey-pod sconces holding candles were affixed about six feet up the columns and provided a flickering orange illumination.

At the far end of the room, a man sat in a carved wooden chair. He was dressed in a simple white shirt and a brown wraparound skirt, and his feet were bare. His skin was the dark brown color of the monkey-pod carvings on the wall. His face was narrow, with wide set brown eyes under dark brows, a slightly fleshy nose, and thin lips. Except for a small tuft of hair at the point of his chin, his face was as smooth as the polished wood it resembled. His hair, tightly curled – what Morgan remembered from his childhood as being called nappy – and cut close to his skull, was black with flecks of white here and there. In front of him was a low wooden table upon which were several shallow bowls also carved from monkey-pod. In the bowls was an assortment of items, including the polished bones of some small animal, now yellow with age, and small stones of various colors. Four chairs had been placed in front of the table, two on either side, facing each other.

The place smelled of candlewax and cinnamon, a not unpleasant combination.

As they walked forward, Morgan took it all in, his eyes wide. Sensing his confusion, Kabbah leaned in close, and in a whisper, said, "The paramount chief is neither Christian nor Muslim," he said. "He follows the traditional beliefs because he is the one who dispenses justice to all under his rule, and only the traditional faith reconciles the differences among the other religions."

Morgan nodded his understanding. It made sense. As the top dog over people of different, and sometimes competing, religions, this allowed the chief to be impartial.

When they reached the chairs, they stopped. Kabbah put his hand to his heart and bowed. The chief, who sat as still as a carved wooden statue, unmoving except for the occasional blinking of his eyes, inclined his head a fraction of an inch in acknowledgement, his gaze locking with Morgan's.

"Papa Changa," Kabbah said. "I have brought the American ambassador, David Morgan, for an audience with you. With him is one of his associates, Lee Kennedy."

"Welcome David Morgan and Lee Kennedy," the chief said in a voice that seemed to echo off the walls. "I am Idoma Changa, son of Imosa Changa and Animata Bundura, by the will of the people, the five hundredth paramount chief of the Chiveru people. Please be seated and enjoy the hospitality of my humble hut."

Kabbah pointed to the front chair on the right, indicating Morgan should sit there, while he took the seat facing him. Kennedy sat next to Morgan. Morgan gave Kabbah a questioning look. Kabbah raised an eyebrow and smiled, inclining his head forward slightly to indicate that it was okay for Morgan to speak.

"Paramount Chief Changa," Morgan said. "I, uh we, are honored to have been invited to visit you here in Ovimbi." He bowed slightly as he finished. Kennedy copied his movement.

"You have had a long journey," Changa said. "Let us first have refreshments." He clapped his hands and two bare breasted girls, probably no more than fifteen, entered from a door to the left rear, one carrying a large wooden tray laden with pineapple, an orange fruit that looked like mango, and peanuts – or, as the locals called them, groundnuts, and one carrying a tray holding a large plastic container, four glasses, and four porcelain saucers. The nuts, from the smell wafting from the trays as the girls approached, had been roasted. The girls put the trays on the table in front of Changa, bowed and left as quickly as they'd come.

Changa stood and put three saucers and three glasses near his guests, taking a saucer and glass for himself last. He then pushed the tray of fruit toward Morgan, and lifting the plastic container, poured a yellowish liquid into the four glasses. As he poured, Morgan detected a sweet and sour odor from the container. He recognized the palm wine Susan Pinchon had warned him about just before their departure from the embassy.

"It tastes like a mixture of sour fruit juice and kerosene," she'd said. "Not too strong, but it's deceptive. Two glasses of the stuff will knock you on your kiester, and you'll wake up the next morning with a headache that feels like a symphony orchestra is practicing off-key in your skull."

He picked up the glass, but held it, waiting for the chief to drink.

"Sir, I want to thank you for seeing me," Morgan said. "I know it wasn't easy to arrange this visit."

Changa looked at Morgan and laughed – a throaty chuckle. "It was not as difficult as you might imagine, Ambassador Morgan," he said. "Even though the national electric grid does not serve us out here in the hinterlands, we are still able to communicate quite effectively with our brethren in Mabuntu."

Seeing the look of confusion on Morgan's face, Kabbah leaned forward. "Paramount Chief Changa has a shortwave radio that is powered by car batteries," he said. "I have one in my apartment in Mabuntu, which, thanks to the lack of reliability of our national power, is also powered by batteries. We talk frequently. It was just a matter of a brief radio conversation to arrange the visit."

Morgan smiled and shrugged. He should have known, he thought. In the U.S., when the power fails, people are lost. In underdeveloped countries, they make do.

Changa raised his glass. "Now, I would like to propose a toast to our visitors." He took a long drink from the glass, and wiped his lips daintily with his palm.

Morgan took a tentative sip. Pinchon had been right – it had a sweet-tart flavor overlaid with the acrid taste he remembered from when he'd failed to remove his mouth from the hose fast enough when he'd siphoned gas from a friend's car in college. He forced himself to swallow, wincing as he did so.

"Palm wine is, like American beer, an acquired taste," Kabbah said. "You will not offend if you do not drink much. In fact, since you are unaccustomed to it, I recommend that you *not* drink too much."

Thankfully, Morgan put his glass down. He noticed that Kennedy had put his glass to his lips, but didn't drink. He too put his glass back on the table. Changa watched them with a half-smile, like a doting grandfather, as he filled three saucers with fruit and groundnuts, and then pushed them across the table.

"I think you will find the fruit and nuts to your liking," he said. "Please, have a small bit of nourishment."

Morgan picked up the fruit that looked like mango and took a small bite. It was tart, juicy, and delicious. Kennedy took a handful of groundnuts, filled his mouth, smiled, and began chewing.

"Best roast peanuts I've had in a long time," he said around a mouthful.

Changa and Kabbah drank more of the palm wine, and picked at the fruit and nuts, watching Morgan and Kennedy out of the corner of their eyes.

They ate in silence for several minutes. When the saucers were empty, Changa pushed his saucer and glass aside, and sat back in his chair.

"Ambassador Morgan, I know you must be wondering why Ali wanted you to speak with me," he said. "How much has he told you about the Chiveru?"

"Quite a bit, actually," Morgan said. "I'm interested, though, in your thoughts about what is going on in your country at the moment."

"That is what I like about you Americans," Changa said. "You get straight to the point. We could learn from you." He smiled down at Morgan. "Yes, I am familiar with your culture. I was not always a chief, you know. I was made chief ten years ago when the former chief died. At the time I was a graduate student at the University of Pennsylvania. I lived in the U.S. for nearly eight years."

"With a U.S. college degree, you could do almost

anything," Morgan said. "Why did you come back to Naganda?"

"It was my duty. The late chief was my father, and I was the eldest son, so when he died, I was next in line. My eldest son – and, I have six sons – will replace me. That is the way it has always been, and it is the way it will always be. The world changes, but some things live on. The Changas have been chief of the Chiveru people for as long as anyone can remember."

He spoke with conviction, but Morgan detected a note of sadness in his voice. He couldn't even imagine what it must have been like for a young man, educated abroad, to have to come back and surrender himself to ancient traditions as Changa had done.

"As chief for ten years, you must have seen many changes."

"Yes, many changes," Changa said. "But, few of them have really affected the people here all that much. Their basic nature remains the same. Some of the young ones leave for the city – but, many come back when they find they don't like the customs of their city cousins. Others are born, live, and die without ever crossing the border of Chiveru Land. I have introduced a few changes. The shortwave radio, for example. Before that, the only way we had of communicating was runners from village to village. I also introduced trucks, which enable our people to take their produce and handicrafts to distant markets. We are better off now than we were ten years ago, but only marginally."

"The chief is being modest," Kabbah said. "He has introduced many modern innovations into Chiveru society. It is true that people still cling to tradition, but they are the traditions of family, clan, and birthplace – many, no most of the houses in the villages here have battery-powered radios, and more and more people are visiting other parts of the country."

Changa smiled modestly.

"I am particularly grateful to your government, ambassador," he said. "For sending your Peace Corps volunteers here to teach our women better health practices. More of our babies are now surviving thanks to their efforts."

Morgan was happy to hear that the Peace Corps was achieving results here. "That's great," he said. "I'd like to meet with the volunteer while I'm here."

"Unfortunately, she's traveling to the more remote villages at the moment," Changa said. "She conducts classes for the women on how to stay healthy during pregnancy. I'm afraid she won't be back for several days."

"Is it safe for her to travel? I heard that there's a band of armed white men roaming around up here."

"Ah yes, the white mercenaries," Changa said. "We have nothing to fear from them."

"How can you say that?" Kennedy asked. "Didn't they kill some of your villagers?"

"At first, I thought so, but we have been watching

them from a distance for some time. They know we're watching, but do nothing. They are well-disciplined. When the second hunters approached them, they warned them off, but in a polite way. Why would they kill the first, and not the second? No, someone else killed my hunters. These white men are strange, but not wanton killers."

It doesn't worry you – armed white men wandering around your territory?" Morgan asked.

"Yes, it worries me, but they have not threatened anyone. The forest belongs to everyone. If they wish to stay there, as long as they do not harm anyone, they are free to do so. I worry more about the other – the ones who kill. It violates our culture."

"Do you have any idea who *they* might be?"

Changa shook his head. "No, but we continue to search for them. I do not think they, like the white men, stay here. Instead, they come and go. I think they might be poachers, after the chimpanzees that live in our forests. In Liberia there is a thriving market for chimpanzee meat."

In just a short time, he'd assessed Idoma Changa as a decent, dedicated leader, interested in bettering life for his people, unlike many African leaders who were only interested in enriching themselves. It would be a shame, he thought, if there *was* oil under his land, and he and his people failed to benefit from it. But, like Morgan, Changa had problems enough on his own turf.

"Tell me, chief," he said. "If oil was found here in your land, do you think it would benefit your people?"

Changa frowned at him, and stroked his chin. "So, you have heard what the English scientist discovered?"

"You know about the geologist?" Morgan asked.

"There is little that happens in my land that I do not know about, ambassador. I know the Englishman came with his instruments and maps, poking around and doing seismic surveys – and, I know he thinks there is oil here. You ask if I think it will benefit my people. My answer to that is – if those who lead our country were honest men, there might be some local benefit. But, with the exception of Musa Gweru, who I believe is honest and sincere, we are led by a band of thieves who will take what money the oil company decides to give to Naganda, and it will end up in Swiss bank accounts, or in new mansions and fancy cars for them and their wives and mistresses."

"You say Gweru is honest," Morgan said. "If he is in charge, why not approach him and ask that he ensure a fair distribution of the wealth?"

"Ah, there's the rub," Changa said, and waved his arms in a dramatic flourish. "*If* he was truly in charge, I might just do as you say. He is not in complete charge, however, so talking to him would do no good."

That was a new wrinkle. Morgan hadn't heard anyone else suggest that the head of the military junta wasn't in control.

"If he's not in charge, then who is?"

Changa looked at Kabbah, his gaze stern. "You did not tell him, cousin?"

"I wanted him to first hear it from you, cousin," he said. Kabbah turned to Morgan. "Yes, ambassador, the chief and I are cousins. I note you looked surprised when he called me that. I apologize for not telling you that from the outset. As to the other – he is correct. Musa Gweru is merely a figurehead, although I'm not sure he realizes it. The real power in this country is in the hands of his uncle, Gideon Banda, and his wife, Amata. You've met Banda, and I have no doubt you have come to the conclusion that he cannot be trusted. The man is greedy and evil. But, compared to Amata Gweru, he is a saint. She seldom appears in public, but Banda is with her every day, and nothing happens in this country unless the two of them approve it. There is a rumor that Gideon and Amata are lovers, but so far they have been discrete, so there is no proof."

"How do you know all this?" Kennedy asked.

"Some of the servants at both Banda's and Gweru's mansions happen to be Chiveru who moved to the city. They tell me things. Most of them are gardeners or maintenance workers, so they don't get inside the houses, but they've reported that when Musa travels outside Mabuntu, Amata sometimes spends the night at Gideon's house."

Morgan made a whistling sound and looked at Kennedy who had a wolfish grin on his face. "This just gets better and better," Morgan said.

"Yeah, there's something under every rock," Kennedy agreed.

Kabbah frowned at them.

"Sorry, no insult intended," Morgan said. "It's just that every time I talk to someone since I've been in this country a new potential problem crops up." He looked up at Changa. "Tell me, sir, what would be the reaction to someone asking you to relocate this village?"

Changa's expression didn't change, but when he spoke, there was deadly earnestness in his voice. "The only way this village will be moved is if I'm first taken out as a corpse," he said. "And, the same goes for every man, woman, and child here. We Chiveru are a peaceful people, but we were not always so. If anyone tries to move us, there will be war."

"Shit," Morgan thought. *"This just keeps getting worse."*

"Have you heard something about Ovimbi being moved, Mr. Ambassador?" Kabbah asked.

Morgan hesitated, and then decided against sharing this bit of information. No sense causing a panic – or a war – until he knew how things would work out with Petrolux's efforts to get at the oil. "No, not really," he said, regretting having to lie to two men he considered honorable. "But, if the oil deposit is in close proximity to the village, drilling operations could pose a danger to the residents. Often, companies will ask that dwellings close to their work sites be relocated. When that happens, of course, they pay the costs."

"It is not about the money," Changa said, and now he was scowling. "No one in Ovimbi is moving."

Chapter Twenty-One

Despite his anger at the subject Morgan had introduced, Changa was still the gracious host. He had two rooms in the rear of the large building prepared for Morgan and Kennedy, and invited them to join him and Kabbah for a sumptuous dinner that evening. The next morning, after a breakfast of rice gruel and tea, they said their goodbyes and started the trip back to Mabuntu. Kabbah was staying on a few days with his family, so, with the driver, George Toko, there would only be the three of them in the vehicle.

Changa had insisted on giving Morgan and Kennedy a gift before they departed – as was his tribe's custom. The problem was, his gift was a goat for each of them. Even if Kennedy hadn't objected on security and sanitation grounds, Morgan had no wish to spend several hours cooped up in a Land Rover over bumpy roads with two goats in the cargo area. Still, he didn't want to offend Changa by being disrespectful of his customs. He accepted the goats, and then asked

Kabbah to ensure they were delivered to the Peace Corps volunteer in the village. That was an acceptable solution to everyone – Changa complimented Morgan on his diplomatic solution.

The rain had come during the night, and by the time they got on the road at 9:30, everything was already bone dry, and the dust had coated the green foliage alongside the road in a yellow cloak. A rooster tail of yellow dust fluttered behind them as Toko navigated around livestock and people in the road.

Thirty minutes outside Ovimbi, they were finally alone on the road – no vehicles, no livestock, and no pedestrians – driving through an area with tall trees on both sides of the road, extending back as far as they could see. In some places, the limbs arched over the road, meeting in the middle, and forming a shadowy tunnel through which they drove. Thick vines curled around the trunks of some of the trees like large boa constrictors. Brightly colored birds darted across the road. At one point, they saw a family of baboons, foraging for food along the right side of the road. The big alpha male of the group stopped and stood erect, glaring at them with his fangs bared, as they passed, while the rest continued to scratch in the grass and dirt for food, ignoring them.

They came to one of the north-south rivers, which had cut a fifty-foot-deep, hundred-yard-wide channel that was spanned by a single lane wooden bridge just over a hundred yards wide. Toko eased the Land Rover onto the planks of the bridge and slowly began to cross. In the seat beside him, Kennedy looked out his window at the swiftly rushing river tumbling over giant boulders below them. Morgan, in the back seat by himself, kept his eyes on the road ahead. Even though he'd been a paratrooper in the army, and during his Special Forces training had been required to rappel from heights of up to 100 feet, he'd never been comfortable with high places – as a kid, he'd never joined his cousins who loved to play on the roof of their two story house in western Maryland.

The Land Rover was less than ten yards into its journey when the dark blue pickup appeared at the far end of the bridge. The normal practice was for arriving vehicles to wait at the side of the road if there was a vehicle already on the bridge, but the pickup drove onto the span and headed for them. Toko blew the Land Rover's horn, but the pickup not only kept coming, but seemed to pick up speed.

"Damn," Kennedy said. "That son of a bitch looks like he's planning to ram us. George, get us the fuck off this bridge!"

Toko had already seen the danger. He stopped blowing the horn, and brought the vehicle to a stop. Ramming it into 'reverse', he began backing it up, his eyes on the rearview mirror and the bridge ahead. When he felt the rear wheels bite the dirt of the road, he picked up speed until they were ten yards from the bridge. He then took his foot off the gas pedal, yanked up on the handbrake, and whipped the steering wheel to the right. This caused the front of the vehicle to whip sharply left as it spun on an axis with the rear as a focal point – the J-turn maneuver Toko had learned during a VIP driving course at the Diplomatic Security Service training facility in Virginia a couple of years earlier. Kennedy, who had braced himself as soon as he saw what Toko intended to do, smiled his approval. Morgan had been caught unawares by the maneuver was tossed against the right door, but otherwise unhurt.

Once the vehicle was facing in the opposite direction, Toko shoved the gear into 'drive' and stomped on the accelerator, pressing Morgan against the back seat as they shot forward.

"A little warning next time, please," Morgan said.

"Sorry, sah," Toko said.

"Mr. Ambassador," Kennedy said. "Would you reach behind you and get me my green bag? George, we've got to get off this damn road before they catch up to us."

Morgan looked out the rear window as he retrieved the bag. The pickup was halfway across the bridge. He saw flashes of light from the vehicle's right side, and then heard a 'thunk' below and behind him – the unmistakable sound of a bullet hitting metal. He turned and passed the bag to Kennedy.

"He's right, George," Morgan said. "They're shooting at us."

Toko sat like a rigid wooden statue, his hands at the 3:00 and 9:00 positions on the wheel, his eyes darting from the front window to the rearview mirror, and his jaw rigid, as he steered the nearly three tons of vehicle over the rough dirt road.

"Shit, if we drive into a populated area, innocent people are likely to get hurt," Kennedy said. He opened the green bag, and withdrew two Colt Commanders and four clips. He inserted a clip in each weapon, and passed one weapon and a clip across the back seat to Morgan.

"George, first chance you get," he said. "Pull off the road and into the trees. We'll make a stand there. Three against two, the odds are with us."

Morgan took the pistol. He put the clip in his pants pocket where it could be easily reached. Kennedy put the other weapon on the seat between himself and the driver. Toko glanced down quickly and smiled.

"Yes, sah," he said. "They taught me how to shoot this one at the school."

"I thought so – the way you handle this vehicle." Kennedy smiled back at him. He looked up at the rearview mirror. "Shit, they're off the bridge. We've got to get the hell off this road."

Toko glanced to his left. "Coming up," he said, and jerked the wheel left, causing the Land Rover to fishtail as the front whipped left. He brought it under control, and skillfully avoided crashing into a tree as he plunged them into the forest that lined the road.

A hundred yards into the forest, they came to a small, semi-circular clearing. Toko stopped the vehicle.

"Okay," Kennedy said. "Let's find a good defensive

position."

"I have a better idea," Toko said. "You and the ambassador find a place to hide. I will draw our pursuers away from here."

"No," Morgan said. "We should all stay together."

"I don't like the idea all that much, either," Kennedy said. "But, he's right. It would buy us some time."

"Do not worry, Mr. Ambassador," Toko said. "I know the bush. I will be fine. Once I've led them far enough away, I will circle back and find you."

"Okay, but be careful," Morgan said.

Kennedy checked the magazine in his Colt and then got out. Morgan got out on the right side and stood next to him. Toko picked the third pistol up from the seat and got out on the left side.

"Try to cover your trail if you can," he said. "We want them to follow me."

He then smiled and turned, plunging into the bush. He made lots of noise as he went, breaking branches and kicking at the undergrowth.

"Okay, now we've got to find a place to hide," Kennedy said.

He spun around and began picking his way carefully away from the vehicle. Morgan followed, trying not to disturb the surroundings. A hundred yards into the bush, they found a large boulder sitting between two large trees, with a low hill behind it. They both agreed that it would make a good defensive position. They eased behind the boulder. There was enough room for three people, and they had a good view and field of fire to their front and to the sides. The hill protected their backs. Sitting, with their backs against the tree, they could see over the boulder by raising their heads a little. They sat back and did what soldiers have done for ages – they waited.

It seemed like they'd been sitting for hours, with nothing for company but the raucous sound of the jungle birds swooping overhead or perched in the trees. Around them this deep in the forest, away from the road, the foliage was a deep green, and the ground beneath the towering trees was thick and brown from decaying vegetation. The temperature had soared, and the trees trapped the humidity, soaking them in sweat very quickly. Morgan batted at the mosquitos that were attracted to their body heat, and tried to remember if he'd taken his malaria pills for the week yet.

There was a rustling sound, causing both of them to reach for their weapons, and then the brush to their right front parted and George Toko, his face gleaming with sweat, stepped out into the clearing. He spotted them behind the boulder and rushed over.

"I led them a few kilometers in that direction," he said, pointing back the way he'd come. "But, it will not work for very long. They will soon know that I have tricked them."

Kennedy made a grunting noise as Toko slipped behind the boulder and knelt between him and Morgan. "Well, they'll have to come at us from the front," he said. "Did you get a look at them? It looked like only two men in the pickup. If that's the case, we stand a chance against them."

"Yes," Toko said. "It was only two, but they have automatic rifles."

"Just means we have to shoot first, and not miss," Kennedy said.

They sat back and waited – and waited. Morgan knew that Toko was right. Their pursuers would eventually discover they'd been led astray, and decide to search in the opposite direction. It was just a matter of time until they stumbled upon this hiding place.

After crouching behind the boulder for an hour, Toko jerked his head up and peered at the woods some fifty yards in front of them.

"I hear something," he said.

Kennedy, who was looking in the same direction, grunted in agreement. Morgan, too, had heard a sound that hadn't been made by birds – it was something larger moving through the thick foliage. They focused their attention in the direction of the sound, their weapons at the ready.

Morgan felt transported back to his days in Vietnam – waiting to ambush a Viet Cong courier, he and his men had crouched in the jungle much like they were doing now – having mentally catalogued the natural jungle sounds, when the man neared on the trail, he'd made a sound much like what Morgan was hearing now. It was a sound that you not so much heard as felt, a disruption in the natural flow of sounds that just pricks the edge of your consciousness. He held the Commander in an easy grip, not too loose, not too tight, his finger resting against the trigger guard, and looking past the front sight at the spot in the brush where his instincts told him his target would appear.

He'd only been off by a few feet. The brush parted about six feet to the right of where he'd been looking. A burly black man dressed in a green military uniform devoid of insignia stepped out into the clearing. He was carrying an AK-47 assault rifle across his chest. He stopped and looked to his left and right. Then he turned and said something Morgan and the others could not hear. He was immediately joined by another black man, this one of smaller build and dressed in brown pants and gray shirt, wearing a wide-brimmed hat with a battered crown, and also carrying an AK-47. The two men conferred in hushed tones. They appeared to be arguing, probably over the direction to go, as the burly man kept pointing toward the boulder, while the smaller man pointed off to the right. Finally, the burly man seemed to have prevailed. They turned and headed straight toward the boulder.

"Take aim," Kennedy said quietly. "I've got the guy on the right. George, you and the ambassador take the other one. Wait for me to fire, and then empty your clips into the bastards."

The wait was agonizing. The two men were taking their time crossing the clearing. But, Morgan knew that Kennedy was right to wait. Even an expert marksman has difficulty hitting something with a handgun from a great distance. Worse, he was about to use a weapon he'd never fired before. He didn't know whether it pulled to right or left, so would have to adjust after the shooting started, when his adrenalin was pumping, and the target likely shooting back. It would probably *take* the whole clip to bring the man down. He took slow, deep breaths to calm himself, and aimed the Commander at the center of his target's chest, just above where he thought the solar plexus would be, and let his finger rest lightly against the trigger.

At the edge of his vision he saw Kennedy tense slightly. He knew the man was about to fire, so he brought his attention back to his target, raising the Colt slightly, and bracing it by cupping his right hand with his left.

There was a sharp cracking sound from somewhere off to their left – a sound like fireworks – and, the man Morgan had been aiming at suddenly crumpled to the ground.

"What the -" Kennedy said.

"What just happened?" Morgan asked. He saw that the other man was also sprawled on the ground.

"The shots came from over there," Toko said, pointing to the left of the clearing. "I heard five or six shots."

They waited, but there was no further sound. "Who do you think it was?" Morgan asked no one in particular. "Could it have been someone from Ovimbi?"

"I don't think so," Toko said. "Chiveru people don't normally have guns."

"Could it be the army or police?"

"If it was either of them, why haven't they shown themselves?" Kennedy said.

"You think it's safe to move?" Morgan asked.

"Whoever that is, if they wanted to kill us, they've had plenty opportunity and we're still here. So, yeah, I think it's safe. In fact, I think the best thing we can do right now is get the hell out of here."

They moved from behind the boulder. Morgan felt a tingle in his shoulder blades, feeling that some unseen marksman was aiming at him, but no shots came. They walked past the two dead men who lay face down on the dark earth, their blood soaking into the thirsty soil. It took them a few minutes to reach their vehicle - and a bit longer for Toko to maneuver it around and headed back to the road. He had to squeeze past the pickup, a rusty old Ford, which had been stopped a few feet behind the Land Rover.

Toko then retraced their route. When they burst from the brush onto the road, he had to swerve at the last minute to miss crashing into the green army jeep parked half-on, half-off the road. He drove between the jeep and an old U.S. Army surplus two and a half ton truck, finally coming to a stop on the other side of the road. Gideon Banda and a Nagandan army private sat in the jeep. Banda had a scowl on his dark face. The deuce and a half was filled with soldiers who looked with mouths agape at the embassy vehicle that had come crashing from the forest.

Morgan stepped from the Land Rover, brushing the dust from his clothing. Kennedy got out and stood next to him.

"You think these guys shot our attackers?" Kennedy asked him in a voice barely above a whisper.

The Nagandan soldiers were armed with old Enfield rifles, and Banda had a Webley MK V1, World War I vintage revolver in a hip holster. Though the jeep and truck were covered in a thin patina of dust, the men didn't seem to be as dusty as they would have been if they'd been in the brush.

"Somehow, I doubt it," Morgan said. "The shots sounded to me like AK-47's or M-16s – I remember that sound from Vietnam. These guys have Enfields, and they make a completely different sound. Besides, if it had been them, why wouldn't they have shown themselves?"

Banda stepped from the jeep and walked toward them. His scowl had deepened.

"Excellency, I heard shots in the trees," he said. "In the direction from which you've come. What has happened?"

Morgan gave him a brief account of what had happened. He turned and ordered four soldiers to follow the back trail and check it out. They were back within thirty minutes, carrying the two corpses, the men's weapons slung over their shoulders.

When the soldiers had laid the dead men in the ditch beside the road, Banda walked over and looked down at them. He knelt and peered closely at the burly one. Then he stood and walked back to Morgan and Kennedy. His expression now was one of worry.

"I recognize the big man," he said. "He is a Ganda sergeant who has been absent from his unit in Mabuntu for over a month. Do you have any idea why he would want to attack you, Excellency?"

"No, I don't," Morgan said. "Nor do I know why he would be here in Chiveru Land."

Creases appeared on Banda's forehead. "Yes, that could be a problem," he said. "The Chiveru do not like outsiders in their land. They barely tolerate infrequent visits by the police and army. You know, Excellency, you should coordinate your future trips outside the capital with me, so that we can provide security. I suspect you will hear from the foreign ministry about this."

Morgan had no doubt that he would. He also had no intention of having his travel controlled by the ministry. He was more concerned, though, about the impact this incident would have on intertribal relations.

"What will you do about this?" he asked Banda.

"You need not worry about it, Excellency. Go on

back to Mabuntu. My men and I will . . . clean this up."

Chapter Twenty-Two

Because of the ambush and the meeting with General Banda, it was dark by the time they arrived back in Mabuntu. Morgan had Toko drive to the embassy. He called in the duty communicator, and he and Kennedy drafted and sent cables of their respective reports of the trip – his to the country directorate, Kennedy to DSS. He then had Toko drive him to the residence before dropping Kennedy off at his place.

Morgan knew the cables would arrive in DC late on Friday, just before close of business, and wondered if they would elicit some kind of immediate, panic response. They had put IMMEDIATE precedence on them rather than the NIACT, or Night Action Required, precedence, simply because the attack on Morgan merited it. To his surprise, he went the entire weekend without a call.

The first thing on Monday morning he called Pinchon, Breedlove, Chambers, and Kennedy to the executive conference room to brief the first three on the trip. Kennedy had already filled Chambers in on the highlights, but she listened carefully and took notes as Morgan talked nonetheless. Breedlove took notes, and regarded Morgan with a somewhat disapproving and judgmental expression. Pinchon simply sat looking amazed until he'd finished his story.

"And, people think the life of a diplomat is an endless round of boring cocktail parties," Pinchon said. "You three are incredibly lucky."

"What I don't understand," Chambers said. "Is who came to your rescue, and why they didn't identify themselves. Are you sure it wasn't Banda's men."

"Yeah, pretty sure," Morgan said. "For one thing, the shots we heard came from a different weapon than the kind Banda's men were carrying."

"How can you be sure of that?" Breedlove asked.

Morgan gave the political officer a steely look. "I got shot at enough in Vietnam, son," he said. "I know the sounds that different weapons make."

"For the record, I agree with the ambassador," Kennedy added. "I don't know who it was, but it wasn't the Nagandan army."

"Whatever," Breedlove said. "This just shows that traveling to Chiveru Land was a bad idea."

Morgan tapped on the table. "Now there, son is where you're wrong. I wasn't too hot on going at first, but now I'm sure it was the absolutely right thing to do. We know more now about the mess here than we've ever known before."

"Sir, just *what* do we know?"

Breedlove was skirting dangerously close to insubordination. Morgan saw his frustration, but his mind was racing. He'd been running events through his mind non-stop, and had just had an epiphany of sorts.

"For one thing, I think I know who saved our asses." All eyes were on him. "Think about it, people. It wasn't the army, and the Chiveru don't have that kind of firepower. Who else do we know does? Come on, people . . . the white mercenaries. They would have the firepower, and we know they're in the area."

"Damn," Kennedy said. "Why didn't I think of that? It makes perfect sense."

"Oh, come on. You don't believe this malarkey about white men with guns running around Chiveru Land, do you?" Breedlove's voice dripped with sarcasm.

"Yeah, I believe it," Morgan said. "And, I think I know why they're there."

Again, all eyes were on him. Alison Chambers' brows arched upwards. But, before anyone could ask a question, Mary Sung walked into the conference room.

"Mr. Ambassador," she said. "The foreign ministry just called – the minister wants to speak with you, and they said it's urgent."

Morgan had been expecting that call. He looked at his watch – 9:00. The ministry worked slower than he'd anticipated.

"Okay, Mary, have George bring the car around front. I'm on my way down. I'll fill you all in on my thoughts on the mercenaries when I come back – Susan, you're with me."

When they arrived at the foreign ministry, they were met at the bottom of the steps by a skinny, baldheaded man that neither of them had ever seen before. Unsmiling, he greeted them, and then curtly told them to follow him. He spun on his heels and led them through the reception hall, into the back room, down a long hallway to a dusty staircase, and up two floors. When they came out of the staircase, he pointed to a set of double doors to the right. When he didn't move to open the doors, Morgan stepped forward and pulled on the rusty brass handles. The doors creaked loudly as they swung open. He turned and looked at Pinchon. Their escort had disappeared.

"That is the strangest reception I've ever gotten here," Pinchon said.

"Somehow, I don't think this is a friendly social call," Morgan said.

He walked into the room. It was a large room, with four high windows on the far wall, their glass panes so encrusted with dust and flyspecks, very little light came through. A large wooden table ran down the center of the room. Wooden chairs with high backs and tattered leather seats were placed around the table. At the far end of the table away from the door through which Morgan and Pinchon had come, was a single chair that was distinguished from the others by being set on a platform that raised it higher by six inches, so that whoever sat in it would be looking down at everyone else.

Sitting in the high chair was Gabriel Simbawashe. In his dark, almost black, suit, and with the scowl on his dark face, he looked like some vengeful judge about to pass sentence on a condemned man. In front of him was a single sheet of paper, which he stared down at, only looking askance at Morgan and Pinchon. At the side of the table, about halfway down, two glasses and a pitcher of water sat in front of two chairs. Morgan assumed this indicated where he and Pinchon were to sit, so he proceeded directly there and took his seat, looking up impassively at Simbawashe.

The foreign minister tapped a dark, pudgy finger on the paper. He then looked up at Morgan.

"First, Excellency," he said. "Allow me to apologize to you for the incident and express my happiness that you were not hurt."

"Thank you, Mr. Minister," Morgan said. "It was quite -"

"But," Simbawashe said, cutting Morgan off mid-sentence. "If you had bothered to inform this ministry of your trip early enough, we would have been able to arrange security, and this might not have happened."

The man's tone, which had at first been

sympathetic, was now like a teacher counseling an underperforming student. Morgan felt a hot flash of anger, but took a deep breath to keep from losing control.

"I doubt very seriously, minister, that notifying you earlier would have prevented this."

"Nevertheless, you know you're supposed to inform this ministry by diplomatic note whenever you travel outside the capital. The note from your embassy didn't arrive here until after you'd departed."

"I don't recall that I was to provide notification *before* traveling, minister," Morgan said. "Or, are you suggesting that I need the ministry's *approval* before I can travel?"

Simbawashe's mouth gaped open. He stared down at the paper. When he looked up, the scowl had deepened. "Of course not, Excellency," he said. "I merely suggest that you should consider taking advantage of our security when you travel. As you've seen from this trip, some areas of Naganda can be dangerous. Might I, uh, ask . . . why did you decide to visit Chiveru Land?"

Morgan sensed that they were now at the point of discussing the *true* reason he'd been summoned. They wanted to know what he'd discussed with Changa, or maybe, what he'd learned. He smiled.

"As ambassador to Naganda, I feel it necessary to know as much about the country and its people as possible. This trip was the first step in my education."

"I am assuming that you met with the paramount chief?"

"Yes – a fascinating man."

"What did you talk about?"

Blunt, unsophisticated – not a good technique to elicit information, Morgan thought. They must be desperate. Too bad. "Now, Mister Minister, surely you understand that I cannot divulge confidential conversations. If you want to know what the chief and I talked about, you should ask him."

Simbawashe sat back in his chair as if Morgan had slapped him. His bloodshot eyes wide and his lips turned down in an angry expression. He opened his mouth, and then snapped it shut, and closed his eyes.

"Very well, Ambassador Morgan," he said after a few minutes. "In the future, though, if you wish to travel to Chiveru Land, please notify this ministry at least two days in advance."

"Mr. Minister, do you require other members of the diplomatic corps to make such notifications?" Morgan knew the answer to that. The Chinese and Russian ambassadors, he'd been told, traveled anywhere they wished, and were not required to make any notification. Nor did the other African ambassadors have to notify the ministry when they traveled. Only the western embassies – the enemies of socialism – had the notification requirement placed upon them. Morgan had bridled at it, but had decided not to make an issue of it until now.

"What does that have to do with anything?" Simbawashe asked. "We impose this requirement for your safety."

"Of course you do," Morgan said. "But, as you can see, I can take care of myself. If you've nothing else, Mr. Minister, I have important work to do."

With that, he stood and headed for the door. He heard the scuffing of a chair on the floor as Pinchon hastily rose to follow him.

Outside in the corridor, as they got their bearings, Pinchon began laughing quietly. "They didn't teach us that in the DCM course," she said. "At the end there I thought he was going to have a stroke. I don't think any ambassador has ever spoken to him that way."

"If they're going to start jerking us around and controlling my movements, he'd better damn well get used to it," Morgan said, and there wasn't a trace of humor in his voice.

Chapter Twenty-Three

August 2, 1978,
Bureau of African Affairs Conference Room,
Washington, DC

Mid-week in DC, hump day, when government bureaucrats are working full tilt to get their desks clean by the end of the next day, Thursday, so they can leave early on Friday and get a jump on the weekend. Summer had hit the city hard, with humidity in the mid-eighties, and mid-day temperatures approaching the hundreds.

The air conditioning in the conference room was straining to keep the temperature in the windowless room at a comfortable level.

Six men sat facing each other across the long wood conference table.

Jason Symington sat in the center, flanked by Greg Wells to his left and Ed Harris on the right. On the wall behind him, looking down benevolently was a print of an oil painting of the Ethiopian Emperor Haile Selassie. Directly across from Symington was Lawrence Collins, CEO of Petrolux. To Collins' right was Philip Dawson, the Chief Financial Officer, and on his left was Winston Geddes, Petrolux's chief counsel. The Petrolux team was dressed in gray three-piece suits with pearl shirts and red ties. Collins had dark brown hair, combed straight back along his oval skull, and a patrician look in his brown eyes. He looked at Symington down a long, narrow nose, with an expression of someone smelling something unpleasant. Symington, in his usual blue suit, white shirt, and red, white, and blue tie, looked back and tried to copy Collins' expression, but had the feeling that he was losing on points.

The Petrolux CEO had asked for the meeting – actually, demanded it – to discuss the company's plans in Naganda. His expression, and the dour expressions of his companions, told Symington that all was not as the company executives desired, and he had a sinking feeling that David Morgan was the root cause of that displeasure. Wells had shared Morgan's cable with him, and while he was rightly worried about Morgan's safety, he was alarmed at his insinuation that Petrolux might be involved with the alleged white mercenaries. He felt like he'd been left in the middle of a frozen lake and that the ice around him was perilously thin.

"Gentlemen," he said, opening the meeting. "Welcome to the Bureau of African Affairs. How can we be of service to you?" He knew the greeting sounded hollow and meaningless, but couldn't think of a better way to get the conversational ball rolling.

Collins continued to look at him in a way that caused him to cringe inwardly. When the man spoke, it was as if his voice came from somewhere else.

"You could be of service," he said. "By ensuring that your ambassador in Naganda doesn't interfere with our business affairs there, and instead does the job he's supposed to do."

"I'm afraid I don't understand. Ambassador Morgan met recently with your representative in Naganda." He turned to Wells. "He's reviewing how he can advocate for the company, correct?"

The desk officer looked at his boss. "Yes, he is," Wells said. "There was, though, some problem with the company's proposed plans. They apparently involve relocating an entire village in a sensitive area of the country."

Collins' face darkened, and his thin lips turned downward.

"Quite often our operations involve some relocation of locals. We compensate the affected populations quite well."

"But, according to Ambassador Morgan, the people in this case don't want to relocate."

Collins leaned to his left and conducted a hasty whispered conversation with the skinny, pale skinned man who hadn't spoken since entering the room. He then turned back, directing his comment to

Symington.

"I'm assuming you're the senior man here," he said. "So, I know you'll understand our situation. We've invested several million dollars in exploration costs already, and so far we've been able to keep news of our find from our competition. We need the U.S. Government to encourage the Nagandans to cooperate if this project is to be successful."

"We, of course, support American business interests," Symington said. "But, if there's a local cultural problem, our hands could be tied."

"I think more is being made of this local *problem* than is necessary. It's strange, don't you think, that this only came to light after your ambassador visited the area?"

"What are you implying?"

Collins made a sniffing sound. "Ben Holder, our man in the field, informs us that Ambassador Morgan didn't seem too enthused with the proposal when he first brought it to the embassy. Then, your ambassador goes trundling off to Chiveru Land, and the next thing we know, the locals suddenly don't want to move."

"I think you're misrepresenting Ambassador Morgan," Symington said. "He's a professional who would never shirk his duty."

"How is it that you know about Ambassador Morgan's travels?" Greg Wells asked. "It wasn't covered by the media."

Collins looked flustered. He had another whispered conference with his counsel. "Uh, well, Ben Holder has a lot of connections in Naganda. He's one of our best field men. He told us."

"Did he also tell you that Ambassador Morgan's vehicle was attacked on the way back, and that he and his party were saved by some mysterious armed men who failed to show themselves?"

"That's out of line, Greg," Ed Harris said, speaking for the first time. "There's no call for that tone of voice."

Symington held up a hand. "Perhaps the tone could use some improvement," he said. "But, like Greg, I'm curious to know what your man in the field has told you, and just what he might be up to."

The advantage, which had been entirely on the corporate side of the table, had suddenly shifted. Collins' cheeks had pink blossoms, and his patrician stare had the look of someone who just picked up a bag of dog poop.

"You understand, of course . . . I can't divulge proprietary information. Suffice it to say, we are only interested in developing a promising oil deposit, and it would benefit the people of Naganda and help supply this country's energy needs. We could go to the Commerce Department, but they don't have a man in your embassy, so we've come to you for help."

"And, just what would that help consist of?"

"If your embassy could convince the Nagandan

government to grant Petrolux development rights, I assure you, everyone will benefit."

"But, that would require the relocation of people from their traditional lands," Wells said. "That won't go down well with the Chiveru. It could cause intertribal conflict."

"I think your Ambassador Morgan might be overstating that situation a bit."

While Morgan might not have been on Symington's Christmas list, and he knew that Ed Harris actively disliked him, he was not about to let this outsider get away with criticizing him.

"I strongly disagree with that characterization, sir," he said. "In fact, I'm somewhat offended by it. Ambassador Morgan is a professional Foreign Service Officer, and he would not do what you suggest. If he says moving those people would cause problems, I believe him."

"Ambassador Morgan says one other thing that's interesting," Wells said. "He says that there's a band of white mercenaries in Chiveru Land. He suspects *they* intervened when he was attacked, and he believes your Mr. Holder knows something about them. Would you care to comment on that?"

The lawyer leaned in and whispered something in Collins' ear.

"I have no idea what you're talking about," he said. "I assume from your tone that you have no intention of advocating for Petrolux in this case?"

"Not at all, Mr. Collins," Symington said. "As soon as we know precisely what is going on, we will advocate strongly for you – as we do for any *legitimate* American business operation."

Collins stood, and the other two followed suit. "Very well, then. I guess this meeting is at an end."

"Mr. Wells will escort you gentlemen out," Symington said. "You'll be hearing from us."

When Wells had led them out, Harris turned to Symington. "You know you just pissed off one of the most powerful men in America? That's not exactly a good career move."

Symington shrugged and smiled a wolfish smile that caused a shiver up Harris' spine. "He might be *one* of the most powerful men in the country, Ed – but he's not *the* most powerful."

"B-but, you're risking your career to defend Morgan. He's not even one of us."

"And, just *who* are 'us'?" Symington asked coldly. "Don't tell me you're -"

"No, no," Harris said, realizing that Symington had misinterpreted his meaning. "I mean, he didn't grow up in the Africa Bureau like you and I did."

"He's still an FSO, and as far as I'm concerned that makes him one of the only 'us' that really counts. Besides, he has some pretty powerful support – more powerful than our friend Collins by far."

Symington stood and walked from the room, leaving Harris sitting there looking bewildered.

Chapter Twenty-Four

August 4, 1978,
U.S. Embassy, Mabuntu, Naganda

Morgan went into the embassy earlier than usual for a Friday. But, he was scheduled to attend a reception that evening, and planned to leave early, so he wanted to get ahead on his paperwork, so he had Toko pick him up at 5:30, and by 6:30 was immersed in the pile of paper that Mary Sung had dumped into his inbox as soon as he came in. He'd never ceased to be amazed by the woman. He hadn't told her he'd be coming in early, but she still beat him in by at least half an hour. She also waited until he left in the evening before leaving herself. He suspected sometimes that she spent most of her waking hours at the desk just outside his office door, something he'd have to talk to her about. He knew she didn't have much of a social life, but didn't want her to spend all her time chained to her desk. The problem was, she'd been the same way in Dagastan, and when he'd suggested she take some time off, she gave him a frosty look and said weekends were enough for her.

At 7:45, the urge for a second cup of coffee hit him. He got up and went to the little alcove behind Sung's desk where a refrigerator, sink, and hot plate were installed for use by those in the executive offices. A large, cafeteria-style coffee pot dominated the counter next to the sink, and the smell of fresh-brewed coffee filled the space. Morgan took the cup that Sung had marked with a tape gun for 'Ambassador Only!' and filled it to near the brim. Holding it carefully, he started back to his office.

"You know I could get your coffee for you," Sung said without looking up from her typewriter.

He knew she'd be happy to do it, but in the army he'd learned that the best commanders were the ones who did little things like that for themselves. That habit had followed him into the Foreign Service, along with the custom of 'feeding the men first,' which meant that any goodies that came the organization's way were shared with the staff before the boss got any. This had been a standing joke between them since she'd come to work for him in Dagastan, and she seemed to get great pleasure in picking at him about it.

"When I become an incapacitated old man, I'll be happy to have you fetch my coffee for me," he said - which was his usual response to her little jape.

She laughed, still not looking up. Her thin fingers

fairly flew over the keys. He was always amazed at how she could carry on a conversation and continue to type whatever document she was working on, never missing a beat at either task.

Just as he was about to enter his office, he looked left through the open door, into the hallway that stretched to the far end of the building. Along this hallway were the offices of the political section and his administrative officer's staff. Normally at this time of morning it would be empty, but near the middle, in front of the political section, he saw Alison Chambers and Tom Breedlove. They seemed to be having a heated conversation. Breedlove was waving his finger in Chambers' face, and even from the distance, Morgan could see that her face was red. He couldn't hear what they were saying, but from their postures, it was a conversation that he was sure shouldn't be taking place in a hallway. He placed his cup on the corner of Sung's desk and headed toward them.

As he came near, he caught the tail end of whatever Chambers was saying. "– because I work for the ambassador, not for you." Her voice was low, but filled with anger.

Breedlove raised his finger again, waving it in front of her eyes. "I'm the political counselor," he said. "And if I -"

"What's going on here?" Morgan asked in a low, gruff voice.

They turned to face him. Both their faces were red now.

"Tom wants me to stop working on the research project you assigned me," Chambers said.

"I think it's a waste of time to -"

"Let's take this into my office," Morgan said. He turned on his heel without waiting to see if they would follow. They damned well better, he thought.

Once they were inside his office, he closed the door and turned to face them.

"Now, what the bloody hell do you two think you're doing? Arguing in the hallway like school kids, for Christ's sake," he said. He kept his voice even, but his cheeks were warm. "You first, Alison – what's going on?"

"Just what I said – Tom wants me to stop researching what the Chinese are up to."

"I think her time would be better spent checking on our Russian friends," Breedlove said. "If there's something sinister going on, you can bet they're at the bottom of it."

"She told you that I wanted that research done, didn't she?"

"Well, yes, but -"

"No buts," Morgan said. "I don't disagree that we need to keep an eye on the Soviets, but ignoring the Chinese is just as dangerous in my book. You can work the Russian angle, while Alison continues to look into what the Chinese are up to.

Breedlove opened his mouth to speak, but Morgan's cold glare left no room for argument. He snapped his lips shut.

"Good," Morgan continued. "Now, Alison, you go on back and get to work." They both started out, but he laid a hand on Breedlove's arm. "You wait, Tom." When Alison had gone and the door was again shut, Morgan looked the political counselor directly in the eyes. "Now, let's get one thing straight – when I give someone a job to do, any changes to that tasking will come from *me*. Do you understand that?"

'Y-yes, sir," Breedlove said. "I just think we're wasting time with the Chinese. They're not really significant here."

"And, you base that thought on what evidence?"

"Uh, well, it's common knowledge. They tend to support wars of national liberation. Now that Naganda is independent, there's not much for them to do but build a few roads that become quagmires during the first rainy season, and buildings that eventually crumble and collapse. It's the Soviets we have to watch out for, and all our resources should be targeted at them."

"Were you ever in the army, Tom?"

"No, what does that have to do with anything?"

"If you had been," Morgan said. "You'd know it's bad tactics *and* strategy to ignore any potential adversary. It's the enemy you know least about who is the most dangerous. Right now, that's the Chinese. I don't intend for us to get caught with our pants down. Now, get back to your office and dig into the Russians until you know more about them than they know about themselves. Alison, meanwhile, will do the same with the Chinese. Oh, and while you're at it, I hope you haven't forgotten to find out what Holder and Petrolux are up to."

"Whatever you say, sir," Breedlove said. "You're the boss."

"And, you'd better hope I don't have to remind you of that fact again."

Chapter Twenty-Five

At 8:00 that evening, when everyone but the Marine guard at Post One had left the embassy, and the building was quiet except for the hum of the air conditioner and generator that kept all the systems running, and the creaking and moaning of settling boards, Tom Breedlove sat in his office, dark but for the circle of orange light from his desk lamp. He carefully dialed the series of numbers that went automatically through the embassy switchboard, into the international phone system, and to a desk in the State Department's African Affairs Bureau.

Holding the phone cradled in his shoulder, he listened to the whirrs and growls, and then the clicking and buzz of the phone at the other end ringing.

"Ed Harris here." The Naganda country director's voice sounded like he was speaking from the bottom of a well with a chorus of crickets singing in the vicinity.

"Ed, this is Tom Breedlove. Do you have time to talk?"

"Just a minute." There was a rustling sound, then a dull thud. "Had some people in the office," Harris said when he came back on the line. "What do you want to talk about?"

Even though he knew he was the only one left on the floor, Breedlove peered nervously toward the door.

"The . . . last time I was in Washington . . . you told me to give you a call if I . . . needed help or . . . had a . . . problem."

"Sure," Harris said. "What's the problem?"

"What isn't the problem, you mean. Look, it's bad enough I have to put up with a woman as DCM, but the ambassador . . . well, I think I'm probably in hot water with him, too."

The line, except for the crackling of static, was silent for a long moment. "Hey, Tom," Harris said finally. "You have to just give Susan time. She's actually a good officer. As to a problem with Ambassador Morgan, what brought that on?"

It tumbled out of Breedlove like water gushing through a break in a dam – his feeling that Morgan was wasting energy and resources on the Chinese instead of focusing on the Soviets, his obsession with the story of white mercenaries, and his use of Chambers, who was not even a Foreign Service Officer, to undercut his position as political counselor. "I'm afraid I told him I thought this business about the Chinese was wasting time," he said. "He acted calm, but I know he was pissed. What should I do?"

"Well, to start with, Tom, you'd better never forget – Morgan *is* the ambassador. He might not be an Africa hand like you, but he's got some pretty strong backing here in DC. So, pissing him off isn't a wise career move. I'm here to support you as much as I can, but you have to tread carefully."

"I know, I know," Breedlove said. "Hell, I knew I'd screwed up as soon as the words were out of my mouth. Do you think I should go to him and apologize?"

"You could do that, or you could let your actions speak for you."

"Meaning what?"

"Morgan was in the army, and he's all about this gung ho teamwork shit. So, you become the consummate team player. Go beyond what he asks you to do, volunteer to do things."

"Even if it means wasting my time chasing ghosts?"

"You think doing what it takes to get a good performance evaluation is a waste of time?"

"Oh, right. I see what you mean."

"And, while you're at it," Harris said. "Keep notes on everything that Morgan says or does. Sooner or later he's bound to trip up. Oh, and it's not such a good idea to call me too often – only if it's truly important."

"Got it," Breedlove said. "Thanks, Ed – I owe you

one."

The sound of the dial tone told Breedlove that Harris had broken the connection at his end. He put the phone gently back into the cradle, and sat there staring across his desk at the shadows outside the ring of the desk lamp's illumination. Despite what he thought of them, he knew that neither Morgan nor Pinchon were fools. He would have to be at his best in order to convince them that he'd had a change of attitude – especially with Pinchon. He was old school, and believed that women were ill-suited to diplomacy. Oh, they made good consular officers, especially when dealing with American citizens in trouble, because of their ability to empathize. But, when it came to making the hardheaded decisions in other areas, he believed they were too emotional. He'd never worked for a woman before, and hoped never to again. If only, he thought, he could survive his current situation. As these thoughts tumbled through his mind, he never considered the reality of his situation. Susan Pinchon had never acted emotional in his presence – had, in fact, been considerably more detached and hardnosed than he himself was capable of being. Even Alison Chambers, when he was hectoring her and waving a finger in her face – her only emotional response was a red face and the whispered warning that if he didn't get his finger out of her face, she'd cut it off and shove it down his throat. His mind edited this out because it was not part of his world, and he had an amazing ability to see only what he wanted to see.

He was confident that he'd be able to fool Morgan. If his attitude toward women was matched by his views of military people – while women were too emotional, he thought soldiers were too rigid and one-dimensional. They didn't appreciate the nuances of a diplomatic situation. He had no doubt that Morgan was like that. Harris was right. If he just started playing the game – saluting and saying 'yes, sir' to everything Morgan wanted, he'd be okay.

If he had any doubts that he was doing the right thing, they were small and hidden somewhere deep in the back of his mind.

Charles Ray

Chapter Twenty-Six

While Breedlove was engaged in his phone call, Morgan was at UN House, a four-story white brick block-like building adjacent to the restricted area of the city, where he found himself surrounded by Nagandan officials and colleagues of the diplomatic corps, all wanting to know all the juicy details about the attempt on his life. For people who had experienced the bloodless coup by the Gweru junta, the idea of a diplomat actually being shot at was a novelty. Morgan had no doubt that his heavily edited version of the incident would feature in dozens of cables to their capitals – no doubt stressing the cowboy nature of the Americans who seemed to always be in the middle of violence at home and abroad. A Nagandan official from the ministry of economics and trade cornered him to ask for his assistance in obtaining a student visa for his nephew – a request he skillfully deflected by advising the official to call the embassy's consular section.

Morgan tolerated the endless questions with good humor, but his attention was focused on a small

Chinese man dressed in a dark gray tunic and trousers, of the kind favored by the late PRC Communist Party Chairman Mao Zedong, who stood alone in a corner of the large reception hall near the hors d'ouevres, holding a cocktail glass which he looked at occasionally, but who didn't seem to be drinking. Rather, he seemed to be carefully watching everyone else, his unblinking almond-shaped eyes cataloguing all that he saw. Morgan didn't stare directly at him, but from time to time, out of the corner of his eye he noticed that he seemed to be the man's main focus.

He had never met Wu Changwen, the ambassador from the People's Republic of China, but he recognized him from the biographical report Carlton Raine had given him that morning when he'd informed him that he was attending the reception and the Chinese ambassador was likely to be there. Wu looked exactly like the photo in the report – a portly Asian of middle height, round-faced with perpetually frowning lips and a flat nose and high cheekbones, his broad forehead extended upwards into a receding hairline. His hair, what was left of it, was glossy black and combed straight back on his skull. A long-time party member, now in his mid-fifties, Wu had joined China's diplomatic service after graduating from Beijing University. He'd served in a number of foreign postings, including China's embassy in Moscow as a junior political officer, before being assigned to Naganda as ambassador.

Alison Chambers had given him background information on the PRC, gleaned from reports she'd received from her former colleagues in the Bureau of Intelligence and Research at the State Department. According to the INR report Morgan had read, the PRC was currently in the midst of a leadership struggle that had been going on since Mao's death in 1976. The main contenders to control the country were Hua Guofeng, Mao's anointed successor, who wanted to institute Soviet-style economic planning and kept Mao's cult of personality alive, and Deng Xiaoping, a, reform minded member of the Communist Party who wanted to strengthen China by adapting to modern standards. Both Hua and Deng, as Mao had become, disliked their giant neighbor to the north, the Soviet Union, but unlike Mao, were willing to turn to a Soviet enemy, the United States. Wu, both Chambers and Raine had told Morgan, was a staunch Hua supporter, and if, as it seemed likely, Deng replaced him as the paramount leader of China, would likely be replaced as ambassador unless he proved himself valuable. While he was in Naganda, though, it was extremely likely that he was still following many of the customs and practices typical of Chinese Communist diplomats for decades – meaning he was probably assessing the various parties contending for control of the country, deciding which benefited China more, and throwing his support to that faction. Morgan could only guess what he'd do if there was a leadership change in China, but guessed that it still wouldn't be good for Naganda, or for the U.S.

Trying not to be obvious about it, Morgan slowly worked his way to the hors d'ouevres table. Stopping a few feet from Wu, he spooned black caviar and minced onions onto a wedge of black bread. When he nibbled at it, the salty caviar, tangy onion, and yeasty black bread made him wish for something to wash it down with, so he grabbed a glass of vodka from a passing waiter. The acrid bite of the vodka complimented the flavors of the food.

"It is not as good as a Chinese banquet would be," Wu said in almost unaccented English. The man had silently moved closer to Morgan. "Our *bai jiu* is far superior to this Russian swill. Have you ever attended a Chinese Banquet, Ambassador Morgan?"

Morgan had no idea what *bai jiu* was, but if it was similar to vodka, would be willing to give it a try. He wasn't surprised that the man knew his name. He no doubt had researched Morgan as thoroughly as he'd been checked.

"No, Ambassador Wu," Morgan said. "I've never had the pleasure."

"You might have a chance to do so, soon. Ever since your President Nixon visited my country in 1972, it has been clear that our two countries will exchange full embassies in the near future. Now that you have severed relations with the breakaway province of Taiwan, there are no more barriers."

Unfamiliar with the current state of US-China relations, Morgan decided it would be best not to discuss that issue. He could, though, talk about events in Naganda.

"I would love to attend a Chinese banquet. Do you

hold them here in Mabuntu?"

"As a matter of fact, we do," Wu said. "In October we celebrate the establishment of the People's Republic. Last year, your predecessor did not come. I hope you will accept my invitation this year. We will have a fifteen course dinner, complete with *bai jiu*, and our best beer, *qing dao,* which is better even than your American beers."

"I certainly hope to be able to attend," Morgan said, hoping that answer would be acceptable.

Apparently it was. Wu smiled.

"Tell me, Ambassador Morgan," he said - his voice low. "What do you think of the situation here in Naganda at the moment?"

"I haven't been here long enough to really understand the situation all that well, other than it's pretty complicated. I'd be far more interested in hearing our views."

"You are correct – it is a very complicated situation," Wu said. "Not only must Chairman Gweru contend with the supporters of the man he ousted, but he has problems within his own group and of the two, I believe his internal problems are far more dangerous."

"What kind of internal problems does he face?"

Wu moved closer to Morgan, so close that Morgan could smell the vodka on his breath, and see that what had looked at first like a black mole at the corner of his mouth was actually a piece of caviar. "I do not have all of the details," Wu said. "But, I have it on good authority that the chairman wishes to steer Naganda on a neutral course to enable it to concentrate on improving the economy. There are some within his group, though, who wish to forge a closer relationship with the Soviet Union. I think you would agree that such an outcome would not be good for your country . . . or mine."

"I suppose you're right. A neutral Naganda would probably be in everyone's best interests."

Morgan had no doubt, though, that it wasn't a neutral Naganda that Wu was interested in.

"Of course . . . a neutral Naganda," Wu said. "The former ruler, for all his faults, was very strongly anti-Soviet." Wu let that sentence hang in the air, looking at Morgan with a question in his eyes.

"But, from what I've learned, he was bankrupting the country. That wasn't good for the people, don't you agree?"

"As I said, he had his faults. But, in the greater scheme of things, it was preferable to Soviet control of the country, which is precisely what our Russian friends intend if they have their way."

"So," Morgan said. "What we should be working toward is a Naganda under Nagandan control. Free to determine its own destiny."

"Yes . . . a free Naganda is what we all want. You must excuse me now. I have another engagement. I look forward to seeing you at my reception." As Wu turned to walk away, his expression was completely unreadable, and that worried Morgan.

Charles Ray

Chapter Twenty-Seven

On the way home from the reception Morgan turned on the back seat light and made notes of his conversation with Wu in the small spiral notebook he kept on the back seat. When he'd finished, he tore out the pages on which he'd written, along with the two blank pages following so that no one could use the pencil rubbing technique to see what he'd written if the notebook was lost or stolen. Just as he settled back in the seat, his emergency radio crackled. The call was from Post One, informing him that a Miss Loewenthal had called from the airport and said she'd come in on the last flight from Europe. He thanked the Marine and ordered Toko to turn left to the airport instead of right to his residence.

His weekend, instead of being two days of sitting around listening to the radio and reading old newspapers and magazines, as he'd originally planned, was forty-eight hours of sheer physical exhaustion as he and Monika Loewenthal experimented with different ways to give each other pleasure.

When he dropped her off at the airport early on Monday morning, they lingered in the parking lot for a long time, hanging on to each other tightly. The scent of her perfume was still in the car when Toko pulled in front of the embassy at 7:30. The driver smiled broadly as Morgan took a deep breath before getting out.

He breezed through the Monday morning pile of paper on his desk, still wearing a silly grin. Mary Sung reminded him that he should maybe grin a little less as they walked to the conference room for country team meeting. That snapped him back to reality, and he managed to get through the forty-minute meeting without his mind wandering to Loewenthal more than once or twice.

After the regular meeting, he asked Pinchon, Breedlove, Raine, Kennedy, Brennan and Chambers to remain behind. When everyone else had gone, he had Chambers close the door.

"I want to fill you in on what I picked up at the UN reception Friday night," he said after she'd resumed her seat. "And, compare notes on what we all think's going on here."

He proceeded to recount his conversation with the Chinese ambassador.

"Looks like you were right about the Chinese," Breedlove said. "They're clearly up to something."

Morgan looked at his political officer with narrowed eyes, but an otherwise neutral expression. He'd noticed how Breedlove had gone out of his way during the country team meeting to be cordial to Chambers, and how he'd nodded approval at almost everything Morgan had said. He liked team players, but Morgan wasn't impressed by butt kissers, which was how Breedlove was coming off. In addition, he found it hard to believe that the man had had a change of personality that quickly. He mentally resolved to watch Breedlove even more closely.

"You were right about the Russians as well," Morgan said, throwing the man a bone. Breedlove fairly beamed. "Both are up to no good, and we've got to find out what before it hits the fan. Alison, how about you filling us in on what you've learned about the Chinese?"

Speaking without notes, Chambers gave an in-depth briefing on the Chinese presence in Africa in general - and Naganda in particular. She apologized to Morgan for repeating much of what she'd already told him, but the others in the room hadn't had much exposure to the Chinese, and she felt they needed the background information to better understand the situation.

Essentially, she said, after Mao's disastrous Cultural Revolution, and the upheaval of the leadership struggle in China, the country had embarked on a course of economic development, which needed massive amounts of raw material to support its growing industrial base. Africa, with its abundant minerals, was a prime source, and the Chinese were switching from support for national liberation movements to wooing governments of the newly independent African states for access to resources. In many cases, they were butting heads with the Soviets who were still trying to build a stable of client states in Africa in their competition with the U.S. and the West.

"Your assumption that the Chinese are cool toward Gweru and the junta is, I think, correct, Mr. Ambassador," she said, summing up. "They were strong supporters of Saidu, and were among the last countries to recognize Gweru's group. Furthermore, we don't know yet if they're aware of the oil find – but, if they do, you can bet they'll be looking for a way to get a piece of the action."

"Thanks, Alison," Morgan said. He pointed at Breedlove. "Tom, what have you got to add to that?"

"First, I'd also like to thank Alison," Breedlove said. He cleared his throat. "I've always known the Chinese were interested in Africa for its resources, but I never understood they were in competition with the Soviets. I've always assumed they were a junior partner in the world Communist movement."

"The Korean War should have taught us the fallacy of that view," Morgan said. "MacArthur assumed the Soviets were so busy with their own problems, they'd never allow the Chinese to intervene, and everyone in Washington held the same belief. The Chinese, though, had their own ideas, as they proved when their forces poured across the Yalu and kicked our butts all the way back to the 38th Parallel. The fact is, the Chinese and the Russians have never really got along all that well, and China doesn't think of itself as *anyone's* subordinate."

Breedlove sheepishly admitted that it had been a revelation. He then went on to explain that the Russians didn't so much need African resources as they merely wanted to make it more difficult for the Free World to get at them – in particular, their aim was to frustrate the United States. For their part, many of the African leaders had drifted into the Communist camp in their efforts to get out from under the yoke of European colonialism. Even some of the African elites who had been educated in Europe and the United States had taken to Communism after experiencing racial inequality during their studies, and in some cases, seeing firsthand the unequal distribution of wealth in the capitalist countries.

While Naganda, like the rest of Africa, had been colonized by Britain during the rush for colonies after 1879, and had been just as mercilessly exploited as the rest, no real armed resistance had formed. As they'd done in Sierra Leone, the British colonial administrators had confined themselves and their direct administration to the capital – meaning that most of the development of industry, infrastructure, education, and health services had been confined to Mabuntu – and had left traditional rulers in nominal charge in the Ganda, Buntu, and Chiveru tribal lands. Because most of the resources that the British were interested in, gold and diamonds for the most part, were in Ganda and Buntu lands, the Chiveru, who accounted for no more than ten percent throughout the country's history, had been left to themselves other than having to pay hut taxes like everyone else. The country's topography and distribution of resources didn't lend themselves to large scale mining or agricultural operations, so Nagandans hadn't faced the forced labor or conscription problems that had provoked insurrection in many other colonies. There had been agitation for, first equality, and then independence, by the elites who, after 1912, were able to go abroad to study. After World War II, its economy and military strength drained by the war, Britain had begun divesting itself of its colonies, and had eventually granted Naganda independence.

Britain's post-independence support, because of its own situation, hadn't improved the country's situation, and the Soviet Union had stepped in, building roads, helping to organize the national army, which during colonialism had been little more than a native constabulary, and providing some budgetary support, in exchange for resources. The Russians hadn't helped Naganda develop an effective industrial sector, leaving it dependent upon export of raw materials. By the late 1960s, whether from guilt, or fear of the Russians, the British increased their support to the country, in particular training and equipping the army on the British model. The U.S., wary of Soviet intentions in Africa, provided health and education assistance, and deployed Peace Corps volunteers to the countryside.

"Saidu, while not what I would call a puppet of the Soviets, was always a bit warmer toward them than us," Breedlove said. "His former army chief, Julius Bongo, was lukewarm toward the Russians, because he felt their military support was inferior to that from

Britain. Truth be told, many believe he'd really rather have gotten U.S. military support, but we never did much in that regard. Anyway, with this oil discovery, I fear everything's changed. There's likely to be a mad scramble by various Nagandan factions, with the Chiveru getting the short end of the stick because they're outnumbered."

"The Chinese will be in on that scramble," Chambers said. "To feed their growing industrial development – and, they're likely to do anything to get what they want."

"And," Morgan added. "I don't see the Russians standing idly by and letting that happen. Ian, what are you hearing from your military contacts?"

"Well, I'm still picking up rumors of a countermove by Saidu supporters – apparently Bongo's in it up to his thick neck," the defense attaché said. "But, I can't get any real details."

"Some of my sources report that Bongo has been meeting on the sly with the Chinese ambassador," Carlton Raine said. "I couldn't get any more details than Colonel Brennan here, but the rumors are that the Chinese are not only supporting his efforts to put Saidu back in power, but they're providing weapons and equipment to his people."

"Damn," Brennan said. "That must be those crates our attaché saw coming through Conakry."

"Did he ever find out what was in them?"

"Not definitely, but a guy at the docks said he

thinks the crates contained some kind of vehicle."

"Maybe trucks," Breedlove said. "The Nagandan army is woefully short of transportation, so if there's a breakaway faction, they'll need transportation."

Brennan nodded. "Makes sense – those crates were heavy enough, they could have contained trucks."

"It would help if we knew where they were being stashed," Raine said. "I'll get my sources looking."

"That's good," Morgan said. He turned to Kennedy, sitting to his left. "What about security, Lee? Should we be taking any extra precautions?"

"I don't see any concrete signs of danger at the moment," Kennedy said. Morgan knew that with his daughter Rachel not due to leave for school in Switzerland for another two weeks, Kennedy was acutely sensitive to any danger to the embassy. "But, I'm keeping a close watch. We should, though, caution people to keep a ready bag packed in case things suddenly change."

"Okay, then," Morgan said. "Let's get to it."

He sat there alone for a few minutes after everyone else had gone.

Chapter Twenty-Eight

August 17, 1978,
Somewhere in the forest in
Chiveru Land

The sun was high in the sky, but only a few slivers of sunlight penetrated the leafy canopy of the trees to make sparkling circles on the dark earth of the forest. Ten hammocks with ponchos tightly strung over them hung from the trees. Nine men in dappled brown and green military uniforms crouched on the decaying humus near nine of the hammocks, cleaning their weapons – an assortment of AK-47 assault rifles and MKII Sten submachine guns – their eyes constantly scanning the surrounding forest. Two men sat in a small clearing nearby, a small fire between them, the smoke a small, curling white column snaking up toward the leafy canopy. A tripod assembly held a coffee pot over the fire. The rich smell of brewing coffee filled the clearing, competing with the odor of wet foliage, rotting humus, and moist dirt. The forest was alive with sound – the tweeting of birds and the barking of monkeys high in the trees. One of the men was dressed in a stylishly tailored brown safari suit that had dark circles of sweat at the armpits, while the other wore a dappled green military uniform that was devoid of insignia. Despite the fact that little sunlight penetrated the foliage, the heat in the clearing was like a steam bath.

Benjamin Holder brushed at a large dragon fly that landed on the epaulet of his safari suit, and frowned across the fire at the uniformed man. Dale 'Junkyard Dog' Callahan, a retired U.S. Army Special Forces major, looked back, his face blank and unreadable. Callahan was in command of the nine men, all veterans of U.S. Special Forces or the British SAS, hardened combat veterans all who had fought by his side all over Africa, and who looked like they were itching for a fight.

"Do you think it's a good idea having a cook fire going?" Holder asked. "The smell carries a long way."

Callahan took a K-bar knife from his belt and scratched at the rotting vegetation near his leather and canvas combat boots. "It took us a while to find this spot," he said. "But, it's unlikely anyone will spot us here. Except for the occasional hunter, the natives don't come here much."

"Speaking of the natives, you were supposed to remain out of sight. There've been reports of a band of white men up here."

Callahan picked up two metal cups from the ground, turned them upside down and banged the bottoms with his knife. He then filled them with coffee and passed one to Holder.

He blew on the steaming liquid and then took a drink. Placing the cup on his knee, he fixed Holder with a cold stare. "Look, we had to cross two countries and nearly half of this place after we crossed the border, just to get here. Crossing a few palms took care of border crossings, but up here in this jungle, you didn't really expect that ten white men would go completely unnoticed, did you?"

Holder took a tentative sip of the coffee. He made a wry face and put his cup on the ground.

"I suppose it was a bit too much to expect that you'd never be spotted, but you weren't supposed to kill anyone – you weren't to do anything but stay hidden until I gave you orders."

"Yeah, sorry about that," Callahan said. "But, I really felt we had no choice but to take those two guys out."

"Dammit, what do you mean? You could have just melted into the forest. Killing those natives when you did – well, the timing was just poor."

"Poor timing? What the fuck are you talking about? I might be a gun for hire, but I'm still an American, and I ain't about to stand by and let some jungle bunny kill the American ambassador."

"Wha-, so, it was you guys who came to Morgan's

assistance. How in hell did you know it was him, anyway?"

"I saw the embassy plates on the car and two men, a white and a black got out – we might be up here in the sticks, but I keep track of what's going on." Callahan's voice had a tinge of sarcasm. "Don't worry, they didn't see us."

"Yeah, well I suppose that *was* the right thing to do," Holder said. "Can't have the American ambassador killed just as we're about to make the biggest deal of my life. But, that's not the killing I'm talking about. Why did you kill the other natives?"

"What other natives? We only killed the two assholes that were shooting at the ambassador."

Holder looked skeptical. "Some locals were shot a while back near where you guys were spotted. You telling me you didn't do it? Who else up here has weapons?"

Callahan wiped the K-bar blade on his pants leg, and pointed the wickedly sharp blade at Holder. "Sounds like you're calling me a liar, Holder," he said. "You wouldn't be doing that, now would you?"

"No," Holder said. His face paled and his eyes focused on the blade. "I'm not calling you a liar. I'm just asking who else up here has anything other than shotguns or spears. People in Mabuntu have heard the tales of white mercenaries up here in the forest, and they think you did it."

"Well, we didn't do it." Callahan slid the knife back

in its scabbard. "I think I know the incident you're talking about, though. Some woman out gathering wood spotted us, and ran off screaming like she'd seen ghosts." He chuckled. "I guess a bunch of white dudes in the woods up here *do* look like ghosts. Anyway, we were un-assing the area when these other locals in uniform came up from the south. They had weapons."

"Locals in uniform? You mean Nagandan soldiers?"

"Nah, I don't think so. They were a ragtag bunch, and they had AK's, not the Enfields the Nagandan grunts carry. They didn't have rank insignia, and were completely undisciplined as far as I could see. If any local villagers were shot in that area, my guess is these dudes did it."

That brought Holder up short. He stared at Callahan, his mouth agape. It was one thing to have to worry about a bunch of hired guns he'd sent up here – at least they were professionals – but, if there was another force running around Chiveru Land with guns it could upset all his plans. He would never admit, even to himself, that he didn't really have a concrete plan; more a hope that he would be able to determine the course of events, and move things to Petrolux's – and his – advantage. He'd been toying with the idea of having the mercenaries stage some kind of incident that he could use to convince the government to move in and relocate the residents of Ovimbi. If Callahan and his men hadn't intervened when Morgan was being attacked, he would have had his incident all tied up with a shiny red ribbon – of course, he'd never say that to a super patriot like Callahan. Not, mind you, that he had anything against Morgan. The man seemed okay for a government bureaucrat. But, his death, or serious injury, would have been a means to a lucrative end for him and his company. It might still have worked if Banda and his troops hadn't appeared on the scene. With the commander of Nagandan forces as a witness, there was no way Holder could spin a story against the Chiveru. He wondered if Banda's presence had anything to do with the other armed men. The situation was beginning to get complicated, and in danger of spiraling out of his control. He might be forced to speed up his timetable – if only he was sure of what should be done. Then, an even more frightening thought exploded in his brain.

"What's the danger that these other armed men will run across you and your men?" he asked.

Callahan laughed. The sound of his mirthless chuckle sent shivers up Holder's spine.

"The danger," Callahan said. "Is that there'll be a few more bodies for the locals to bury. We counted about twenty of these yahoos, and like I said, they were an undisciplined lot. In a fight they wouldn't stand a chance against my men."

"I would rather you avoided a confrontation."

"Don't worry - we're not going looking for a fight. Just telling you what'll happen if they happen to accidentally stumble into us."

"Okay. I want you to stay alert," Holder said. "Things are reaching a critical point, and I might have a mission for you in a few days."

"We're *always* alert. That's how we've survived so many wars. Now, a little advice from me – if you don't want people to notice us up here, you might want to consider not driving up in that shiny car of yours, parking it on the road, and meeting with us face-to-face. We have the shortwave. You could send messages using that code I gave you."

"Yeah, I know. I'll do that from now on. I just wanted to talk to you directly about this to reassure myself."

"Quit being such a nervous Nellie," Callahan said. "You're paying us good money for this job, and you can be confident that we'll give you your money's worth. But, if you should have to come up here again, could you at least bring a couple cases of beer with you."

Charles Ray

Chapter Twenty-Nine

Morgan was having a great Friday morning. For some reason, the overnight traffic from Washington had been light, and there were no pending crises for him to confront. Moreover, he didn't have any evening events and his calendar for the weekend was clear.

He was sipping at his second cup of coffee and catching up on back issues of the *Washington Post*, when Carlton Raine tapped on his door and walked in without waiting for an invitation. Morgan looked up, down, and then back up again. The man looked terrible. His eyes were bloodshot and had large puffy bags under them, and his brown chin was dotted with black and gray stubble. His clothing, light brown cargo pants and a dark brown shirt, were rumpled and sweat stained, and looked like he'd slept in them.

"I'd say 'look what the cat drug in'," Morgan said. "But, I'm not sure any self-respecting cat would get near you. You look like shit warmed over."

Raine made a growling sound, but smiled. "I feel like shit," he said. "I've been up all night."

"So, that means you could use a cup of coffee," Mary Sung said from behind him. She stood there holding a cup from which white vapor and a rich aroma arose.

Raine turned slowly, breathing the aroma in. "Mary, you're the only person I know who can sneak up on me like that – and survive the experience," he said. He took the cup from her and drank deeply.

"That's because you like my coffee," she said. She turned on her heel and went back to her desk.

"You know," Raine said. "If she wasn't so devoted to you, I'd damn sure try and recruit her for the agency. Might do it anyway before I leave here."

"Good luck with that," Morgan said.

A standing bit of patter since their days together in Dagastan, Morgan was never sure that Raine wasn't serious. Mary Sung, who spoke Mandarin, Cantonese, Thai, Lao, and Vietnamese, in addition to her native English – she'd been born in Washington, DC – had one of the sharpest minds Morgan had ever encountered. But, she was never happier than when she was sitting behind a desk pecking away at a typewriter. She'd often told Morgan that when she retired from the Foreign Service, she was going back to DC's Chinatown and buy herself a nice condo and raise orchids.

Raine turned one of the chairs near Morgan's desk around, and straddled it, putting his coffee on the corner of the desk and propping his muscular arms on the chair back.

"I got some news for you," he said, his bloodshot eyes boring in on Morgan. "And, you're not gonna like most of it."

"In that case, you might as well give me the bad news first," Morgan said.

"Okay, the countercoup," he said. "Bongo has reportedly recruited around a hundred Ganda men, some of them deserters from the army, and has them holed up in the southwest of Chiveru Land."

"A hundred doesn't sound like much against the entire army."

Raine laughed harshly. "You forget, buddy – Gweru took over with nothing more than a pickup truck full of pissed off soldiers who wanted better pay."

Morgan winced at the thought. The Nagandan army had zero combat experience, and most of its senior ranks were occupied by officers interested mainly in what they could loot. As much as it pained him to admit it, a hundred determined arm men *could* probably pull off a takeover – especially if the rumors of dissension in Gweru's ranks were true.

"According to Ian Brennan Gweru is pretty popular with the rank and file," he said. "He should be able to rally enough men to beat down a hundred rebels."

"Ah, that's where the bad news gets worse," Raine said. "If they were facing guys armed with the same weapons, there's no doubt he could. Trouble is,

Bongo's guys have Gweru outgunned."

"Shit! How badly?"

"Pretty bad, according to one of my sources who happens to travel to the wilds up north to poach monkeys. He says he saw tanks the last time he was in the boonies, two of them. What he described was more like armored personnel carriers, but they had machine guns mounted on them. I'm gonna check it with Ian, but it sounded like a version of the Soviet BTR-60PB, an armored APC. Each one carries a 14.5 mm and a 7.62 mm machine gun and 16 armed troops. The Nagandans don't have armor, and only a few old .50 caliber machine guns. Against the BTR, they'll be cut to pieces."

"How in hell did they get armored vehicles up there?" Morgan asked.

"I think we know what was in those crates that came through Conakry."

"There were more than two crates, though."

"Yeah, meaning they probably have more than the two APCs," Raine said.

Morgan dropped his head into his cupped hands. This was rapidly becoming a situation that was out of control. If Bongo moved, and Gweru resisted, it would be a slaughter, and he knew well that in conflict on that scale there were always civilian casualties. It would be a mess.

"Soviet APCs? Sounds like our Russian friend's

been pulling one on us," he said.

"Not necessarily," Raine said. "In addition to the Soviet Union and the Warsaw Pact, a lot of the Communist world has equipment either directly from the Soviets, or they make domestic versions. The Chicoms and North Koreans make a lot of hardware that's a direct knock-off of the Russian version. Remember, Ian said the crates had Chinese markings on 'em."

"That's pretty ballsy, even for the Chinese. The world's not gonna look too kindly on them being party to a massacre."

"It's not only ballsy, but brilliant," Raine said. "My source said he didn't see any kind of markings on the APCs. They look like Russian, and without markings, Ivan's gonna be blamed for it. They'll deny it, but no one will believe them. The Chinese can sit back and smile, and when Bongo takes over, swoop in and clean up."

Morgan shook his head. "It can't get much worse than that."

"Oh, it can, bubba, it can definitely get worse," Raine said, stabbing a long, dark finger at Morgan's desk. "Remember the reports of white mercenaries up north?"

"How could I forget that? Are they involved in this, too?"

"No, my source doesn't think so. He accidentally spotted them when he was moving away from the

APCs. They seemed to be avoiding them as well. He counted ten of them, dressed in military uniforms and armed with automatic rifles, probably AKs, but he couldn't be sure. He said they moved through the bush like they knew what they were doing, but Chiveru Land is only so big – two armed groups skulking around the woods are bound to run into each other sooner or later."

"Great, the only thing to make that any worse is the damned mercenaries turn out to be American soldiers of fortune."

"There's a good chance that they are – or Brits," Raine said. "As you might imagine, my guy didn't stick around long enough to ask to see their passports."

Chapter Thirty

After Raine left to write up his report before going home to shower and change, Morgan had Sung summon Maya Livingstone to his office. The few remaining pieces of paper in his inbox were now forgotten. His first priority was to take care of any Americans who might be out in the countryside, in harm's way, and at the top of that list were Livingstone's Peace Corps volunteers.

If fighting broke out between the factions, the volunteers would be even more vulnerable than the local villagers, standing out like pimples on prom night, and wouldn't necessarily know where to go to get out of the way of the fighters. He was going to make a suggestion to Livingstone, one that he knew she would be likely to object to. He had the authority to do more than merely suggest, but he hoped it wouldn't come to that.

He was going over in his mind what he'd say to her when she appeared in his door. Today she was wearing a one-piece, flower print wrap around dress and head wrap, in yellow, red and green, after the style of the Ashanti of Ghana. She wouldn't pass for a local, and Morgan wasn't all that impressed with Americans who 'went native,' but he had to admit that she made a striking figure.

"Come on in, Maya," he said, getting up and walking over to the sofa. He offered her a seat on the sofa, and took his usual chair, the one nearest the wall and just off center from where she sat.

When she crossed her legs, the wrap around parted, revealing an expanse of cocoa colored thigh, which she didn't seem to notice. Morgan slowly looked away to avoid causing her to notice that he'd seen. Thankfully, she put her hands on her lap, blocking the view. He made an effort to keep his gaze on her face.

"What can I do for you, Mr. Ambassador?" she asked.

"I'm concerned about the volunteer you have in Chiveru Land," he said. "Uh, Ms. Tyler -"

"Taylor, Rebecca Taylor," she said. "What's the cause of concern?"

He wasn't sure how much he could, or should, share with her about the situation just yet. Not that he didn't trust her - but until he knew enough to tell the entire staff, he felt more comfortable keeping it within the core security group.

"Actually, I'm concerned about all of your volunteers. But, with the reports of mercenaries near

Ovimbi, and my being ambushed near there, I'm not sure it's a good idea to leave her up there all alone."

"The people in the villages up there love Rebecca. They wouldn't let anything happen to her."

Under ordinary circumstances that might be so, but if a war erupted, there was likely to be general panic. One lone white woman could get crushed in the stampede.

"My gut tells me that all of the volunteers should be pulled back to Mabuntu for a while," Morgan said. "But, I definitely think you should bring Taylor back."

She looked suspiciously at him. "Is there something you're not telling me?"

He might withhold information, but he wouldn't lie. "Yes, right now there is. I wish I could tell you, but the situation's still too murky. I promise that I'll tell you everything I can in due time. For now, though, can you just trust me?"

"Okay, I'll pull Rebecca back. She won't like it, but I do trust you. Lord knows, I don't know why I should, but I do. I'll go up first thing tomorrow and bring her back."

"Get Lee to go up with you," Morgan said.

She got up and started out. At the door, she stopped, looking strangely at him. Then, just as quickly and quietly as she'd arrived, she left.

Morgan breathed a long sigh. In his mind, he could

hear the whistling sound of the bullet he'd just dodged.

Chapter Thirty-One

August 20, 1978
A farm just outside Mabuntu

Sundays in the countryside, whether the area was predominantly Muslim or Christian, tended to be days of rest – a holdover from colonial times when Sunday was the only time workers in mines or other British-run concerns were given time off to be with their families.

In the Baptist, Episcopalian, Anglican, Presbyterian, and Catholic communities, people were gathered in small churches, the men seated to one side and the women and children on the other, listening to preachers and priests extol the virtues of hard work and probity in their native languages. The Protestants tended to worship in churches made of wood, while their Catholic counterparts seemed to prefer stone buildings. The Apostolics, a totally native African sect that wore white robes and eschewed buildings, preferring to worship in the open, gathered in handy fields, usually under a large tree, again, with men and women separate. In the Muslim communities, because Sunday was not considered a holy day, the men gathered in small groups to talk and drink tea, while the women prepared the staple food, casaba flour formed into a mixture the color and texture of library paste, and boiled. Called *fufu*, it was served with stringy green vegetables fried in palm oil, groundnut stew with bits of chicken in it, or fish. The palm oil stained everything it touched orange, so most of the villagers had orange-ish lips and fingertips. Once their church services were done, the Christian communities would break down along similar lines, with the men sitting around drinking palm wine and discussing weighty events, while the women prepared the daily meal.

In a house on a farm on the northeastern outskirts of Mabuntu, a farm that had once cultivated massive quantities of maize, but whose land now lay fallow; two men sat facing each other across a carved monkey pod coffee table. On the table was a large silver tray inlaid with the British royal crest, a silver tea urn, and silver containers for sugar and milk. Arrayed around the tray were china cups and saucers, each with its own tiny silver spoon.

The two men eyed each other warily. Though they belonged to the same tribe, they could not be more dissimilar, and had no trust or love for each other. They had been thrown together by circumstance.

Six feet tall, Julius Bongo had cut a fine figure as a

young officer in the Nagandan Colonial Constabulary, and subsequently as a rising star in the newly independent state's army. But, as he'd risen in rank, finding himself more and more immersed in the country's political maneuverings, his midsection had expanded, until now he was a six-foot-tall, graying man with skin so dark the shadows were blue, bloodshot eyes with yellowing corneas, and a stomach so large he could no longer look down and see his feet. The once-chiseled features of his ebony face were now puffs and folds of fat, and his thick lips were now curved into a perpetual scowl. For all of the deterioration, though, he still looked good next to the man sitting across from him. Joshua Saidu had always been chubby, but the years spent in idleness as president of Naganda after independence had turned his chubbiness into an obscene obesity. Almost as dark as Bongo, in the sarong he wore, he looked like a dark parody of an Asian Buddhist statue. His piggy eyes, as bloodshot and yellowish as Bongo's, were almost hidden in the folds of flesh of his forehead and cheeks. He matched Bongo's scowl.

Saidu poured himself a cup of tea, and spooned a large quantity of sugar into the cup. He then added milk until the mixture was almost white. He lifted the cup to his fleshy lips and with a loud smacking sound, drank. Bongo winced inwardly. He also fumed. According to the customs of the Ganda people, a host was supposed to offer his guest refreshment before partaking himself. This, he thought, was just another example of Saidu's perversity and showed how much the man had strayed from his cultural roots. He retained none of the finer cultural traditions of his people, and hadn't picked up any of the good parts of British culture. He was, in a word, a fat, slobbering brute. But, he'd been president, and the Ganda, strangely, supported him – or at least, a large number of them did. In order to get his own position back as head of the military, he had to put this buffoon back in office. He sighed and poured himself a cup of tea, adding a small amount of milk and sugar. He then sipped slowly, and quietly – tacitly rebuking his leader's lack of manners. Saidu didn't seem to notice.

"Is everything prepared?" He speared Bongo with a commanding glare as he put his cup down. "There can be no mistakes made. We must move swiftly, and strike hard."

"Yes," Bongo said. "All is in readiness."

"Our friends delivered as promised?"

Bongo chuckled. "Yes, and it will look like the Russians were behind it. I must say, they have a deliciously wicked sense of humor, those Asians."

Saidu's fat face creased with worry lines. That, Bongo knew, was his greatest fault. The man was indecisive and insecure, which was why he'd abdicated so quickly when Gweru and his troops came roaring up to State House. Sneak up behind him and say 'boo,' and he'd piss his pants – or worse.

"You are sure there are no problems?" Saidu said. "I would hate to see something go wrong at the last minute."

"I assure you, sir – *nothing* will go wrong. I have one hundred men armed and ready to move on my signal. By this time next week, you will be back in State House."

The worry lines eased, and Bongo breathed deeply. He saw no reason to tell the fat fool about the group of white men who had been reported in Chiveru Land. They were a minor annoyance in his view. The reports said there were only ten of them, and even with their automatic rifles, they would be no match for his hundred Ganda fighters armed with some of the best weapons the Communist world had to offer.

"Very well, General, no *Field Marshal* Bongo," Saidu said. "I think this calls for a celebratory dinner."

He clapped his pudgy hands, and a door across the room opened. Two young Ganda women, clad only in thin sarongs wrapped around their waists and ending at mid-thigh, walked in bearing large trays of meat, vegetables, bread and fruit. They were followed by a thin, elderly man who carried a tray upon which was a large bottle of Johnny Walker Black whiskey, a bucket of ice, and two glasses. Bongo smiled. Saidu was a fat fool, he thought, but you had to give him credit for knowing how to throw one hell of a party. The food would be delicious, the whiskey the finest available, and the two serving girls would make a fine dessert.

Neither man noticed the glare on the face of the man carrying the whiskey.

Chapter Thirty-Two

Morgan had only been asleep for two hours when the strident ringing of his front doorbell woke him. He reached over and flicked on the bedside lamp. The clock read 1:30. Damn, he thought, has the shit hit the fan already? That was the only reason he could think of for someone being at his door at that hour. It had to be an embassy American. They were the only ones the guards would admit without calling him first.

He pulled on a robe and padded down the long hallway to the front door. Looking through the peephole, he could see Carlton Raine standing in the glow of the security light. He swung the door open.

"Blood," he said. "What's brought you here this late – or early, depending upon which day you wish to consider."

Raine, who had earned the nickname 'Blood' early in his agency career on several rather dangerous direct action missions, didn't smile at Morgan's lame attempt at humor.

"Can I come in, Dave? I just got some news that you need to know before you set foot in the embassy this morning."

Morgan stepped aside to let him enter. "Come on and sit down," he said. "What's your news?"

"Are we alone?"

"Sure. I give the residence staff the weekends off, and they don't come in this morning until six."

"Okay, then," Raine said. "No need to sit, I won't take up much of your time, but there's something you need to think about today. I have a source close to Saidu, and he called me around midnight. Bongo was at Saidu's farm today, and my source overheard them talking about the move on Gweru. It's happening before next Sunday – probably Saturday because everyone's out getting liquored up before having to go to church on Sunday, and the city's practically shut down."

Even though the news didn't surprise Morgan, it still gave him a chill. "Shit, that doesn't give us much time to get prepared," he said. "Did you find out where they're likely to strike?"

"No, the source didn't overhear any details of the operation . . . he did hear one other thing, though – the Chinese did supply Bongo. I mean, we already knew that, but this just confirms it."

"I'll have Susan convene the emergency action committee first thing. In the meantime, we need to try and get as many details of what these idiots have planned as we can. I'll see you in the embassy at 0800 – uh, I mean 8:00 am."

When facing an emergency Morgan tended to drift into thinking like a soldier. He'd have to watch himself. Except for Raine and Kennedy, no one else on the embassy staff had any military experience. What he needed most of all now, in addition to maintaining his own calm, was to keep them focused and on track.

"See you then," Raine said, and left.

Morgan locked the door behind him and padded back to his bedroom. If he was going to remain calm and in control he'd need his rest. He had a feeling he wouldn't be getting much sleep for the next several days.

Charles Ray

Chapter Thirty-Three

At 8:00 am on the button, Morgan was seated at the head of the big table in his conference room. He'd slept until 6:30, and after a light breakfast, arrived at the embassy at a quarter to eight.

To his right sat, in order, Susan Pinchon, consular chief Hector Gonzales, PAO Richard Weir, administrative officer Albert Pembroke, and Mary Sung who took notes. On the left were Tom Breedlove, Carlton Raine, Lee Kennedy, Alison Chambers, Ian Brennan, and Maya Livingstone. Breedlove had looked at Livingstone with a frown when he entered, but had said nothing. Morgan knew the political counselor was wondering why the Peace Corps country director was invited to an emergency meeting.

"Thank you all for coming," Morgan said. "Some of you are probably wondering what this is all about." He paused and took a sip of coffee. "We're facing an emergency situation, and it'll take everyone working together if we're to get through it in good order. I'd like Carlton to fill us in on what we learned over the weekend."

Raine gave a brief, sanitized version of what he'd told Morgan earlier that morning. "The bottom line," he concluded. "Is that Saidu's people plan to move against the junta this coming weekend. Our best estimate is that it'll be Saturday."

"Thanks," Morgan said. "Now, Colonel Brennan, would you share what you've learned?"

Brennan sat up straight, and began reciting a summary of the attaché office's information as if he was giving a military briefing.

"We've learned from some of the younger officers that former army commander Bongo has recruited some of the Ganda noncoms and rounded up young men from Ganda Land. He can field about a hundred. According to our sources, they're holed up in Chiveru Land for some reason, and we've confirmed the information Carlton's people dug up – they've been armed by the Chinese with a couple of armored APCs and two light amphibious tanks. In addition, they got AKMS assault rifles and ammo."

"My source didn't know about the tanks," Raine said. "What model?"

"I'm not absolutely sure," Brennan said. "But, from the description, I think they're the PT-76. They also got two Zil-131 trucks, enough transport to move a hundred fighters with no problem."

"Must have been Bongo's goons that attacked us," Kennedy said. He looked from Raine to Brennan. "How do you guys think this'll go down?"

Raine inclined his head toward Brennan. Morgan smiled. He knew that Raine had as much, if not more, combat experience as the colonel, but he was willing to defer to his military colleague. That was why the two men worked so well together – professional and personal respect.

"This is just guesswork," Brennan said. "But, in order to take over the country, they have to control the capital. That means neutralizing the battalion that's guarding the city – not a big problem considering it has no armor, and only has two .50 caliber machine guns to back up the Lee-Enfields they carry. The big problem will be getting to the city. I'm guessing they'll split up and hit it from at least two, probably three directions. Considering where they are, that means axes of advance the northeast, due north, and northwest."

"Why wouldn't they just push straight in *en masse*?" Breedlove asked. "You just said they have the advantage in firepower."

"Moving four armored vehicles and that many men in a single column over this country's roads would be a tactical nightmare," Brennan said. He tried to keep his voice level, but the look of disdain on his face was apparent. "They'd be unable to mass fires, would be in danger of getting strong out over a distance that would make it impossible to support each other, and since a force of that size would hardly go unnoticed, the folks here would know about them long before they ever reached the city. In order to achieve tactical surprise, they're likely to split into smaller groups, and move overland to get to the outskirts of the city."

"I think you're right," Raine said. "That's the way I would do it."

"That means the entire northern area of the country could become a war zone," Kennedy said. His face was grave.

Morgan saw the stricken look on Livingstone's face. Most of her volunteers were in the north.

He pointed a finger at the consular officer. "Hector, how many Americans do we have in the northern part of the country?"

"We have an estimated 200 Americans in the whole country," Gonzales said. "Mostly missionaries, and mostly in the north and northeast."

"How difficult is it to contact them?"

"We have wardens with shortwave radios in the key areas," he said. "I can contact them, and have them contact everyone in their network. The whole thing will take about a day. What do I tell them?"

"That's what I brought you all together to decide. We don't have a lot of time," Morgan said. "We need to focus on how to get Americans in that area out of harm's way without causing a panic in the process." He turned to Pinchon. "Susan, I want you to convene the full emergency action committee. I want to know where every American is, how we make contact with them, and how we can move them to safety. Lee, I'd also like your recommendations on securing the embassy and our residences. I'd like something by noon at the latest, so we can catch them in Washington before they go home for the evening."

Livingstone raised her hand. Morgan acknowledged her with a lifting of his brows.

"I suppose you'll want me to pull all of my volunteers into Mabuntu?"

"I think that would be prudent," Morgan said. "Work with Lee on getting transportation.

She looked hesitant.

"Is there a problem with that?" he asked.

"Uh, yes," she said. "I went to Ovimbi after we last spoke, to bring Rebecca Taylor back, but she wasn't in the village. They weren't worried because she often spends days traveling to the remote villages. I really couldn't tell them why I was back so soon – mostly because I didn't know anything. The problem is, I still haven't heard from her."

Morgan looked around the room.

"Okay, an additional task," he said. "Determine Rebecca Taylor's whereabouts and get her to Mabuntu. Any questions?" No one spoke. "Right then, I'll get out of your way and let you get to work."

He got up and walked slowly out. This was for him the hard part – had always been – turning things over to subordinates and stepping aside. His inclination was to dive in and start working on every little detail, but he knew that here in the embassy, as in a military unit, when the guy in charge micromanages, subordinates don't develop their potential, and eventually, things get completely fouled up. Every person in the room was a professional, skilled in their areas of expertise, and if he provided them with enough guidance, the resources to accomplish the mission, and the knowledge that he trusted them to get it done, it would be done. As he took the long walk back to his office, the words of an old sergeant major he'd served with came back to him, "A good commander tells his troops what he wants them to do, gives 'em the ammo and supplies to do it, then gets the fuck outa their way so they can get to it."

It wouldn't be easy, but he'd force himself to stay in the balcony and let his players tune their instruments in the orchestra pit without his interference. A nagging little voice in the back of his mind, though, was saying, "At the opera, nobody really gets killed."

Chapter Thirty-Four

BT

210945Z AUG 78

FM AMEMB MABUNTU
TO SECSTATE WASHDC IMMEDIATE
INFO   CDRUSEUCOM/J3/   STUTTGART   GE
IMMEDIATE

STATE FOR UNDERSECRETARY FOR MANAGEMENT,
BUREAU OF AFRICAN AFFAIRS, BUREAU OF
CONSULAR AFFAIRS, AND DIPLOMATIC SECURITY
SERVICE

EUCOM FOR OPERATIONS OFFICER

UNCLAS – FOR OFFICIAL USE ONLY

SUBJECT: CURRENT SITUATION IN NAGANDA

1.   SUMMARY: EMBASSY HAS LEARNED FROM

RELIABLE SOURCES OF PLANNED MILITARY MOVE AGAINST CURRENT GOVERNMENT, SUPPORTED BY EXTERNAL PARTY. PC VOLS BEING PULLED BACK TO CAPITAL, AND AMCITS IN RURAL AREAS IN NORTH AND NORTHEAST BEING ADVISED TO RELOCATE TO CAPITAL. WATCHING SITUATION, AND IF IT APPEARS TO BE DETERORIATING, WILL REQUEST NONCOMBATANT EVACUATION (NEO) VIA NAGANDA INTERNATIONAL AIRPORT. FOR NOW, REQUESTING AUTHORIZATION TO FUND VOLUNTARY DEPARTURE OF NONESSENTIAL PERSONNEL. END SUMMARY.

2. EMBASSY HAS LEARNED FROM MULTIPLE SOURCES OF A POSSIBLE ARMED MOVE AGAINST THE GWERU GOVERNMENT BY A GROUP LOYAL TO FORMER PRESIDENT SAIDU. THE GROUP IS BEING ARMED AND SUPPLIED BY FOREIGN ELEMENTS (DETAILS REPORTED SEPTEL). WHILE A DEFINITE TIME OF THIS OPERATION IS NOT YET KNOWN, INFORMATION INDICATES IT IS LIKELY TO OCCUR ON OR ABOUT AUGUST 26.

3. ARMED GROUP IS REPORTED TO BE IN NORTHEAST AREA OF NAGANDA. AMBASSADOR HAS ORDERED THE RELOCATION TO MABUNTU OF ALL PC VOLUNTEERS LOCATED IN NORTHERN NAGANDA. WARDEN NOTICE BEING ISSUED TO AMCITS LOCATED IN NORTH, ADVISING THEM TO ALSO MOVE TO MABUNTU IF POSSIBLE, AND IF NOT POSSIBLE, TO FIND A SAFE AREA UNTIL SITUATION RESOLVED.

4.   SECURITY SITUATION IS UNKNOWN AT THIS TIME, BUT THERE IS STRONG LIKELIHOOD THAT IT COULD DETERIORATE. IF THIS HAPPENS, EMBASSY WILL REQUEST NEO. GEOGRAPHIC CONSTRAINTS MAKE EVACUATION THROUGH NAGANDA NATIONAL AIRPORT BEST CHOICE. RUNWAYS AT AIRPORT WILL SUPPORT LANDING BY AIRCRAFT UP TO C-5, WITH LIKELIHOOD OF NEED FOR A FORCED ENTRY AND SECURITY TO MOVE EVACUAEES FROM ASSEMBLY POINTS TO AIRPORT.

5.   COMMENT AND ACTION REQUEST: IN ORDER TO MINIMIZE SECURITY RISK, EMBASSY IS REQUESTING DEPARTMENT AUTHORITY FOR VOLUNTARY DEPARTURE OF DEPENDENTS AND NONESSENTIAL EMBASSY PERSONNEL.
MORGAN

BT

As Morgan read the copy of the already transmitted cable, he tried to imagine the reaction when it hit desks in Washington. He had worked with Pinchon, Breedlove, Raine, and Brennan to draft and send a more detailed classified telegram (the Septel referred to in this cable) outlining what they knew about the planned countercoup, and the Chinese involvement in arming Bongo's force.

Even with the weight of evidence in that missive, though, he knew there would be resistance to his proposal for sending nonessential personnel out of country. In addition to the cost of transportation, there would be daily payments to those who departed – in all likelihood to Stuttgart, but some would opt to return to the U.S. Perpetually underfunded, the State Department was always hesitant to take on new operations because it meant siphoning money from someone's pet projects somewhere else. It wasn't a decision he'd made lightly either. If it was approved, and the countercoup didn't take place, he'd be on the shit list in Washington for a long time, and it would likely reflect poorly in his next performance evaluation. He was, though, sure of himself. There was just too much evidence to ignore, and he wouldn't be able to live with himself if he took the timid route and waited until the bullets started flying before asking for authority to take action to protect the people for whom he was responsible.

Kennedy and Chambers had already taken action. They'd called the school in Switzerland and arranged for Rachel to go early. She was due out on the evening flight to Amsterdam, and excited at the prospect of traveling to Europe on her own. Morgan had suggested that one of the adults accompany her, but both had resisted. Kennedy maintained that Rachel was a mature and responsible teenager – a contradiction in terms to Morgan, but he accepted his security officer's assurance – and besides, when things started popping, both of them would be needed at the embassy.

He was fortunate that there weren't many other children at the post – only Gonzales, Weir, and Pembroke had their families with them. They too arranged for their families to return to the states, banking on Washington agreeing to the voluntary departure, but willing to go out of pocket rather than expose them to danger unnecessarily.

He initialed the top left corner of the cable and tossed it into his outbox. There was little for him to do now but wait.

Charles Ray

Chapter Thirty-Five

August 21, 1978, office of
Deputy Assistant Secretary of State
Jason Symington, Washington, DC

Jason Symington looked up as Ed Harris came rushing into his office without knocking. He was about to chastise the man, until he saw the harried look on his red face.

"What is it, Ed?" he asked, trying to keep the anger from surfacing. Sometimes, the man simply forgot his place.

Harris held up several sheets of letter sized paper. "Did you see these cables from Mabuntu?"

A flicker of annoyance crossed Symington's face. It was nearly five, and he was getting ready to go to a meeting with the assistant secretary. He'd planned to come back to his office afterwards to read the late traffic.

He took a deep breath. "What is it about?"

"It's Morgan," he said. "He's asking for voluntary departure for nonessential personnel and dependents. Do you have any idea what a move like that will cost?"

He didn't, but he wasn't about to admit that to a subordinate. More interesting, though, despite Harris not mentioning it up front, was why Morgan would want to do it.

"Why is he asking for voluntary departure?"

There was a flicker of confusion on Harris's face, then embarrassment. Hah, thought, Symington, you realize you screwed up. Should have thought about it a bit more before you burst in here mouthing off. He smiled.

"Uh . . . he's saying there's gonna be a countercoup . . . something about the Chinese supporting it," Harris said. Then he placed the cables on Symington's desk. "Here, you can read it for yourself."

Sighing, Symington picked the documents up and started to read, thinking that if Harris wasn't such a self-absorbed idiot, he'd have prepared a summary brief and presented it properly. Or better, he could have sent the young desk officer, Greg Wells, in to do it. Now there was an outstanding officer, he thought, if only working for this dipshit doesn't ruin him, or make him decide to quit and go work elsewhere.

First he read the unclassified situation cable with the departure recommendation. He saw nothing in it, really, to be alarmed about. Yes, it would be costly to evacuate a few people, but not as costly as dealing with the fallout if a dependent was injured or killed. He then pushed that message aside and lifted the one with the red-bordered cover sheet – a highly classified message, which he quickly saw contained the details of just who (the damned Chinese) had armed the plotters, how they were armed (he didn't understand the designations of the weapons and vehicles, but took the embassy's word that they were lethal), and what was known about the possible timing, and route of march of the force. As far as he could see, David Morgan had pretty much covered all his bases, and made a prudent decision. On the other hand, he had to deal with Harris and his ilk on a daily basis. It was important that he do well in his current job if he was to have a shot at a higher position – like assistant secretary, or even a senior director position at the National Security Council – and people like Ed Harris could make or break him.

He carefully put the cable on top of the other one and looked up at Harris who was swaying, almost hopping, from side to side.

"Okay," he said. "A partial evacuation of the embassy dependents and some of the staff will cost – what – maybe a hundred thousand or so? What about the cost of someone getting hurt in the melee of a coup – especially a family member, and word got out that we wouldn't let the ambassador take action to protect them?"

"B-but, this'll mean shifting funds from some pretty important projects. I think Morgan might be overreacting to this anyway."

Symington's right eyebrow arched up. *"Overreacting? He has information from multiple independent sources, information through both of his intelligence agencies at the embassy, that indicates something is about to happen. Are you truly such a brain dead moron?"* It gave him pleasure to think that, but he would never say it. Instead, he looked at Harris with a benign smile on his face. "Maybe so," he said. "But, he *is* the man on the ground. I think we should give him the benefit of the doubt."

He spoke softly, but his tone was definite. The slumping of Harris's shoulders told him the man knew he was defeated. But, even a defeated rabbit, in the claws of a predator, has one last bite.

"Okay," Harris said. "But, you'll have to be the one to explain to the seventh floor why we're spending this much money."

Before Symington could think of a suitable response, the direct line on his desk – the one that only a handful of people knew the number to – rang. He raised a hand at Harris for silence, and lifted the receiver with the other.

"Symington," he said simply.

"Jason," the stentorian tones of Senator Jonathan Appleby came clearly over the line. "I hope I'm not interrupting anything important."

Symington sat straighter. Appleby was one of the few people who had his direct number, and *the* most important of that few.

"Not at all, sir," he said. "Could you give me a moment?" He put a hand over the mouthpiece. "We'll talk later, Ed – I have to take this call." When Harris had slunk out, he removed his hand. "Now, sir, how can I be of service?"

"It's how *I* can be of service to you," Appleby said. "I'm calling to help you avoid making a big mistake."

"I don't understand, sir."

Even in the privacy of his office, Symington was reluctant to use the man's name or title. It was always 'sir.' Nothing had ever been made explicit, but he knew that it was important to keep his relationship with Appleby quiet – his true relationship, which was not State Department official and senator. Of course, if pressed, he would have found it difficult to characterize that relationship. In public, Appleby was the senior senator from North Dakota, a member of the Democratic Party, and staunch supporter of the president and his policies. In private, and Symington thought, in actuality, he was the head of a shadowy, anonymous group of powerful men who met in secret, made strategic phone calls at just the right time, and made decisions that somehow found their way into the public policy process with the origin removed. While the bureaucracy could impact one's career, Symington knew that Appleby's organization could truly make – or break – a career, and he suspected that they held the power of life or death in their hands.

Within the State Department's Foreign Service

contingent such an organization also existed – although one without quite the same degree of power and influence. The White Dragons were a group of senior Foreign Service Officers, most from Ivy League, upper middle class backgrounds, who thought of themselves as the heart and soul of the institution, and who had managed over the years to gain control of enough key positions within the department to help each other advance. Symington had been recruited into the group by a former ambassador for whom he worked as political counselor, and was now considered one of its senior members. Appleby's group had coopted the White Dragons years earlier, and Jonathan Appleby himself identified select dragons, who he then pulled into the workings of the larger organization. Symington's chest swelled at the thought that he'd been one of the few so selected.

"Listen, Jason, and you will understand," Appleby said. "I've been informed that David Morgan, your ambassador in Naganda, is facing a potential crisis and is asking for authority to draw down the American presence. I've also heard that some in your bureaucracy oppose this move."

Symington wasn't surprised that Appleby knew this. The man had his tentacles in every department in Washington.

"Uh, yes," he said. "There's some concern that Morgan might be overreacting, and there's also the cost of moving that many people and paying them per diem for an undetermined period."

"Let me assure you that he is *not* overreacting. The threat is real, and the action he's recommending is not only prudent, but brilliant."

"So, the Chi-, er, foreign presence, in Naganda is real?"

"It is very real, and the skeptics over there in Foggy Bottom would be wise to start paying attention to him about it."

The way was now clear for Symington. His support for Morgan would piss the bureaucracy – especially Ed Harris – off, but it didn't matter. He had support where it counted. And, for reasons he couldn't understand, so did David Morgan.

Charles Ray

Chapter Thirty-Six

August 24, 1978
Foreign Ministry, Mabuntu, Naganda

The summons to the foreign ministry hadn't come as a surprise to Morgan. He had been a bit surprised at how quickly Washington had responded positively to his request for authority to drawdown nonessential personnel and send dependents away. But, he'd acted quickly, and the last of the family members and junior American staff had boarded the last flight out the night before. There was no way moving even this small group would go unnoticed, and he was sure the Nagandan government would be curious about it, and would probably be upset about it.

Sitting in the foreign minister's meeting room, with Simbawashe glaring at him, he could see that there was more upset than curiosity.

"Would you care to tell me, Mr. Ambassador, why

you're evacuating members of your embassy staff?" The minister's dark cheeks were suffused with red, giving him an almost comic appearance.

Morgan had given a lot of thought to how much of his knowledge of the developing situation he would share with Simbawashe. With probably less than 48 hours until it hit the fan, he saw no justification for withholding any but the most sensitive details.

"I have it on good authority, Mr. Minister," he said. "That certain elements loyal to your former president are planning to attack Mabuntu in the next few days. I decided to remove family members and certain members of staff out of harm's way, which is my obligation as ambassador. I have also advised Americans living in rural areas to consider relocating for the time being."

Simbawashe's look of anger changed to one of shock.

"Where did you learn this?" he asked.

"It doesn't matter where the information came from really – I think it's reliable. I'm not certain what the security situation will be, so I'm taking the prudent course. Are you telling me that no one in your government is aware of anything?"

"Ah . . . well, we know there are a few malcontents among those who were formerly in government . . . but, it is not likely that they would try anything so rash."

Simbawashe's eyes darted from side to side as he

spoke, and he'd laced his fingers together. He fidgeted in his chair. Morgan knew he was lying, but not sure what part of his statement was false. He couldn't share any classified information with him, but he was curious as to just how tied in he was with the junta.

"What can you tell me about these . . . malcontents, Mr. Minister?"

"Uh, I'm afraid that information is sensitive, Excellency – you understand, or course." Morgan took that to mean he didn't know anything. "You can rest assured, however, that our leader has the situation under control."

"In that case, sir," Morgan said. "You can understand why I must take the actions I'm taking. It would be derelict of me to leave the families of my staff exposed to possible danger. They will be returning, though, as soon as we are assured of their safety."

The minister had a pained look on his face now. His fleshy lips quivered. "Will you . . . be closing your embassy? That would send a devastating signal to the people of Naganda if you Americans left."

As much as Morgan would have liked to reassure the man, he would not – could not – blatantly lie to him. "We're remaining open . . . for now," he said. "Whether we remain so will depend entirely on how events unfold."

Thoroughly beaten, his plan to call Morgan in and browbeat him in shambles, Simbawashe looked like a large, dark inflatable doll that has sprung a slow leak.

He sat shrunken in his chair, staring at the floor. Morgan almost felt sorry for him, but he realized that there was nothing more he could do. He again reassured him that if the situation didn't become desperate, the embassy would remain open, and if there was no violence those who had departed would return. In a subdued voice, Simbawashe thanked him and sat there staring at the wall as Morgan departed.

Chapter Thirty-Seven

When Morgan arrived back at the embassy, Mary Sung met him near Post One.

"You have visitors," she said. "The British, Canadian, and French ambassadors heard about our dependents leaving, and they've come to talk to you about it."

"Damn," Morgan said. "I'd hoped to be able to know more about the situation before having to deal with my diplomatic colleagues. Where did you stash them?"

"I arranged with Richard to put them in the USIS conference room. He and Tom are keeping them company until you arrive."

He would like to have had the opportunity to talk more with Raine and Brennan, but it would have to wait. He knew that once word got out that the Americans were leaving – even a few of them – it would send ripples through the diplomatic community. If it had just been the British and Canadian ambassadors, he could have had a candid conversation with them because of the information sharing agreements with their countries, but despite being an ally, no such agreement existed with France, so he would have to choose his words carefully. Furthermore, he'd have to be careful not to say anything that would cause panic. He'd had the two week charm course for first time ambassadors before leaving Washington, but it hadn't prepared him for situations like this. He would literally be making it up as he went along.

"Okay, Mary," he said. "Tell Susan to join us."

She went to the elevator, and he started down the hallway behind Post One toward the conference room that the public affairs people used for their public programs. The one advantage it had was that because it was accessible to the public, sensitive discussions weren't allowed. If they pressed him for information he couldn't divulge, he could use that as an excuse for not sharing.

When Morgan entered the room, Richard Barton-Kettering, Andre LeFarge, and the Canadian ambassador, Christine Chretien – a tall woman with ash blonde hair, narrow shoulders, and long, athletic legs, who favored pants suits to dresses – sat at the far end of the conference table huddled in conversation with his political counselor and public affairs officer. Chretien was the first to notice his arrival.

"Ah, David, you survived being summoned a second time to the foreign ministry, eh?" She stood and hugged him when he'd crossed the room.

The two men warmly shook his hand. All three had worried looks on their faces.

"You were called in because of the departure of some of your staff, *n'cest pas*?" LeFarge got right to the point.

Morgan motioned them to be seated. As Breedlove and Weir rose to leave, he indicated that they too should stay.

"Susan Pinchon will be joining us shortly," he said. "Yes, Andre, the departure of family members and some of the staff was the good minister's motivation for the summons."

"Do you mind sharing with us why you sent them away?" Chretien asked.

Before Morgan could respond, Pinchon walked in and took a seat next to Breedlove.

"Thanks for coming, Susan," Morgan said. "I was just about to respond to Christine's question about why we sent dependents home. It's simple, really – it's because we have credible information that a countercoup is in the works."

"I have been expecting it to happen for some time," LeFarge said. "But, it is likely to be another comic opera takeover like the last one, do you not think?"

Here, Morgan knew, he would be treading on treacherous ground. He would have to choose his words carefully.

"We don't think so. For one thing, the last coup was a spur of the moment thing, and Saidu fled in panic. I don't see Gweru running away, for one thing, and the other is, we're told this thing has been in planning for some time."

LeFarge's forehead wrinkled. "Who is behind this alleged coup – Saidu?"

"Who else?" Barton-Kettering said. "And, I've no doubt that our good friend Julius Bongo is up to his puffy neck in it as well."

Barton-Kettering's intelligence people were as good as Morgan's, so he probably knew almost as much about the situation as Morgan did. He had the added advantage that everyone looked at the Americans, assuming that with their technology they knew everything, and often ignored the British who had been in the spy business before there was a United States of America, and had networks all over the globe – especially in their former colonies.

"We can't confirm it," Morgan said. "But, it does seem to be Saidu loyalists."

"Surely Gweru has most of the army behind him," Chretien said. "The way Saidu and Bongo mistreated the military, I doubt that more than a few score retain any loyalty to them."

"The word we get is that they've recruited Ganda tribesmen."

"Oh, pah, then it will be a debacle," LeFarge said. "What chance do untrained men have against an army, even one as incompetent as the Nagandan army?"

Morgan looked at Pinchon and Breedlove. Both inclined their heads slightly. He took a deep breath.

"We've also heard that the plotters have received external support, and are better armed than the army. I can't give you details." He hoped they'd interpret that as him not having the information. "But, rumors are they have some fairly modern automatic weapons that give them a firepower advantage over the Nagandan Enfields."

Barton-Kettering nodded as he spoke. So, the British had probably heard of the Chinese support for the plotters too.

"Well, we're fortunate that, unlike you, we don't have many family members to worry about, and we're so small, everyone is essential," Chretien said. "Am I to assume you don't plan to close the embassy?"

"Not unless the situation looks to really go south," Morgan replied.

"You will keep us informed if you see that happening, eh?"

"You know I will."

Charles Ray

Chapter Thirty-Eight

Leaving Breedlove and Weir to escort the ambassadors out, Morgan headed for the elevator. As he neared Post One, he noticed Hector Gonzales in an animated conversation with Lee Kennedy in the side passage.

As he neared them, Kennedy looked up. "Mr. Ambassador, Hector's just brought me some disturbing news," he said. "Why don't you tell the ambassador what you told me, Hector?"

"Some of the missionaries have started drifting into town," the consular chief said. "One of them just dropped by my office a few minutes ago and told me that one of the locals in his church said he saw the Peace Corps volunteer assigned to Ovimbi kidnapped by a bunch of armed men."

Morgan appreciated Gonzales's ability to deliver the meat of his subject without a lot of preamble or rambling, and his relative calm as he did so. Given what he'd learned, he could have been forgiven for being excited.

"When and where did the kidnapping take place?" Morgan asked.

"Sometime yesterday morning, about ten klicks outside Ovimbi. He said the man told him that there were six men and two strange looking vehicles in a clearing near the road. He'd taken to the bush to avoid them, when he saw the woman Rebecca Taylor walking along the road from the other direction. When she saw the men she turned to run, but they caught her."

"Damn," Morgan said. "I wonder if it was the mercenaries."

"No," Gonzales said. "The man who talked to the missionary was Chiveru, and he said the men he saw were Ganda."

Carlton Raine, who had just come through the front entrance, walked up as Gonzales finished speaking.

"What's happening?" he asked.

Morgan repeated what he'd just heard. "This is not good," he said. "If word gets out that we've an American – and a Peace Corps volunteer to boot – taken hostage by the coup plotters, the shit will truly hit the fan."

"That's for sure," Raine said. He looked at Kennedy, whose face was set in angry lines. "Are you thinking what I'm thinking, Lee?"

The security officer nodded. Morgan wasn't sure he liked where this was going. He *knew* what they were thinking, because as Gonzales was talking, he'd had the same thought himself. The problem was, they weren't equipped for it.

"I'm not sure this is a good idea," he said.

"We can't just sit on our thumbs and do nothing," Kennedy said.

"Besides," Raine added. "I think the two of us could pull it off."

The two men looked angry, but it was a controlled anger – and was overshadowed by the determined set of their faces. At times like this, Morgan's instincts, honed by his years in the military, and his combat experience, warred with the caution he'd been taught since joining the Foreign Service. Rebecca Taylor was one of *his* people, and he'd been taught never to leave anyone behind. During his time in Vietnam, he'd seen commanders put an entire unit at risk to try and recover one man cut off behind enemy lines – and, never had one of the men in the unit hesitated. Sometimes you have to take chances, and now was one of those times. The old Morgan won the internal struggle.

"Okay," he said. "What's your plan?"

"We'll start by getting as precise location of the kidnapping as we can," Kennedy said. "Then, we'll work from there."

Gonzales repeated what he'd been told about where

the incident took place.

"That's about three to three and a half hours' drive," Raine said. "If we get started now, we can get a search started before dark."

He and Kennedy turned to Morgan.

"You'd better get started," Morgan said.

Chapter Thirty-Nine

Raine and Kennedy, after changing into dungarees and heavy shirts, stocked one of Raine's vehicles – a Land Rover with a souped-up engine and heavy duty tires – with C-Rations from Kennedy's stock of emergency rations, two M4 carbines – a lighter version of the M16 rifle – and ten clips of ammunition. Both men also carried Colt Commanders in hip holsters. They left the embassy just before noon, and made good time on the road northeast from the capital, arriving in the vicinity of the incident just before 4:00 pm.

Raine pulled the Land Rover off the road, and they got out and walked toward the clearing in the trees. They'd come to the right place. It would have been hard to miss. The ground was torn up where tracked vehicles had run back and forth over it. Here and there were scuff marks in the earth from boots as well. Walking around, they discovered that the vehicles had gone further into the trees to the east.

"Won't be hard to follow this trail," Raine said.

"Looks like tank tracks, and they've cut a pretty good trail, so we can follow in the Land Rover."

They got back into the vehicle, and Raine wheeled it around and began following the trail through the trees.

"This engine's pretty loud," Kennedy said. "You sure we'll be able to sneak up on 'em?"

"Good point." Raine rolled the window down. "If they have their engines running, they'll never hear us, and we'll hear them from a long way off."

"And, if they don't have their engines running, we could run right up their asses before we know it."

Raine shrugged. "Well, reach back there and get an M4, slam a clip home, and keep your eyes open."

Kennedy laughed, but he reached over the seat and did as suggested. With the carbine cradled against his right shoulder, he peered out the front and right windows of the car as they bounced from rut to rut through the forest. He hadn't been in the field like this for a while, but Kennedy found his tracking skills slowly coming back as the time passed. He could tell from the condition of the broken bushes, for instance, that the trail they were following was at least a day or so old, because the stems were dried out. In places, the vehicles they were following had scraped the trunks of trees, and these scars, too, didn't look as if they'd just been made.

Neither man talked. Raine concentrated on keeping out of the deeper ruts, and Kennedy kept his eyes on their surroundings, especially the trail ahead of them.

They couldn't miss the trail, though. The grass was beaten down, and the ground chewed up by the tracked vehicles that had run over it. Trees closed in on either side, and the canopy overhead shut out most of the sunlight, making it so dim in some places that Raine turned on the headlights. Suddenly, Kennedy saw an arc of light about a hundred yards ahead.

"Looks like we're coming to another clearing," he said.

Raine slowed the vehicle. Then, he brought it to a stop and turned off the engine. The only sounds they heard were the raucous cries of birds and the barking of monkeys off in the distance.

"I don't hear anything," Raine said. "Let's move forward."

Restarting, he inched slowly forward, straining his ears to hear any other sound over the growl of the engine. As they neared the clearing, he stopped again, but left the engine running. He heard no other sounds.

As they inched into the clearing, he realized that he'd heard *only* the sound of their engine the last time he stopped. He hadn't heard the birds and monkeys. That could only mean one thing. They were halfway into the clearing when he realized his mistake.

The tank tracks curved around to the right, and as he began to swing the Land Rover in that direction, what he saw ahead caused him to gasp, and to gape. Sitting on the trail, its 76mm gun aiming directly at them, was a PT-76 tank. He slammed on the brake, jerked the gear lever into reverse, and jammed his foot against the gas pedal. But, as he looked back through the rear window, he slammed the brakes again.

"What the -" Kennedy started to say, but he too looked back. "Shit."

"Shit is right," Raine said. "And, we're deep in it."

Behind them, next to a wide, freshly made gap in the bush, another PT-76 sat, and its gun was also aimed at them.

Chapter Forty

August 23, 1978,
The Committee Headquarters,
Washington, DC

Not far from the White House, on a narrow east-west street, sat a three-story, red brick house, surrounded by a high, red brick wall. Built around the turn of the century, it was set upon a little hill from which it had for decades looked down upon its neighbors. But then, Washington had started changing. The sprawling complex that was George Washington University was closing in from the west, and at the other points of the compass, higher buildings were being constructed to serve as office complexes. The house looked like a relic from a time long past, clinging desperately to its position, almost in defiance of the changes going on around it.

As the sun sank lower in the west, the higher buildings cast their long shadows over the house. Even the street lamps seemed dimmer than they had in the past. Passersby hardly gave the place a glance. There was no number or name on the gate, and as the sky dimmed and the city lights came up, the only light inside the compound was a very faint purplish-orange glow from one window on the second floor.

That window, covered by heavy violet drapes, was in a room that contained only a large circular table, around which sat twelve high-backed carved wooden chairs. Table and chairs were completely unadorned. The room was lit by a chandelier suspended from the ceiling over the center of the table. The twelve bulbs were just enough to light the table, leaving the rest of the room in gloomy shadow.

Only four chairs were occupied. In one, his back to the window, sat Jonathan Appleby, dressed in black – black coat, white shirt, and black tie – with his snow white hair combed straight back, he looked like an old fashioned fire and brimstone circuit preacher. To his right sat another man, smaller, with thinning white hair combed ineffectually over the bald spot on the top of his narrow skull, also wearing a black coat, white shirt, and black tie, and to his left, a portly man with dusty brown hair, flecked with gray, with heavy jowls and fleshy lips, like the others, dressed in black coat, white shirt, and black tie. The three of them were the apex and legs of a triangle, the base of which was the man who sat across the table facing them. Lawrence Collins, the CEO of Petrolux, was wearing his trademark three-piece gray suit, only this time with a dark blue tie. His normal patrician look, though, had been replaced with the look of a condemned man about to hear sentence passed. In most venues, he considered himself the man in charge, the alpha male

– but, here he was definitely at the bottom of the food chain.

Everyone was silent while the fifth man in the room, an elderly black man with an impassive brown face, dressed in a black tail coat, white shirt and bow tie, served brandy and cigars. When he'd placed a snifter of brandy and a Cuban cigar with a small box of wooden matches and a cutter in front of each man, he quietly withdrew, making not a sound as he crossed the wooden floor, silently closing the door without even the click of a latch, and disappeared into whatever recess he occupied when his services weren't needed.

Appleby took his time preparing and lighting his cigar. When he'd lighted it and blown out rings of blue-white smoke, the others followed suit. He then lifted the glass, sniffed appreciatively and then sipped. The others followed suit. Collins's hands shook as he held the snifter.

Finally, Appleby cleared his throat – a signal that it was time to get down to business.

"Very well, gentlemen," he said in the voice he often used to mesmerize his fellow legislators. "It's time we got down to business. Mr. Collins, why don't you start by telling us what Petrolux is up to in Naganda?"

His hand in mid-air moving his cigar toward his trembling lips, Collins paused. He looked at the cigar, and down at the table – anywhere but into the piercing gaze of the man across the table from him. He felt a pressure on his bladder. God, he thought, I hope I don't have to piss.

"Uh, well," he said. "A rather large deposit of oil has been located – or that it, a possible, but our source of this information if most reliable – and we're attempting to broker an arrangement that will allow Petrolux to . . . exploit the find."

The ascetic looking man to Appleby's right put his cigar in the crystal ashtray at his elbow and leaned forward. "Your man in the field, Mr. Holder is it, is a, uh, rather uncontrolled sort, is he not – given to undertaking operations without always clearing them with corporate?" His voice belied his appearance – it was as deep and commanding as Appleby's.

"Ben's a good man," Collins said. "He does what's necessary to get the job done."

"Regardless of who gets hurt in the process," Appleby said.

"You have to understand, gentlemen, we explore for oil in some rough areas of the world. It's not always possible to avoid some level of injury. But, we try to keep it to a minimum."

"Do you call uprooting a whole people minimum injury?" The jowly man asked in a nasal voice.

Collins looked confused at first, and then he made an 'O' with his lips. "Oh, you mean the need to relocate the people in this little village in Naganda – Ovimbi, I believe it is – that could be done relatively easily, and Petrolux would pay for it."

"He's not referring to the physical impact," Appleby said. "You'd be uprooting their culture. I'm led to believe this village is central to the Chiveru culture, the resting place of most of their ancestral spirits, and that they would resist moving."

"I suppose there would be some resistance. But, these people are less than five percent of the country's population. Surely you wouldn't expect the other ninety-five percent to be deprived of the benefits of this find because of a few native superstitions?"

"If it was only that simple, sir. This could cause intertribal warfare. Is there no way to do this without moving that village?"

"But, more than seventy-five percent of the deposit is underneath the village."

The portly man leaned as far forward as his ample girth would allow. "So, that means you can drill in the area where the remaining twenty-five percent is located?"

Collins leaned back. "Well, we could, but in order to get at the rest we'd have to slant drill, and that increases our cost substantially."

"What you're really saying," Appleby said, his voice dripping with sarcasm. "Is that it would cut into your profit margin."

"B-but, if our price to extract the oil goes up, so do the prices Americans have to pay at the pump."

"Come now, sir – we all know that the American consumer pays less per gallon for his fuel than anyone else in the world, except for a few people in countries where energy is government subsidized. We also know that you'll raise the price at the slightest excuse, cost of production be damned. So, here's what Petrolux is gonna do." Appleby used the voice he used on the Senate floor, a booming baritone that commanded attention, and brooked no resistance. "You're gonna tell the Nagandans that you'll drill for the oil without them having to move a whole buncha people; you'll make sure to give the government a decent cut of the income from that oil; you'll build a few schools and clinics, and improve the roads in your area of operations; and, you'll pull those damn mercenaries out that your man Holder sent into the area."

The color drained from Collins's face, and he recoiled as if he'd been punched in the gut. He knew that Appleby and his shadowy group were deeply embedded in the nation's decision making process, and anyone opposing them would be in for a rough time – government contracts would suddenly be renegotiated, or bids rejected. For a major company, having Washington pissed at you wasn't good for the longevity of company executives. His board of directors wouldn't be happy at the reduction of the profit margin from the Nagandan field, but it would be preferable to the potential loss to the company's overall operation if he defied Appleby. He'd also heard stories of others who'd defied the man suffering unfortunate accidents. He didn't know if they were true, but wasn't inclined to test that.

"Very well, sir," he said. "I suppose we can do that."

"Ain't no suppose to it," Appleby said. "It's that way

or no way."

After a visibly shaken Collins had departed, the three men sat in companionable silence, sipping expensive brandy and smoking banned Cuban cigars, attended to by an elderly black man, who moved about the room as silently and smoothly as the tendrils of smoke from the cigars.

Chapter Forty-One

August 24, 1978,
American Embassy,
Mabuntu, Naganda

Morgan was sitting at his desk, looking at a draft memo from his administrative officer relating to management controls of the embassy – and failing for the third time to focus on it – when Alison Chambers rapped on the door and stuck her head into his office.

"Mr. Ambassador, do you have a minute?"

He looked up and smiled. "Please, Alison, come in," he said. "I need a break from this cursed report anyway."

He pushed the memo aside, and motioned her to the chair near his desk. She had an excited look on her face.

"I've been reaching out to women locally," she said. "As you might imagine, given the structure of this country's society, women tend to band together just to survive being ignored by their husbands and the culture at large. At any rate, one of the women I met just happens to have a cousin who works in the Gweru household. She's Amata Gweru's personal maid, and is, like most of the domestic help here, treated as a piece of furniture. She hears and sees almost everything that goes on there, and what she heard recently is earthshaking."

"Let me guess," Morgan said. "She knows that Amata and Musa Gweru's uncle are having an affair."

"Oh, just about everyone but Musa knows that." She laughed. "Actually, I think he suspects, but because he loves his wife, and his uncle is his oldest male relative, with his father deceased and all, he just looks the other way. This kind of affair is not uncommon here. No, what my friend's cousin heard is much worse than that. It seems that the first lady doesn't think her husband has the right stuff to be this country's leader, but her paramour does. They're planning to use Saidu's move against him to get rid of him."

"By get rid of, you mean- "

"I mean, kill him. Banda knows more about this planned countercoup than he's sharing with Gweru. He even has an idea of the timing. When Bongo's troops move on the city, he plans to kill Gweru and blame it on Bongo. Gweru is popular with most of the rank and file, and Banda hopes to parlay that into enough force to defeat Bongo's hundred, and, of course, he will step in to fill his slain nephew's shoes."

Plots within plots. Morgan shook his head in wonder. It was amazing that Naganda had stayed intact as long as it had. The plan to return Saidu to power was bad enough, but if general fighting broke out between his forces and whatever force Banda could muster, it would embroil the entire country in a war that no one would win – least of all the people.

"That puts us in a dicey position," he said. "I took a chance and dropped hints about the countercoup to Simbawashe, but I don't know whose side he's on in all this, so I have no way of knowing if any of this has gotten to Gweru."

"So, what do we do?" Chambers asked.

"What I probably should have done in the first place," he thought. But, if he did what was on his mind, Washington would likely be very unhappy. He could even get canned for it. He didn't want to take the rest of his staff down with him. "I'm thinking on it," he said. "But, I think it's best that you not know, so if you're ever asked about it you can honestly say you knew nothing."

Chambers frowned and leaned forward. "Dave, you're not planning to do something foolish, are you?"

"Not only foolish, but possibly dangerous. You go on back to your office, and let me worry about it."

She sighed. "Is there any way I can talk you out of

it?"

She was smart – he knew that – which was why he'd wanted her as his special advisor in the first place. But, this was one thing he'd have to do alone – for everyone's sake.

"I have no idea what you're talking about," he said. "Now, get out of here. I have some thinking to do."

With a final sigh, she rose and walked to the door. At the door, she turned, and he could see tears in her eyes. It was as if she was saying farewell – and that could very well be what it was.

Chapter Forty-Two

Once he was sure Chambers was out of earshot, he walked over to the door. Mary Sung looked up from a paper she'd been proofreading before sending it in to him for approval.

"Mary," he said. "Please hold all calls for the next half hour, and see that I'm not disturbed."

She gave him a strange look, but nodded her understanding. She was smart, too; as smart as Chambers and with many more years' experience. He had no doubt she had an idea of what he was planning, but as long as he didn't tell her, it was just speculation.

Returning to his desk, he fished around in the top left drawer until he found the folded piece of paper Gweru had given him at his credential presentation ceremony. Smoothing it out, he laid it on the desk next to the phone. Lifting the receiver, he slowly dialed the numbers. The phone crackled, clicked, and buzzed before he heard the tone of the phone at the other end ringing.

After six rings, Gweru's voice sounded tinnily in his ear. "Yes, who is calling?"

"This is David Morgan, sir," Morgan said. "Are you free to talk to me right now?"

"Of course, Excellency," Gweru said. "I have been hoping you would call. Would you like to meet with me?"

"I think, sir that it would be a good idea. But, it must be a private meeting – just the two of us."

Gweru might be blind to his wife's dalliance with his uncle, but he wasn't stupid. He immediately agreed, and gave Morgan directions, which he hastily scribbled on the legal pad he kept on his desk. When he rang off, he went out and told Sung to have Toko bring the car around to the back of the embassy, and told her he'd be unavailable for an extended period. If anyone asked his whereabouts, she was to tell them that he was involved in an important private meeting – and, nothing else. Her forehead was creased in worry lines, but she merely acknowledged his instructions, and picked up the phone and called the motor pool. Morgan left, confident that his driver would be waiting for him when he arrived at the embassy's back entrance.

He stepped through the door just as Toko pulled the car up. Getting into the back seat, he gave the driver the directions to his destination.

"That's in a bad part of town, sah," Toko said.

"I kind of figured it would be," Morgan said. "But, I'm meeting someone who wants to keep that meeting secret."

"Oh, then that is the right place for it." Toko laughed and gunned the engine as he pulled toward the back gate.

A few blocks from the embassy, Toko turned right into a narrow lane bounded on both sides by high stone walls that quickly gave way to an assortment of buildings – shacks really – constructed from a variety of materials that served as stores, restaurants, and residences for some of the city's poorer residents. Sullen looking men sat on boxes and stools outside the precariously leaning beer parlors, drinking a noxious looking liquid from plastic containers, while the women plied their trade on the cracked sidewalks. Piles of trash were everywhere. The shiny black car attracted a few curious glances, but most people averted their eyes. Morgan had decided not to fly the flag, so he looked like some important, but unknown, personage – someone the denizens of this district probably didn't want to annoy. Even with the windows up, and the air conditioner going full blast, the humid heat and sour odor of the outside seeped into the vehicle. Morgan had yet to become accustomed to it, but he tried not to wrinkle his nose too much. He didn't want to insult his driver, who didn't seem to notice the smell or heat.

After twenty minutes, Toko made another turn – this time left – into an alley that ran for fifty yards before ending at a large metal gate in front of which stood two soldiers, one with an Enfield held across his chest, and another with an RPG on his shoulder. As the car approached, the soldier with the Enfield came to attention and saluted, while the other ran to open the gate. Toko drove through, and the gate was immediately closed behind them.

They were inside an oasis of green in the gray, brown, and sickly yellow of the area outside the gate. Red, violet, and yellow flowers grew in profusion and the grass was neatly trimmed. They stopped on a graveled area in front of a modest sized house of white painted brick with a bright green metal roof.

Toko got out and opened the door for Morgan. As he stepped from the vehicle, the front door of the house opened. Musa Gweru, dressed in a military uniform without any rank insignia, stood in the doorway. As Morgan approached, he extended his hand. There was a broad smile on his dark brown face.

"Excellency, thank you for coming so quickly. Please come inside," he said. "Your driver will be taken care of."

He stepped aside and let Morgan enter. Once Morgan was inside, he closed the door and led him down a short hallway into a small room containing a sofa, two stuffed chairs, a carved wooden coffee table, and a low chest upon which sat a large television set and a video player. The John Wayne movie, *The Green*

Berets, was playing. Morgan had seen the movie when it had first come out in 1968, and while he'd always been a John Wayne fan, he'd been disappointed by the film when the last scene showed the sun setting in the sea at Danang beach. Anyone who'd been in Vietnam knew the water was east of the beach. That one geographic and astronomical bit of artistic license had spoiled the whole film for Morgan.

Gweru sat on the sofa facing the TV, and pointed to one of the chairs for Morgan. He took the one facing away from the TV.

"Thank you for taking the time to see me," Morgan said.

"It is my pleasure. Can I offer you something to drink – tea, or perhaps something stronger?"

He reached into a cooler beside the sofa and withdrew two cans of Budweiser beer. The cans were covered with condensation from the ice in the cooler.

Hell, Morgan thought, might as well. He took a can. Gweru handed him an opener. He punctured the top of the can, causing a bit of the beer to bubble up as the gas blew out with a 'siss' sound. He handed the opener back to his host, who expertly opened his can. They both took long drinks from the can. Morgan wasn't much of a beer drinker, but the cold malt tasted good after the heat outside.

Morgan put his can down on the coffee table and leaned forward, his hands on his knees.

"I wanted to talk to you," he said. "Because I have

some information that I think you must have."

Gweru took another drink, and put his can down. "You sound very serious. What is this information?"

This is where Morgan was about to take a step on a journey from which there was no return. If he'd read Gweru wrong, it would be a disaster. It was likely to be a bloody disaster even if he'd judged the man correctly. But, he'd come too far to back out. The only thing he could do was plunge in and hope he didn't hit bottom.

"I have no doubt that you know that there are those loyal to the man you ousted who would like nothing better than see you fall as well," he said. Gweru nodded. "Well, I have information that those very people are planning to move against you, and soon."

Gweru inclined his head, a half smile still on his face. "I am aware that there are those who oppose me. I did not know they were actively planning anything. That is disturbing news. I won't ask you where you learned this – I know you will not be able to tell me. But, can you tell me who is heading this effort, and when they plan to make their move?"

Morgan let out a breath. The man was no fool. And, he remained calm as he asked his question.

"I can't be absolutely sure," Morgan said. "But, I think General – former General Bongo – is in charge. He has approximately one hundred fighters, and they plan to attack tomorrow. This is not confirmed, but I think the information is reliable."

Gweru stroked his chin, his eyes narrowing.

"That does not surprise me," he said. "General Bongo never did like me. When we took over, he resigned his commission rather than serve in the army under my command. I assume that Joshua Saidu is also involved. No matter, my uncle is twice the officer that Julius Bongo is, and if he only has a hundred men, Uncle Gideon will make short work of him."

"That . . . could be a . . . problem. You see, I also have information about General Banda that I hesitate to bring up to you, but I think you have a right to know." Gweru's face wrinkled in a querying look. "Are you aware that he is having an affair with your wife?"

The querying look turned to one of sadness. "How does one ever *know* such things? I have not caught them in the act, but, yes, I have suspected it for some time now. You must understand David – may I call you David?" Morgan nodded. "And, please, call me Musa. You see, I am at heart a simple man. Amata, my wife, on the other hand, loves the finer things of life. She wants to spend her time in Europe shopping, while what I want to do is rebuild my country. Uncle Gideon shares her taste for fine wine, expensive clothes, and fancy cars, so I suppose it is only natural that they would eventually develop a closer relationship. I don't like it, but he is my elder, so I must remain quiet. That is the way of our people."

Morgan felt sorry for the man. Thrust into a position he hadn't sought, and having to look the other way while his wife cuckolded him – it would have broken a lesser man. The rest of Morgan's news, though, just might be that final weight that would crack him.

"That's not the end of it," he said. "We've also learned that the two of them plan to use Bongo's move against you to rid themselves of you."

Expressions of anger and confusion warred for control of his face. "You are not saying that-"

"Yes," Morgan said. "We've learned that they plan to kill you when Bongo attacks, and blame it on him. Banda thinks that your popularity with many in the army will embolden them to stand firm and defeat Bongo, and then he – as would be expected of your loving uncle – will step in to ensure your legacy."

Gweru leaned back against the sofa cushion, looking up at the slowly revolving blades of the ceiling fan.

"How sure are you of *that* information?"

"Pretty sure."

"Yes, I am sure you must be, or you would not have taken the risk of bringing it to me. That puts a different light on things."

"Bongo is being supplied by the – an outside force – and, he has tanks and armored APCs. Even with only a hundred men, Musa, that's a formidable force."

"No doubt, but we have the advantage of numbers and we'll be defending our homes, so even though it will be difficult, and there will be many casualties, I think we can deal with General Bongo and his traitors."

"That'll be complicated by your having to watch your back," Morgan said.

"Ah . . . that I will take care of first," Gweru said. His expression now was stony. "Thank you for coming, David. Now, I have many things to do, so you must return to your embassy. I know you have already sent your families away, so now you must take care of those who are left. I cannot guarantee that the streets will be safe for the next few days, but I am confident that you will know what to do. After this is over, my friend, we must get together again, for a happier occasion."

There was nothing else to say. He had no idea what Gweru would do, but the set of his face told Morgan that it wouldn't be pleasant. They shook hands warmly, and Gweru walked him to the door. As Toko drove away, Morgan looked out of the car's rear window. Gweru was still standing in the doorway with a pensive look on his face.

Charles Ray

Chapter Forty-Three

By the time Morgan's car was pulling into the back courtyard of the embassy, Gweru was already making his first move. A few blocks from the embassy he noted trucks disgorging armed soldiers on key street corners, and they looked like they meant business.

Ian Brennan met him at the back door. "Hey, Mr. Ambassador," the defense attaché said as Morgan mounted the steps. "You're back just in time. Something's going down in town, and I don't think it's the countercoup."

"Yeah," Morgan said as he eased past him and into the corridor. Brennan followed. "I saw armed men being positioned at some of the key intersections." He couldn't tell the man that he knew why. The less he knew, the better if things if went wrong. "I think Gweru's got wind of Bongo's plans."

"Yeah, but he's off a day. Besides, what chance do

his guys have with their pea shooters against automatic weapons and armor?"

"I wouldn't count them out so soon. I'm no African hand, but I have studied the history of this continent. Don't forget that in 1879, at the Battle of Isandlwana, the poorly equipped Zulus, with spears, and a few muskets, defeated the British who had breech loaders, cannons and rockets. The key there was numbers, and Gweru has numbers on his side."

"Oh yeah, I remember reading about that when I was going through area studies for this job," Brennan said. "The British suffered their worst defeat in history, until Dunkirk, that is. But, it'll be bloody, you know that?"

Morgan knew – he knew all too well. Not only would the casualties among the combatants be horrific, but there was likely to be a large number of civilian casualties. That thought reminded him that he had two of his staff – no, three counting Rebecca Taylor – out in the bush somewhere who were likely to get caught in the crossfire.

"I think we need to get the Americans in town sheltered in the embassy. That should minimize the danger to them – provided there's no heavy fighting in this vicinity. I hope Carlton and Lee get back here before things get too hot. I've got to get to the consular section, and get Hector working on contacting Americans. In the meantime, I need you to reach out to your military contacts and find out what's going on."

"Will do, boss," Brennan said. He saluted and

walked briskly toward his office.

After stopping at the consular section and giving Gonzales his instructions, Morgan went to his office.

Sung followed him in, carrying a fresh mug of coffee.

"You look like you need this," she said, and went back to her desk.

He sat behind his desk, sipping the hot coffee and looking up at the ceiling. At this point, there was little he could do but wait. The coffee was just about gone when Chambers walked in without knocking. She looked worried, which Morgan understood. Her husband was somewhere in the country and things looked like they were about to come apart. But, she also looked the determined professional she was.

"Mr. Ambassador," she said. "More news about the Gweru family domestic affairs."

"I hope it's not as bad as the last."

She shrugged. "I suppose it depends. I just got a call from my friend – the one whose cousin works for Musa Gweru's wife – and she said, Gweru had soldiers arrest his wife and his uncle. They were taken away somewhere – no one knows where."

"Guess he must have learned what they planned to do." He kept his face expressionless.

Chambers smiled. "Yeah, guess he must have. I wonder how?"

"We'll probably never know," Morgan said. "That's one less problem to worry about, though.

She stood there, looking down at him, her brows creased.

"Is there something else?" he asked, hoping she wouldn't ask him anything more about how Gweru learned of the assassination plot.

"Oh, I was just thinking about Lee and Carlton. I hope they're okay."

"I wouldn't worry too much," Morgan said, thankful that she'd changed the subject. "They're both pretty capable, and I happen to know Carlton took some pretty heavy fire power. They'll be okay."

"They'd better be," she said. "If Lee gets himself hurt, I'll kill him."

Chapter Forty-Four

Sitting in the Land Rover, with the business ends of 76mm cannons pointing at them from front and back, Lee Kennedy and Carlton Raine looked at each other.

"Okay," Kennedy said. "What do we do now?"

"We get the hell out of here."

"You've got to be kidding. Or, haven't you noticed that there are tanks blocking us front and rear?"

"I don't mean that, I mean get the hell out of this vehicle. Grab your weapon, and on my mark, dive out your side. I'll go out this side. When you hit the ground, run like hell for the bush. Those tubes don't track that fast, so if we're lucky we'll be out of sight before they can get a bead on us."

"Shit, I guess it beats getting blown to bits inside this tin can. Okay, I'm ready."

"Go," Raine shouted, as he elbowed open the driver's side door and dove toward the ground.

Kennedy jumped out the other side, hitting the ground and rolling, before getting up into a crouch and sprinting for the bush. He heard Raine's footsteps receding rapidly from behind him. When he made it to the bush he ran another ten yards before he dove beneath a brambly looking plant and crouched, waiting to catch his breath. Looking around, he could only see foliage and the brown-ish gray trunks of trees.

Except for the calls of the birds, all he could hear was his ragged breathing. Then, the near silence was broken by the sound of laughter.

He raised his head slowly, but saw nothing. His curiosity got the better of him. He'd heard no shoots, just the laughter. He rose slowly and retraced his steps. When he arrived at the trail, he gingerly poked his head through the bush. His eyes went wide at what he saw.

Four men wearing floppy campaign hats and brown and green camouflage uniforms with AK-47s on canvas straps hanging loosely around their necks, and a small woman in khakis and a brown cotton shirt that hung loosely on her tiny frame – Kennedy recognized Rebecca Taylor – stood athwart the trail. They were pointing at him and still laughing. To their right, he saw Carlton Raine's head poke from the bushes, an embarrassed look on his face.

"My, my, you guys do move fast," the tallest of the four men said. "I don't believe I've ever seen anybody scoot into the brush that fast before since I left 'Nam.'"

"Just giving you harder targets to hit," Raine said, rising from the bush and brushing off his pants.

"Oh, if we'd wanted to hit you, we'd of done it when you first drove into the clearing," the man said. "Hell, we had you bracketed." He looked closer at Kennedy. "I've you before. You were with the American ambassador a few days ago. You fellas work for the embassy, I take it?"

Kennedy stepped forward. "Yeah, I'm Lee Kennedy, the RSO. That is Carlton Raine," he said, pointing at Raine. He didn't bother further identifying Raine.

The tall man stepped forward, extending his hand. "I'm Major Dale Callahan," he said. "Some people call me Junkyard Dog, 'cause I'm meaner'n one. I guess you could say I'm the commander of this little group. Got six more – three in each tank." He raised his hand after shaking with Kennedy. The hatches to the driver's compartment and turret on each vehicle popped open, and six more smiling faces emerged – one in each driver's compartment, and two in each turret. Callahan identified each, pointing as he did so.

"Mind telling us how you came by these beauties?" Raine asked as he walked up, extending his hand.

"Interesting story, that. There's been a lot of traffic up here of late. Buncha guys with these tanks and some APCs skulking 'round the woods. Completely unprofessional, but dangerous nonetheless. We were keeping an eye on 'em. The tank crews decided they needed some more driving practice, so they took off to this clearing. Fools didn't even take perimeter security along. Anyway, this young lady came along." He put a hand on Rebecca's shoulder. "And, they spooked and grabbed her, so we had to come to the rescue."

"And, a good thing they did, too," Taylor said, smiling coyly up at Callahan. "They were planning to kill me and dump my body in the forest."

"The six of them got dumped in the woods instead," Callahan said. "And, since they didn't need their rides anymore, we took 'em. You have any idea who these dirt bags are?"

Kennedy explained about the planned countercoup.

"I'm surprised they didn't come after you," Raine said.

"They did, but a couple of rounds in the dirt in front of 'em caused 'em to rethink their need for these babies."

"They probably didn't want to throw their timetable off," Kennedy said. "Besides, they still have the APCs."

"Yeah," Callahan said. "They had BTRs, and each one of 'em has two machine guns, a 14.5mm and a 7.62. They pack a lot of fire power. Of course, they don't stand a chance against these PT-76s. One of these 76mm rounds will go through the skin of a BTR like a hot knife through butter. They're incompetent, but they're not stupid. When we popped a couple of rounds in front of 'em, they *di di maued* outa here."

"Shit, they're probably on their way to Mabuntu as we speak," Kennedy said. "We need to get back. Miss Taylor, you'll come with us." He looked at Callahan. "What are your plans, major?"

Callahan looked around at his men. They all had eager smiles on their faces. "Well, we were paid to guard an empty patch of ground up here," he said. "But, if the shit's hitting the fan down south, I don't reckon anybody's gonna be bothering anything up here. Seems to me like you folks in the embassy might need a little extra security."

"You offering? I can't pay you anything."

"We've already been paid, and there's nothing up here to spend the money on. Frankly, I'm getting bored up here with nothing to do, and I've always wanted to see Mabuntu anyway. Why don't you head out – we'll follow you."

Chapter Forty-Five

August 24, 1978,
Washington, DC

The following article appeared on page A-5 of the noon edition of the *Washington Post* on Thursday, August 24, 1978.

Upheaval in Naganda

(Mabuntu, Naganda)   Sources in the West African capital of Mabuntu, Naganda have told the Post that Captain Musa Gweru, head of the military junta that recently overthrew Joshua Saidu, president of the country since it gained independence, has ordered the arrest of General Gideon Banda, chief of staff of the Nagandan armed forces and head of the intelligence service, and Amata Gweru, wife of Captain Gweru, and is charging them with high treason.

Sources say the two, who are allegedly lovers, were

planning to assassinate Captain Gweru and replace him as head of the junta.

This development comes amid persistent rumors of a possible countercoup by forces loyal to Saidu and the former army chief Julius Bongo. A State Department spokesman here in Washington said that the U.S. Government is watching the situation in Naganda closely, and is encouraging all parties to exercise restraint, and to respect human rights and the rule of law. U.S. embassy spokesman Richard Weir, contacted by telephone told this reporter, "All Americans here in Naganda are safe for now, and although the city is peaceful, we continue to monitor it closely." He declined to comment on whether or not the embassy is planning to evacuate Americans from the country.

Nagandan government officials would not return calls, nor has the government made a public statement about the situation.

Chapter Forty-Six

August 25, 1978,
Mabuntu, Naganda

Other than the deployment of soldiers at key points, Mabuntu remained peaceful through the night. On his way to the embassy on Friday morning, Morgan noticed that the checkpoints had been fortified with sandbags and large metal drums, and extra soldiers in battle gear manned them.

He arrived at the embassy at 7:00 am to find that two extra Nagandan soldiers in full battle gear had been added to the police guards that normally provided security to the embassy. The soldiers and police saluted him as his vehicle passed. The embassy security guards at the door looked nervous, but smiled and saluted him. Inside, the Marine at Post One was in combat fatigues complete with a flak vest and helmet, and had a serious, no-nonsense look on his youthful face, similar to the expressions Morgan had seen on the faces of young soldiers about to go into combat in

Vietnam. He only hoped this young man wouldn't have to face hostile fire.

Upstairs, outside his office, Mary Sung sat at her desk, seemingly unfazed by all that was taking place around her. She followed him in, carrying a mug of coffee which she put in the center of his desk, and a stack of paper which mostly consisted of the overnight cable traffic which she placed neatly in his inbox. She left him to decide whether to drink coffee and ignore the inbox, ignore the coffee and concentrate on the paperwork, or alternate sipping and reading. Having heard nothing from Washington overnight – he'd fully expected to get a phone call – he decided that the third option was the best. He needed the additional jolt of caffeine, and he needed to know what was going on in the outside world. What he really needed was something to take his mind off the fact that until the situation developed in one direction or another, there was nothing he could do but sit and wait. Even though he'd gone on many reconnaissance patrols in Vietnam where he'd been required to lie prone under a bush for hours watching a trail, he'd never become good at idly waiting.

The top cable in the stack was a response to their report on the arrest of Amata Gweru and Gideon Banda, thanking them for being so on top of the situation, and alerting them that forces were on alert in Stuttgart and Frankfurt for a possible NEO. The estimated time from his request for evacuation to the two hundred or so evacuees departing Mabuntu, depending upon security at the airport, ranged from twelve to twenty-four, so Morgan was reminded to not delay making that call. He knew, though, that if the military had to do a forced entry in order to conduct the evacuation, it could be longer while U.S. forces assaulted the airport, secured it, then fought their way out and to the embassy, where the Americans who would be evacuated were staying in the basement – in the cafeteria and health clinic, and in hastily erected tents in the rear courtyard. One way or another, the situation would have to be resolved within the next 48 hours, which was how long he estimated the water and emergency rations at the embassy would last.

The rest of the documents were routine messages, and he began working his way through them quickly, marking most of them for shredding.

Ian Brennan rapped on his door just as he was nearing the bottom of the stack.

"Come in, colonel," he said. "What've you got?"

Brennan sat in front of the desk. "I thought you might like an update on the situation in the city."

"I would," Morgan said. "Have Bongo's people arrived yet?"

"Yeah, they hit from the northwest about an hour ago. Gweru had managed to rally a good portion of the army units in town, and they've been resisting well – although, they're taking a lot of casualties. Luckily, according to the guy who called me, Bongo's only got two armored APCs. I don't know why he's not using the tanks – they must have broken down – but, even without them, it's just a matter of time before his guys overrun Gweru's positions. Last I heard, they were only a few klicks from State House. They take that and that's the ballgame."

"Shit, if Bongo takes over, what happens next?"

"There's likely to be general violence," Brennan said. "I hear Gweru has some supporters up country who're moving this way as we speak. If Bongo wins, they're probably gonna take to the bush and keep fighting. The whole fucking country could go up in smoke."

Morgan shook his head. Rebel victory seemed to be a foregone conclusion, which meant that Naganda wouldn't be a safe place for foreigners. Evacuating under such conditions, though, could be more dangerous than staying in hiding, if only he had enough supplies to take care of so many people for an extended period. He wasn't given to second guessing, but he was thinking that it might have been a good idea to call for an evacuation earlier. Now, they would just have to make the best of it.

Alison Chambers rushed into his office without knocking. She had an incredulous look on her face. "You two have to come downstairs," she said excitedly. "You won't believe what just pulled up at the rear of the embassy."

She turned and ran out. After quick, confused glances at each other, Morgan and Brennan hurriedly followed. She'd taken the stairs rather than wait for the elevator, so they followed. She went all the way to the basement level, and as they came out into the cafeteria, through the large glass window Morgan saw a crowd of people waving their hands and talking in an agitated manner. More people crowded around the window and door, staring out.

They caught up with Chambers, and the three of them made their way through the crowd and out the door. When they exited the building, the crowd parted to make way for Morgan, and what he saw caused him to stop in his tracks.

Carlton Raine's Land Rover was parked just inside the yard. Raine, Lee Kennedy, and Rebecca Taylor stood beside it, accompanied by a tall man in an unmarked military uniform. The four of them had broad smiles on their faces. Morgan was glad to see his three people, but he was more drawn to what he saw behind them. Sitting just beyond the gate was a small Russian amphibious tank – searching his memory of Warsaw Pact weapons, he remembered that it was a PT-76 – with another uniformed man sitting on the turret. As he pushed forward, he saw the second tank just behind the first.

"Hey, boss," Raine said. "We're back, and we brought you a present."

Chapter Forty-Seven

Raine introduced the mercenary commander, and informed Morgan that they were the ones who had saved him and Kennedy from their attackers. The sight of the tanks, under the control of Callahan and his men, eased Morgan's mind. Now at least the embassy could be protected. Morgan invited Callahan to his office, and asked Pinchon, Brennan, Kennedy, Raine, and Chambers to join them.

After Mary Sung had served coffee, he had Brennan outline the tactical situation.

"Even with only two APCs, Bongo will eventually defeat Gweru's forces," Morgan said when the defense attaché had finished. "If that happens, this country will explode. I'm afraid there's no way we can safely evacuate at the moment."

"Yeah, you don't want U.S. forces having to come into a situation like that," Callahan said. "That would lead to a mess I don't think our government's up for. We're on our own, ambassador, and you're the president's representative, so you're the man who has to make the call – what do we do?"

Already in it up to his neck, Morgan had an idea that he was afraid would ignite an intense debate and encounter resistance, even from those in the room who he considered his friends. What he was thinking violated every lesson in diplomacy he'd been taught since entering the service. He was not supposed to take sides in local disputes, but remain aloof and objective, and let the locals work out their disagreements among themselves. That was fine when his and other American lives were not at risk. In none of his training since becoming a Foreign Service Officer had he been told what was appropriate in such situations. Left, therefore, to his own devices, he would have to make a decision, and then be prepared to deal with the consequences.

"If we let Gweru be defeated, the country will descend into chaos," he said. "We will all then be at grave risk. So, the only way to ensure our own safety is to make sure this conflict has the right outcome."

Callahan smiled wolfishly. "You suggesting we throw in with the young captain, ambassador?"

"Yes," Morgan said, and then tensed, waiting for an outburst from one of his staff members. They all sat quietly looking at him. He saw no indications of resistance or disagreement. "I think those two tanks you . . . borrowed . . . could turn the tide in Gweru's favor. That is, if you're willing."

"We been sittin' on our duffs out there in the bush for too long. I think a little dust up is just what me and my men need right now." Callahan turned to Brennan. "Colonel, can you give me a map with force dispositions?"

Chambers raised her hand. Morgan acknowledged her. "I'm not posing any objection, or anything," she said. "But, you do realize that this is an act of war?"

Morgan shrugged. "I suppose it is. But, we're in the middle of a war zone, and I think we have a right to defend ourselves. For the record, let it be known that this is my decision, and mine alone, and all of you objected to it."

All heads shook in unison.

"I'm not objecting," Kennedy said. "And, for the record, I don't give a damn who knows."

"You got my vote," Raine said.

"I don't see any other alternative," Pinchon said.

"I wasn't objecting," Chambers said.

"All the way," Brennan said.

"I guess we'll all hang together," Morgan said.

Callahan finished his coffee and stood. "Okay, colonel," he said. "Lets you and me go plan ourselves a war."

Charles Ray

Chapter Forty-Eight

Holding the sketch map that Ian Brennan had hastily drawn, Callahan stood in the open hatch of the lead tank, peering ahead at the maze of narrow alleys that Brennan had neglected to mention.

"Baby Duck this is Junkyard Dog, over," he said into the microphone near his mouth.

"This is Baby Duck," the voice of Liam Dorsten, his second in command sounded cracked and tinny in the headphones covering his ears, despite being only twenty yards behind him. "What's your status, over?"

Callahan scanned left, then right. To the left was a jumble of shacks and a couple of brick buildings. The lanes seemed as narrow and winding as the alleys in front of his position. Off to the right was what looked like an open field with a lot of lean-tos and wooden racks. Looking at the map, he saw that this was the big open air market. Usually packed with people, it was empty now, with only a few stray dogs sniffing around looking for scraps. Off in the distance, the pop of gunfire could be heard, which explained why the streets and market were empty.

"Straight line to objective blocked," Callahan said. "Best route looks to be off to the right, through the market, over."

"Roger that, Junkyard Dog. How far to objective, over?"

"About two klicks, so we move from here in tactical formation. Offset your unit to left, cover left flank. You copy, over?"

"Copy – cover left flank. Wilco, over."

"Moving out. Stay alert and good luck, out."

Callahan slapped the metal of the turret. In response, the engines roared and the tank lurched forward, swiveling on its tracks toward the right. The driver had opened the hatch to the driver's compartment and stuck his head out for better vision. Callahan looked to the front and sides, alert for possible ambushes. The switch on his headset/mike had been set to 'broadcast all' so that his crew as well as the other tank could hear him. Down below, in the cramped compartment, three of his men were crowded around the .76mm gun, ready to fire on his command.

The PT-76 entered the market area, crushing empty fuel drums and reducing lean-tos and racks to kindling with loud crunching sounds, and tearing large gouges in the reddish-brown clay. Once through the market, Callahan ordered a one-quarter left turn, and the vehicle shot across the bumpy macadam street, through a wooden house that was fortunately empty, without even slowing down.

The terrain more resembled Brennan's map now. The compound containing State House, the countercoup force's objective, was less than a kilometer ahead. Even without the map Callahan would have known that. The sound of gunfire was getting louder. He only hoped those up ahead were concentrating on that as well, and wouldn't hear the throaty growl of the tanks' engines until it was too late.

"Baby Duck, Junkyard Dog, over."

"Baby Duck – go." Dorsten's voice was tight – not with fear, but excitement. He sensed that action was near.

"Estimate seven hundred meters to objective," Callahan said. "Remember - target the armor first, over."

"Roger, Wilco – out."

Callahan could hear a bit of tightness in his own voice. He could feel the blood coursing through his veins. His mouth was dry. It was always like this just before going into combat. And then, that first shot's fired and you go on auto-pilot, doing what you've been trained to do, almost without thinking – your only objective at that point – staying alive. If they managed to take out the APCs with their first volley, though, that wouldn't be a problem. Less than a hundred men, armed with AKs against two light tanks, would be like a flock of geese going up against a hunter with a machine gun – feathers would fly and there'd be roast goose for a lot of future dinners.

Beyond the mangled huts the ground seemed to drop off in a slight decline. Callahan signaled a halt. Beyond the rim of the decline he could see a light pulsating haze. He figured this to be the smoke from the APCs which were besieging the State House compound.

The other tank pulled up on line with his vehicle, twenty meters to his left. He keyed his transmit switch. "Hold position," he said. "I'll scout up ahead and get the lay of the land."

Without waiting for a response, he removed his headset and hung it on the hook just beneath the hatch. He grabbed his AK-47 and, making sure the clip was seated firmly and a round was in the chamber, he eased out of the hatch and dropped to the ground, kicking up a cloud of dust. With his weapon at the ready he walked forward, looking right and left and carefully studying the terrain for possible ambushers. Not that he expected one. His observations of Bongo's men in the bush had taught him that they were not professional warriors. They could drive the APCs and fire their weapons, but were completely undisciplined, relying on their superior firepower to overwhelm their intended target. The tanks he'd captured, for instance, had been out with just the crews. Any soldier familiar with the ungainly vehicles knew how vulnerable a lone tank can be. Up against a vehicle it is devastating, but a single soldier with an anti-tank round in his RPG can take one out. When the men had taken the girl Rebecca Taylor, and Callahan smiled as he thought of her, they'd stood around arguing about what to do with her. No one was paying attention to their surroundings, enabling Callahan and his men to approach within ten yards unseen. A few accurately placed shots and Taylor found herself surrounded with bleeding corpses, and Callahan's group found itself in possession of two light tanks.

Nearing the rim, he dropped to one knee and leaned forward. About 500 meters ahead and slightly below him, the two BTR-60's sat about ten meters apart, their machine guns aimed at the high stone walls of the State House compound some 250 meters further along, spitting their 14.5mm and 7.62mm rounds at firing positions along the top. Occasionally, he could see a few soldiers pop up during a lull in the machine gun and fire their rifles at the men lying prone behind a hastily erected earth barrier who fired back with their AKMS assault rifles. None of the fire was very accurate, and the attackers, firing their AKs on full automatic at 100 rounds per minute, were expending ammo at a high rate. No one was watching their rear. Smiling, he turned and walked back to the tanks.

Back in the hatch he put his headset on, and keyed it. "Move us forward until we can depress the tubes on target," he said.

The two machines roared forward until they were sitting on the face of the ramped incline, their 76mm guns pointing downward. Inside each tank, one of the three gun crewman was looking through a scope and giving directions to another who spun a wheel that brought the tube to bear on its target. Callahan had instructed them to fire the first round at the machine guns mounted on top of the APCs, and then follow up with one or two rounds at the undercarriage. When the men had the guns properly aimed, they reported to Callahan.

"Locked on target," the gunner in his tank said.

"Roger, also locked on target," the other said.

Callahan took another look at the scene below. The gunmen behind the berm of earth were grouped closely on either side of the two APCs, so shrapnel from the shells detonating against the side of the vehicles would take out several. This *was* beginning to look like a turkey shoot. He smiled.

"Fire," he said into the mike, and grabbed the rim of the hatch to hold on.

The loud 'boom' from the tanks' guns vibrated inside his skull and made his ears ring, and he was enveloped in a billowing cloud of smoke. The tank bounced back several inches, causing him to pitch forward. Only his grip on the metal hatch had kept him from being thrown to the ground.

As the smoke cleared, he was rewarded with the sight of the mangled machine guns, or what was left of them, on both targets, and several torn and bloody shapes on the ground near the two vehicles.

"Good shooting," he said. "Now, fire at will and finish the job."

The tanks' guns boomed again. He saw an orange flower blossom at the rear hatch of one APC and another at the front panel of the other. White tendrils of smoke shot out from the center of the fiery explosions. More men near the now disabled vehicles were tossed into the air by the force of the explosions, their bodies ripped and torn by the metal fragments whizzing through the air.

There was shouting from those unhurt, and moans and screams from the injured and dying, but they didn't seem to be aware of where this deadly assault was coming from. Some of the men leapt to their feet to run away, only to be cut down by rifle fire from the wall in front of them.

"The vehicles are toast, Dog," Dorsten's voice sounded in Callahan's ear. "Should we drop a few rounds into that mass of men?"

"Fire away," Callahan responded.

In quick succession, each crew fired two shells, walking them in from the right and left toward the center. There was only seconds between the explosion of each pair of shells, and more men died along the berm, their bodies torn apart.

Bongo's men, the few that were left, were now aware of the source of the new attack upon them. A few pointed back up the hill at the black shapes spitting fire and death into their midst. That realization broke their will to fight. Of the original 92 men attacking State House, there was now only twenty who could stand unaided, and many of them were bleeding from minor wounds caused by flying shrapnel. Throwing down their weapons, they began waving their arms and shouting in their native language.

Callahan gave the signal to move and the two tanks jerked forward down the hill. At the same time, the large metal gate in the wall around the State House compound swung open and several uniformed figures emerged. One man, in the center of the group, was unarmed but clearly in charge. The group marched forward. The unarmed man raised his hand and shouted something. The defeated attackers stood and placed their hands on top of their heads.

As the two tanks arrived at the scene, more soldiers were emerging from the compound. A few gave the tanks startled looks, but they were obviously aware of the role the tanks had played in breaking the attack. The unarmed man, on the other hand, looked at the tanks with no expression on his dark face, until Callahan opened the hatch and stood up. Then the man's eyes widened momentarily.

"Would I be having the pleasure of meeting Captain Musa Gweru?" Callahan asked.

"Yes, I am Musa Gweru," Gweru said. "And, who are you?"

Gweru's gaze moved from the man to the vehicle in which he rode.

"Major Dale Callahan, at your service, sir."

Charles Ray

Chapter Forty-Nine

With the countercoup thwarted, and Bongo and
Saidu found cowering in a shed at Saidu's farm and
taken into custody, Gweru moved to restore order to
Mabuntu.

Fortunately the civilian casualties were light – two
drunken men had wandered into the path of the APCs
as they entered the city, and had been crushed
beneath the wheels. Callahan and his tanks had done
far more damage, having demolished nearly an entire
city block in their mad dash to relieve Gweru and his
force, but under the circumstances, the Nagandan
government had decided that the damage was
unavoidable, and that particular neighborhood was
seedy and needed to be rebuilt anyway.

As it turned out, there would be sufficient money to
rebuild that neighborhood and others as well. Two
days after the failed countercoup, Petrolux Corporation
announced a deal with the government to develop the

oil deposit in Chiveru Land, and further that it would use a share of its profits from the operation to help construct or upgrade infrastructure throughout the country.

Petrolux's executive in Naganda, Benjamin Holder, informed Morgan that the mercenary unit he'd hired no longer worked for the corporation. Morgan already knew that, though, as he'd been informed by Callahan that Musa Gweru had hired him and his men to train the Nagandan army.

Appearing in public for the first time since his takeover from Saidu, Gweru announced changes to the Nagandan government and military. A senior general was named to replace Gideon Banda as army chief of staff, and Banda's former assistant in the security service was named the service's head, separating the military and security service for the first time since Naganda became independent. Ali Kabbah was appointed to a constitutional commission, and charged with coming up with a roadmap to elections within a year. Gweru also took the unprecedented step of traveling to Ovimbi to personally apologize to Chief Idoma Changa for the coup plotters using his territory as the launch pad for their attack, and pledging more involvement of Chiveru in his government for the duration of his tenure. He then traveled to Ganda Land to ensure the people there that while his junta ruled all people would be treated equally. And lastly, he toured his own tribal area, Buntu Land, to reassure his people that even though they, like the Chiveru, were a minority, their rights would be respected. As Morgan watched the young captain in operation, he was reminded of a campaigning politician, and wondered what Gweru's future plans were.

After the dust settled, Morgan had Tom Breedlove come to the residence on Sunday for breakfast, and after eating had sat with him on the patio overlooking the green hills east of the city and drafted their report of events. He'd skirted the issue of how the poorly armed Nagandan army had defeated a better armed opponent by pointing out the numerical advantage the defenders had, and the apparent lack of order and discipline of the attackers. Breedlove took notes as Morgan talked, retired to a corner of the patio with a number 2 pencil and a yellow pad, and within an hour had drafted one of the finest reports Morgan had seen in his career. When Morgan mentioned this, Breedlove puffed out his chest and smiled like a kid who's just won the local spelling bee. Morgan told him to go in to the embassy and put the cable in final form, and then send it. When Breedlove asked if he wanted to see it again before it went out, Morgan said, no, Breedlove could release it himself. The man beamed again. With that Morgan knew that they'd turned a corner in their relationship. He'd finally made Breedlove a member of his team.

He spent the rest of the weekend alone, sitting and watching the large vultures circling in the sky, and listening to the sound of women cutting wood in the forest on the hill behind his house.

Waking early on Monday morning, he had a light breakfast and set out for the embassy at 6:30. It was just before 7:00 when he stepped out of the car in front of the building. The soldiers were gone, leaving only the two policemen and his embassy guards outside the building. Inside at Post One the young Marine was back in his dress blue uniform. He smiled and saluted sharply as Morgan walked past. In fact, everyone he'd seen so far, including his driver George Toko, had broad smiles on their faces. And, well they might. They'd faced the abyss and hadn't gone over. The country was not only at peace, but facing the prospect of a better future. It would be an uphill climb, with many false starts and disappointments, but any journey worth taking is like that. Morgan felt confident that they would eventually make it.

As he stepped out of the elevator and headed to his office, Susan Pinchon and Tom Breedlove came out of the political section.

"Morning, Mr. Ambassador," the two said in unison.

Morgan noticed that they seemed comfortable in each other's presence, and that Breedlove stood slightly behind Pinchon in a position of deference. He smiled. Yes, the man was now truly a member of the team.

"Morning, guys," he said. "Fine day, is it not?"

"That it is, sir," Breedlove said. "Susan, I'll have that cable on your desk in an hour, okay?"

"Fine, Tom," she said, patting his shoulder. "No rush, though. Whenever you get it done."

She fell in beside Morgan as they walked the rest of

the way to the executive section. They said nothing. Nothing needed saying. They both knew.

Mary Sung met them at the door, a puzzled look on her light brown face.

"You've been summoned to see the president," she said to Morgan.

"I'll clear my desk and be right with you," Pinchon said.

"No, he was quite specific, he only wanted to speak with the ambassador," Sung said.

"Don't worry, Susan, I'll fill you in when I get back," Morgan said. "Mary, tell George to meet me out front."

"He's waiting for you."

He turned and headed back to the elevator. Shit, he thought, and I haven't even had my second cup of coffee. Wonder what he wants this early on a Monday morning.

Toko made good time from the embassy to State House, arriving at the gates in the wall surrounding the compound ten minutes after pulling away from the front of the embassy building. There had been changes since his previous visit - the bullet holes, pockmarks, gouges, and black smears on the wall and some of the nearby buildings from the recent attack were still visible. Most notable, though, was the fact that the big iron gate wasn't closed and guarded as it had been in the past. Two soldiers stood sentry duty to either side of the opening in the wall, but they only saluted as

Morgan's vehicle went past.

Another two soldiers stood guard at the front entrance to State House. When Toko pulled up in front of the entrance, one of them rushed down and opened the door for Morgan. As Morgan stepped out, the man came to attention and saluted. The other soldier opened the door as he approached, smiling broadly at him as he passed.

Musa Gweru waited just inside the entrance.

"David, thank you for coming on such short notice," he said. He stepped forward and grasped Morgan's hand in both his. "It has been an exciting past few days, has it not?"

Morgan returned the pressure of his grip. "Yes, it has," he said. "It reminds me of something I heard once – in the Chinese language; the wish that you live in interesting times is actually a curse."

"That it is." Gweru laughed. "That it is. It also reminds me that our Chinese friends were behind Saidu's vain effort to regain power."

"How did you learn that?"

Gweru turned and started walking toward the sofa and chairs in the corner, guiding Morgan with a hand at his elbow.

"It is perhaps best that you not know that," he said. "Let us just say that someone who has firsthand knowledge of their actions shared the information with me. I have also learned that the Russians were supporting my uncle. That was most disturbing news."

Morgan didn't press him on his methods of obtaining information. He had a good idea how it was done, and it *was* best that he not know for sure.

"What do you plan to do about it?" he asked.

Gweru motioned him to the chair to the right of the large, high-backed chair that was his, and then sat, crossing his legs. He took his time pouring coffee from a silver urn into a china cup on the table near Morgan. He then poured tea for himself, adding a generous amount of sugar and milk until the dark brown liquid was almost white. He waited for Morgan to take a sip of coffee before sipping from his own cup. He then placed the cup on the table.

"I wrestled with that all night," he said. "Finally, I decided to do nothing."

Morgan's eyes widened in surprise. "Both countries worked to overthrow you, and you're planning to let them get away with it?"

"Yes and no. We have a saying in Africa – when the elephants fight, the grass gets trampled. In this situation, we are the grass. If I move against one or both of them, they are likely to try something else, and we might not be so lucky next time. By ignoring it I leave them wondering how much I know. At the same time, I will continue to pursue the programs we have with each. If they wish to compete with each other, let it be in trying to win me over."

Morgan laughed. It was a masterful move. Having

failed in their efforts to get rid of him, both would now redouble their efforts to gain supremacy of influence in the country by trying to influence the man who survived their plotting and removed both of his main rivals from the game. As long as Gweru was in power that stratagem should work. That left, though, the question of how long he planned to retain control.

"That should work as long as you're in power," Morgan said. "But, what happens after elections – which I assume you still plan to hold – won't they move on the next government?"

"I have given that a lot of thought. I do still intend to see elections held. I think I have a solution, though, that will ensure that the Russians and Chinese are held at bay. I have spoken with al-haji Ali Kabbah, and he has convinced Chief Changa to allow his name to be entered as a candidate for president. I imagine that there will also be candidates from the other tribes, but if the chief runs he will win."

"How can you be so sure of that?"

"In our history the Ganda and Buntu have often fought each other. It was the Chiveru who always stepped in and helped us make peace. Every Nagandan child knows that history, so if a respected Chiveru elder is running for the leadership position, all but the political hardliners will vote for him. As to him being able to keep the Russians and Chinese at bay – you've met him, what do you think?"

Morgan knew he was right. Idoma Changa would be no one's puppet. In fact, it was more likely that it would be him doing the manipulating.

"It just might work," he said.

"I am convinced it will," Gweru said. He picked up his cup and took another sip of tea, smiling at Morgan over the rim. He had a conspiratorial look in his eyes. "There is one other thing. Colonel Callahan told me that it was your idea for him and his men to come to our aid."

"Uh, yes, but it's probably best that we not make that public," Morgan said.

"Yes, I can understand that." Gweru chuckled. "Your government, despite its reputation for - how shall we put it - meddling in other countries' affairs, does not like its diplomats taking such an active part in local events like wars. Do not worry, David, I am taking care of that little . . . problem. Tomorrow I will be making an announcement about my plans to reform the military in the months leading up to the elections. One of those plans is hiring foreign experts to train the army – and, Colonel Callahan and his men are those experts. I will phrase it in such a way that, considering the role they played in stopping the coup, people will think they were hired long before that day. He has agreed to go along with this plan, so your superiors in Washington will never know anything different."

It sounded like a good idea to Morgan, but there was one possible hitch.

"But, Callahan and his men were hired by Petrolux.

What if they say something that casts doubt on your story?"

"I have thought of that as well, friend David," Gweru said. "I met with Mr. Holder of Petrolux. He made a quite generous offer as you know. He is also willing never to mention that the mercenaries worked for him or his company. It seems that there were those in Washington who were not pleased to know an American company was hiring mercenaries to support its commercial operations, so Petrolux is more than happy to forget that episode."

Morgan could scarcely believe it. Everything neatly wrapped up and tied off with pretty ribbons. He wondered about Petrolux. It would have had to be someone pretty powerful to put a scare into an oil company. Strange that he'd seen nothing about it in the official cables or the news summaries.

These thoughts were quickly crowded out, though, by the thoughts of all the work ahead of him. He would have to arrange assistance to the fledgling political parties and the government in the complicated process of campaigning and elections, get monitors for the entire process, and even push for a more robust training program for the Nagandan military, to keep an eye on what Callahan was doing and to ensure the Soviets and Chinese made no inroads in that institution.

The time ahead would be interesting, and with no guarantees of the outcome. Without explicitly saying so, Gweru had assured Morgan that he had no political ambitions himself, despite his political acumen. He worried that the young man, having been the head honcho of the country, wouldn't be able to return to the role of a lowly captain in the army, but felt that Gweru was savvy and able enough to land safely on his feet. Yes, it was going to be interesting times – Chinese curses be damned.

Charles Ray

Chapter Fifty

September 6, 1978.
The Committee Headquarters,
Washington, DC

The small room in the red brick building in the walled compound was full for a change. Every seat at the big round table was filled. A blue haze of cigar smoke filled the air. The aroma of the illicit Cuban cigars was comforting. Large crystal brandy glasses sat in front of each man. The elderly black butler moved around the table, pouring amber liquid into each glass – a precise amount in each, ending with a deft twitch of his wrist to cut off the flow without spilling any of the expensive liquor.

His task completed, he silently withdrew.

Seated at his usual place at the head of the table – and even though the table was round and shouldn't with such distinctions as the 'head' not being a part of the motif, there was no doubt that this was the alpha position in this setting – was Jonathan Appleby. Around the table to his right and left were arrayed a group of men who collectively controlled levers of power in government and industry not just in the United States, but around the globe. These were men who could, with one phone call, topple heads of state or divert the course of rivers.

Appleby lifted his brandy glass and, holding it under his nose, breathed deeply. He then took a sip. An expression of satisfaction crossed his face. Picking up his cigar, he drew in deeply and then opened his lips slightly to let the smoke drift out and curl upward toward the ceiling.

"Well, gentlemen," he said. "We're meeting for a change without a crisis to occupy our attention. The president has declared an emergency and evacuation of Love Canal, but it'll be a while before the media and public pay it much attention, and the near crisis in Naganda has been most effectively handled by our ambassador there."

Directly across the table from Appleby, a tanned man with iron gray hair cropped close to his head, and an erect posture that clearly identified him as a former military man, frowned.

"I don't know if I agree with you about the absence of a crisis," he said. "Let's not forget that in June the voters of California approved Proposition 13. That 60 percent slash in property taxes is setting the state up for a fiscal crisis in the near future, and that will impact on all of us."

"Oh, don't be such a worry wart, Calvin," a tiny man with bulging eyes sitting two chairs to the speaker's left said. "California will survive, and so will we. The president has Begin and Sadat at Camp David as we speak, and it's looking good for the two of them to come to some kind of understanding. If we can calm things in the Middle East, the world will look better for everyone."

"Yes – everyone's waiting for the results of that encounter," Appleby said. "Keeping a lid on the Arab-Israeli conflict means less danger to our oil supply and that'll help offset some of our domestic financial problems."

"I suppose you're right, Jonathan," the man called Calvin said. Last names were never used in these meetings, not for security reasons, but because it was felt that this increased the sense of brotherhood and camaraderie. "Speaking of oil, I understand that your intervention with our friends at Petrolux was successful."

"Beyond my wildest expectations. Not only did Petrolux change its tune about disrupting Nagandan culture, but they threw a few extra things in the pot which will help to ensure the situation there remains stable for a while."

"This new find will really improve Petrolux's market position," the small man said. "I saw in today's *Wall Street Journal* that their stock has already risen twenty points."

"That it did," Appleby said. "Which means that anyone who bought shares before yesterday will see a nice appreciation of their portfolio."

He looked around the table, and was met with smiles and nods. After his meeting with the Petrolux CEO, he'd contacted the other members of the Committee and *suggested* that they buy shares in the company. Through his broker he'd purchased ten thousand shares himself. Legally, what he'd done wasn't really insider trading – but he knew that, like him, everyone else had made their purchases discretely. There was little likelihood any of them would be prosecuted, but no one in the group wanted their activity to become public. Had to keep up appearances. They were effective only as long as they stayed behind the curtain like the wizard in that movie about the little girl from Kansas who got swept away by a tornado.

The man to Appleby's left raised his glass. "I propose a toast to the free enterprise system, may it always be thus."

Glasses were lifted; creating eddies in the cloud of smoke surrounding them. But, the eddies soon disappeared, and they were once again enveloped in an obscuring mist.

If you find the adventures of David Morgan and his friends interesting, you won't want to miss the first two books in the *White Dragon* series.

The White Dragons

David Morgan is the deputy to the ambassador in the country of Dagastan, a country hardly worth living for, much less dying for. But, when something of value is found there, he discovers that there is something that others think is worth killing for. When people start dying, Morgan must work with intelligence analyst Alison Chambers and security agent Lee Kennedy to find the mysterious hands pulling the strings in order to survive.

Paperback - $15.26 Kindle version - $6.95

In the Dragon's Lair

Assassinations and a coup have plunged Dagastan into chaos. David Morgan, along with his friends Alison Chambers and Lee Kennedy must work together to keep peace. Morgan finds himself targeted by the Washington bureaucracy, looking to blame someone for the death of the former ambassador. Behind all the trouble is a group known as the White Dragons, and Morgan must expose them before a hired gun gets to him.

Paperback - $12.98 Kindle version - $6.95

Available in paperback on most retail book sites and for Kindle at amazon.com, amazon.uk, amazon.de, and most other amazon sites.

The Buffalo Soldier series:

Buffalo Soldier: Trial by Fire
Buffalo Soldier: Homecoming
Buffalo Soldier: Incident at Cactus Junction
Buffalo Soldier: Peacekeepers
Buffalo Soldier: Renegade
Buffalo Soldier: Escort Duty
Buffalo Soldier: Yosemite
Buffalo Soldier: Battle at Dead Man's Gulch

Other books by this author:

Al Pennyback mysteries

Color Me Dead
Memorial to the Dead
Deadline
Dead, White, and Blue
A Good Day to Die
The Day the Music Died
Die, Sinner
Deadly Intentions
Death by Design
Till Death Do Us Part
Deadly Dose
Dead Man's Cove
Dead Men Don't Answer
Deadly Paradise
Kiss of Death
Death in White Satin
Death in Taxis
Drop Dead, Gorgeous

Other fiction

Angel on His Shoulder
She's No Angel
Child of the Flame
Pip's Revenge
Wallace in Underland
Further Adventures of Wallace in Underland
Dead Letter and Other Tales
The Last Gunfighters
Frontier Justice: Bass Reeves, Deputy U.S. Marshal
The White Dragons
In The Dragon's Lair
Dragon Slayer

Nonfiction

Things I Learned from My Grandmother About Leadership and Life
Taking Charge: Effective Leadership for the Twenty-first Century
Grab the Brass ring
African Places: A Photographic Journey Through Zimbabwe and southern Africa
There's Always a Plan B
A Portrait of Africa

About the Author

Charles Ray has been writing fiction since his teens. He won a Sunday school magazine writing contest when he was thirteen, and having his byline on a short story published in a national publication forever hooked him on writing. During his time in the army (1962-1982) he often moonlighted as a newspaper or magazine journalist, and was the editorial cartoonist for the Spring Lake (NC) News, a weekly newspaper, during the 1970s. In addition to his writing, he was an artist/cartoonist and photographer for a number of publications, including Ebony, Eagle and Swan, and Essence, and had a monthly cartoon feature and did several covers for Buffalo, a now-defunct magazine that was dedicated to showcasing the contributions of African-Americans to the country's military history.

After retiring from the army, he joined the U.S. Foreign Service, and served as a diplomat in posts in Asia and Africa until his retirement in 2012. He has worked and traveled throughout the world (Antarctica is the only continent he hasn't visited), and now, as a full time writer, continues to globetrot looking for interesting things to write about, draw, or take pictures of.

A native of Texas, he now calls Maryland home.